HIGH
IS
THE
WALL

By Ruth Muirhead Berry

 Muhlenberg Press, Philadelphia

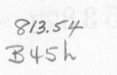

©

1955 BY MUHLENBERG PRESS

Second Printing

33,873
July, 1956

Library of Congress Catalog

Card Number 55-11315

Printed in U.S.A.

UB767

To my children

within and without

the garden wall

Chapter 1

IN the days when they first knew each other, out in California, they walked in the old garden together. The wall was there but they were unconscious of it because they were absorbed in each other. On one side of the garden the wall was so low that Faith could see over it to a glint of the blue Pacific, and a jutting point of whitish land, with three apathetic eucalyptus trees showing against the water. The stems of the geraniums which almost covered the wall were woody with age, yet the flowers bloomed profusely.

Down the center of the garden was a rust-colored path, hard as concrete, leading past a sun dial with a Latin inscription which Neil translated as "Useless without a ray from heaven." Beyond the dial was a wishing well, where people threw coins, and Neil tossed in several silver dollars because, he said, they would be well used, and Faith must know without being told how much he wished for his one great desire.

Beyond the well an arbor of wisteria covered the path till it ended at a high, far wall. Here was a scaly statue in dull red and blue, with a tiny gabled roof over it. When they came to it, Neil crossed himself, which told Faith that the shrine had a special significance.

There was much to see—old blue pottery jars with azaleas, gray olive trees, and green acacias, with rustic seats beneath them. A Brother in a loose robe and sandals walked slowly back and forth. But more captivating to her imagination than all else was Neil, whom she had known but a few weeks, yet to whom she was drawn as steel is drawn to a magnet. Neil was Irish and better looking than any man should be, with deep blue eyes and black, black hair. Faith knew little about the Irish except that they had been persecuted, had kissed the Blarney stone, boasted poets like Yeats and Blake, and sang songs about mother and Killarney. In the small Protestant town back East where she had been reared, almost everyone said one's grandmother had been Irish—on St. Patrick's Day they said it—but few claimed it as a very definite heritage. There could have been some Irish among the railroad workers who went to Athens to Mass at the little Church of St. Aloysius, but Neil was not like these.

The Irish had taken Boston from the Puritans and the Catholic Church in America from the Italians, Faith remembered reading once, and now they were on their way up and up, but she had never really known any of them. Now Neil was eager to teach her of a culture about which she also knew little—a culture shared internationally by all Catholics. He spoke to God in the Catholic language, he said, and Faith thought this was beautiful. Because there was no wall between them then, she loved his saying it, and tried to understand what he meant.

"It's my native tongue," he had continued, "and it's universal. It's the language of the poets and the mystics.

2

I'm sure it's the language He loves most and that He too expresses himself through it."

"How do you know, when you haven't tried any other kind?" she asked.

"Oh, I've been inside other churches with friends and they were bare and ugly, with no meaningful symbolism. It's easy for me to see why God stays there for only an hour on Sundays."

But he had laughed, so Faith laughed, too. Since days were passing and there was not time for them to tell again and again how much they adored each other, not all the differences between them were clarified before Faith had to return to her home in the East.

Cahpter 2

FAITH loved her mother, not with the sentiment of an old song, or with an inward resentment as psychiatrists say is common, but with a healthy give-and-take attitude. She worked for her mother's reconstruction, so to speak, and tried to train her in the way a mother should act. She tried to subdue her mother's enthusiasms, make her avoid reminiscences, and keep her from meddling with the affairs of young people whom she could not possibly understand—for Faith was interested in her mother's good, as well as her own pride.

It was baffling sometimes when other young people followed her mother about, pouring out confidences, laughing at her jokes. There was always a procession of them coming back to introduce a new mate or exhibit a baby. Only she and her brother Steve were interested in forcing her mother into conformity. When they over-stepped their father's patience in this, he would growl genially, "Lay off! Lay off! Your mother may not suit you, but she suits me, and I'm the one who picked her out."

Then her mother would say, "Thanks, John. I do hope you'll be at St. Peter's right hand to interpret me when my time comes." Their father would mutter that she was obviously hoping he would die first, and go back to his study.

But no matter how Faith tried, Margaret McLaren remained a woman who walked a forthright way toward her goal. She could be teased with wisecracks, restrained by criticism, or hurt by neglect, but she would not appreciably change the direction of her course. She went her way with a free-swinging stride and granted others the same privilege. Faith had felt little restriction in the home, but it was a home permeated by her mother's spirit and affected by her strong convictions.

Today, for the first time, Faith feared her mother's opinion. It was so important for her to like Neil and approve of him for a husband. She had talked of him when she returned from California, but only as a wonderful date—the grandest man she had ever seen, and so good-looking! And now he was back in Athens, his home town, only fifty miles from Avalon, where Faith lived. He would come over to see her and meet her people and, when the way was prepared there would be time enough to tell them that he was a Catholic.

It was hard to guess how her mother would react to his Catholicism. People called her broad-minded but Faith knew this wasn't the right word. Her mother had deep, sturdy notions about the way people could approach God, but her opinions wouldn't fit exactly into any one set of tenets. Sometimes she attributed her assorted convictions to a Presbyterian grandfather, a Methodist grandmother, a Quaker mother, and long association with the Congregational church. But she was not confused, and she walked an unhampered upward road, gathering grace from every source, and distributing it where she could. She was never deluded by sham, and her eyes were not closed.

Faith read Neil's letter for the fifth time, then put it in the front of her dress. Her happiness had a blinding quality, like hot sunshine. To be loved by a man like Neil Mackaig came to so few girls. She must enjoy it now and put her doubts aside for another time. She broke a lilac bunch from a bush that overhung the gate and sucked the sweetness of several florets. The perfume was overpowering, like her love. It was too beautiful to be endured.

She wondered how her home would look to Neil. An all-over remodeling was needed. She would not have wanted a new place, for their substantial 1900 edition of the comfortable suburban home was still livable. Its wide front porch was always filled with chairs, and the chairs, more often than not, were filled with people— people who came because the McLarens were an interesting family to visit.

The yard was large enough for croquet and a swing. Around its border grew old-fashioned flowers. Other people tried new plants, but Margaret kept the old ones renewed, sometimes adding, but seldom removing anything. The furniture inside was the same. From year to year things were refinished so they did not become too shabby, but there was no plan. When you went to match the cover for a chair, that material was sold out and you started over again. But the sweet-toned piano was covered with good music, and the long shelves in the library were full and inviting. There were new things and old, new information and old, new ideas and old. On such her home was built.

7

When Faith and Steve had come of college age, her father's salary would not cover the expense, so her mother had taken in students, working long, hard hours to make extra money. Still this had not kept her from being president of the Congregational Women's Fellowship, or working with the Red Cross. Now she was talking of running for election to the school board.

"You'd be good," her husband was saying, "You'd put some ideas . . ."

"Don't, Dad!" Steve protested, "Do you want your wife in the role of a Lucretia Mott or Frances Willard?"

Steve sat on the counter space in the kitchen where his mother was rolling cookies. Two years older than Faith, he was teaching school to save money for his master's degree. He affected a high degree of skepticism about all progressive movements, especially if flavored with religious enthusiasm. He insisted he was an agnostic, but open to conviction if anything could be presented on an intellectual level which he could consider.

"He's always looking for a religion worthy of him," his father would say. "His mother and I pray that one day he'll find himself worthy of one of the trodden paths to God." If they were greatly concerned about his attitude, Faith did not sense it. Her father and mother attended the local Congregational Church regularly, but not with rigidity. God could be worshiped outside stated sanctuaries. Still, they believed in assembling together. Faith worked in the church, taught a church school class, and sang in the choir. Sometimes she attended the meetings of the youth group, but it was not always inspiring.

"They are just pooling their ignorance," she would tell her mother. "I don't get anything from it. But I love the church service and it should satisfy you that I go to it." She felt she should return something for her mother's sacrificial work in getting her through college, and she knew her mother regarded church work in this light.

Faith broke in on the matter of the school board, not with words but with a face that could not hide her inner radiance. Steve noticed her at once.

"Ye gods, kid! Have you seen a vision? Mary, after the appearance of Gabriel, could never have looked more uplifted."

For the first time Steve's irreverent remarks jarred her. Usually she thought them funny, but now she hoped he would refrain in Neil's presence. She wasn't sure how a devout Catholic would react to jibes about the Annunciation. But she must tell them of Neil's coming as casually as she could. "You know the man I said was such a wonderful date when I was in California?"

"Do we?" exclaimed Steve. "A demigod, a dream, a magnificent dancer, a songster superior to Bing Crosby, handsomer than Robert Taylor, an escort of the first water, so to speak. Is he to descend upon us?"

"He'll be here Sunday and I do hope . . ."

"That I'll curb my tendency toward facetious remarks, dad will comb his hair, mother can be kept on safe subjects of conversation, and the entire house be refurnished before that time. Is that it?"

"It's too late to redo the house. But I do hope you all will . . ."

"We'll do our best, honey," said her mother. "You make a list of the things I'm not to say and I'll try to keep within bounds if he doesn't stay too long."

9

"Imagine a brain that could anticipate what mother would say," observed Steve.

Margaret McLaren made an unmatronly face at her son. "Hush, Steve," she said, "You know we'll all do our best to have things nice for Faith's friend. We always have, for both your guests. Why don't you ask him to come over on Saturday, Faith, and spend the week end?"

"He can't get away till around seven-thirty Sunday morning," Faith said lamely, hoping they would not guess that Neil would go to six o'clock Mass before leaving Athens.

"There's the first flaw in your superman," Steve put in. "A fellow that can't get up before seven in the morning for a start to see his girl, can't be badly smitten. You'll have to exude more charm, Sis."

"That will get him here just as you should be starting to teach your class," protested her mother.

"I told him I'd get Sally Morris to take it for me that day so we could have the time together. It won't hurt to cut church once," she added pleadingly. "I hardly ever miss."

"Mother can explain it to the deacons," Steve continued, "And no doubt God . . ."

"Don't be silly, Steve," said his mother. "But I do hate to have either of you assume a responsibility and then let it slide. This once, when there's not time to make other arrangements, I don't see what else to do."

The family did make an effort to put its best foot forward. Steve was goaded into mowing the lawn. Margaret planned a dinner of her best company dishes which could be put in the oven and kept cooking during the church service. Faith took the house apart, putting

10

it together in shining and more tasteful fashion. She removed a plaster-of-Paris Buddha which Steve insisted on setting on the library shelves to tease her, as he knew how she disliked it. She took away several worn pillows from the couch and made new covers for others. She spent hours on flower arrangements, trying to get the right effects and to cover up frayed areas. Then last thing, she rearranged the music on the piano so that "O Divine Redeemer" and "Panis Angelicus" were on top and she could urge Neil to sing for her family. She even practiced the accompaniments.

When the table was set with polished silver and fresh linen, with a bowl of pink tulips in the center, it looked almost good enough for Neil himself. Her mother was co-operating as well as such an impulsive person could when strait-jacketed. Her father had promised to keep his study door shut, his hands out of his hair, and not to start a dissertation on the mid-nineteenth century basis for the rise of totalitarianism in Europe (on which he considered himself an authority), even if Steve opened the way with references to Carlyle or Bismarck. Steve would not commit himself, but Faith prayed that he would behave.

Neil arrived in a car three years younger than the one Faith's family owned, and two sizes larger. He came while her father and mother were at church. She was delighted at this because there were no observers of the first joy of their meeting. Also she knew he had a Catholic scorn for the indifference of Protestants to their own worship. While she was at some loss to explain her own compromise in staying at home to greet him, it was good to be able to say, "Mother and Dad are

11

at church. They wouldn't miss it if the roof fell in." It only slightly stretched the facts.

Neil was even more wonderful than her memories of him.

"How could I have met such a girl as you, Faith, on a trip to California, then find she lives within fifty miles of my own home town? It's almost too much good luck. What a girl you are! Lovelier even than I remembered."

"You, too," she whispered in his ear, her face against his coat.

She was overjoyed that he was pleased with her, though her mirror told her that she looked well. The short, informal cut was becoming to her golden hair. Her brown eyes made up for some tiny freckles over her nose and the fact that it was a very short nose at that. Her mouth was small and well-shaped. Today in a semi-tailored green taffeta even Steve said she looked sharp. It was something, with her limited budget, to be able to look much better dressed than she really was.

Steve had gone somewhere with the old car and was good enough to stay away till after the folks returned from church. She and Neil arose from the couch when she heard her father and mother talking as they walked up the path. It seemed disloyal to apologize for one's mother, especially such a remarkable mother as hers. Still, Faith found herself saying, "My mother is an unusual woman. We say she's . . . well, unpredictable. I'm sure you've never met anyone just like her."

"I've never met anyone just like her daughter, that I know," Neil whispered, taking another kiss. Then they stood up and tried to act as though they were watching the goldfish.

12

Her mother was chatting with her husband as they came up the steps. "I really don't have a style any more, John," she was saying. "Nature has confused me. Fat one year and thin the next. Brown hair, then gray. And styles themselves whizzing around in such a dizzy way. Shall I try to set one of those fire-shovel hats over my nose and affect chic, or do I get a floppy one that declares I've outgrown my girlhood and don't know it? Or just a plain, matronly turban, abhorrent from any angle? What do you think?"

"I don't care what kind of hat you wear," her father was insisting, "You would be delightful and stimulating if you wore a brown derby . . ."

"They talk this way all the time," Faith whispered, wondering how it sounded to Neil. "No matter what mother does, father thinks she's perfect."

"We'll be that way, too, Faith. I'll always think what you do is right."

Her parents greeted Neil with warm friendliness, as was their custom in meeting anyone. Her father began visiting at once, skirting questions of European politics, but not discoursing. Margaret excused herself and went to the kitchen, for one of her tenets was that dinner should be served immediately after church in order to have a free afternoon. Faith could remember no deviation from this rule. When Steve came in she left the men to visit and went to put the jellied salad on her mother's best Haviland.

She found herself wondering how a Protestant blessing would sound in Catholic ears, but when the moment came her father used the one she liked best— sonorous and a little grandiose, "Eternal Father, whose gracious gifts . . ." There was certainly nothing in it to insult anyone's conception of God. Even Steve was careful of his remarks. However, Faith kept wishing that she had made a clean breast of Neil's religion, for it kept her on tenterhooks for fear something would be said.

So that afternoon while they were out for a ride, having promised to be home for supper and to have Neil sing for the family, she was glad that he brought up the subject.

"Have you told your family that I'm a Catholic?" he asked.

"No, I haven't. But I think we should."

"Are they . . ." he hesitated. Perhaps he thought *bigoted*, but he finished with "prejudiced against Catholics?"

"I'm sure they're not prejudiced. They both believe very strongly that everyone has a right to his own approach to God. They are always saying it."

"Then what would they mind?" He sensed her reservation.

"You said something once about the Protestant having to sign papers," she went on. "My mother is part Quaker. She doesn't believe in taking an oath or promising anything. I mean like signing a pledge. Though she belonged to the W.C.T.U., she didn't want us to sign a pledge when we were little. She thinks people should know what is involved and be terribly serious if they commit themselves to something. And it should be a matter where one wouldn't likely change one's mind."

"How about marriage? You commit yourself there. Certainly Quakers don't believe in free love."

"I should say not! I can't explain mother's standpoint exactly. Only that she's funny about making a commitment. She believes that God continually reveals himself to people. That there is such a thing as an inner light that guides you if you try to get in touch with it."

"She doesn't think the light zigzags sometimes, leading you first this way and then that, does she?" Neil demanded, smiling but incredulous.

Faith laughed. "It's not that bad. But she believes in growth. And people do change their minds about religion and a lot of things."

"But surely one shouldn't build a life on the possibility of change!"

"It isn't that," said Faith. "It's hard to explain. I know they like you, Neil. They'll think you're just wonderful when they know you. But mother will feel I should be married in my own church, with our own minister. I know she will. If you could be married that way, I'm sure there wouldn't be a word said."

"But I can't, honey. Not even for you, I can't. It would cut me off from the sacraments. Without them, I'm sure I'd be a different person. I doubt if even you would want me then." She could see that he was terribly distressed. His handsome face had lost its smile and the twinkle was gone from his blue eyes. Irish blue, she called them. They were as distinct a contrast to his black hair as her brown eyes were to her butter-colored curls.

"I've been told," he continued, "that there is nothing in Protestant teaching which is radically against a Catholic marriage. As a matter of sentiment your family would like to have you married from your home church. But it's a social, rather than a religious, feeling. And your people would think a Catholic marriage was valid. Usually they get over any prejudice against the promise to bring the children up as Catholics once they really understand it. I've known of whole families who come into the Catholic Church because of it."

"That wouldn't be an argument to use with my people!" Faith stated more flatly than she intended.

"We won't use it, then," said Neil, a bit of his smile coming back. "We'll have to plot our course and handle this thing carefully. But, first, you said your mother was part Quaker. How can you be part anything in religion? Don't you have to be definitely one thing or another?"

"I didn't mean it that way. Among Protestants there are many denominations with their own distinguishing features. Sometimes the difference is a matter of form, or of government. But they go back and forth and exchange ideas. No one thinks anything of it. My mother was reared a Quaker, but her father was Presbyterian, and she went to a Presbyterian college. Then she served as a missionary under the Congregational Boards. She has very positive ideas. My father was reared Episcopalian and still prefers it and goes back when he can to take the Sacrament. When they moved to Avalon there were none of the churches in which either of them had been brought up. There was some Congregational background for each of them so they compromised on it. So you see what I mean."

"Frankly, I don't see. Among Catholics, you have to be one thing or another."

"But in important things the churches I mentioned do agree. We have union services and all that."

Neil did not seem to hear. Either he was unconcerned about the mores of Protestantism or he was thinking of their own problem, for he said, "If you don't mind, darling, I think I'll tell your folks tonight that I'm a Catholic and that I love you. We might as well find out where we stand."

"I'm sure you're right," Faith agreed, "but I hate to have anything come between us and I'm not sure what they'll say."

"It will be less between us if we face it frankly," he said. "And your people will have more respect for me if I'm open and aboveboard."

How fine he is, Faith thought. How could anyone help seeing that he is wonderful?

Before supper Faith persuaded Neil to sing "Panis Angelicus" for which he used the Latin words, and "O Divine Redeemer" which he sang in English. He had a true tenor with an appealing note that made her mother say impulsively, "Oh, that is beautiful. Sing again, please. Do you know 'Come Ye Blessed of My Father'?"

Faith wasn't sure of the status of this song. It was a nuisance to have to be sure of the theology even of songs, but in time she would learn what could and could not be done, and just how strict Neil was.

Finally, Steve left on his date, after expressing pleasure at meeting Neil. It was then that Neil came directly to the point with her parents. He was sorry, he said, that he had to broach the subject when they could not possibly know much about him. He invited them to look into his past, his family, and his prospects. Then he told them that he loved Faith and wanted to marry her. He would do everything in his power to make her the happiest girl in the world. Only one thing seemed to stand in the way of perfect accord and that was their different religions. Since he felt his religion was the best part of him, he would not be himself without it. Un-

17

fortunately, his church would deny him the sacraments if he married outside her doors.

He spoke quietly, but firmly, sitting beside Faith on the old sofa and holding her with a steadying arm. He was much more composed than she and, if he had not already had all her love many times over, he would have had it then. Surely her parents could not help admiring so straightforward, so tactful a person!

She was both relieved and troubled when her father said, with equal frankness, "No one could help but respect the way you have presented your case, Neil. And I hold a double admiration for a man who will state his religious views when they come in conflict with his happiness, or what he thinks is happiness. But there are basic differences between the Protestant and Catholic approach to God. Faith is only twenty-one. That isn't a great many years, but it is a time when romantic love seems to be the paramount thing in life. She should not let this keep her from doing some serious thinking. And you should realize that you are asking a tremendous sacrifice. Because Faith is too young to grasp its significance makes it all the greater chance." Then he turned to his wife. "What do you say, Margaret?"

"Like you, I admire Neil's frankness. But his own church is so afraid of mixed marriages that it has placed all sorts of difficulties in the way of them." Then she turned to Neil. "You know, yourself, Neil, that the Catholic Church is so afraid your faith will be weakened that it will demand that Faith give assurances that this will not happen. But it offers no guarantee that her belief will not be undermined. You're older than she is and, evidently, you know what your church teaches.

She wouldn't stand much chance of holding her own, I'm afraid."

"Mrs. McLaren, I think I can promise, without disobeying my church's regulations, that I'll not interfere with Faith's attendance at her own services. I love her as she is and I'll never ask her to do a thing I'm not compelled to do."

"But these promises are unfair," said Margaret. "They place two people, who should be equally yoked together, in an arrangement where one of them holds a favored position."

"I can't help that, Mrs. McLaren," Neil said earnestly. "These are old, old laws. They may be wrong and I'm not defending them. But my church is an old, old institution and wonderfully wise. If, in time, she decides that these regulations are not good, she will change them, I assume. But the Catholic Church doesn't change easily. That is why so many people find it comforting."

"I like your candor," John McLaren repeated, "but I feel the Catholic determination to protect its members imposes a wrong on the non-Catholic mate. Especially in the matter of children. More than likely they will feel closer to the parent who has the same religion. You are asking for a favored position from the start."

"I doubt if it's that bad," Neil protested. "I've known a number of happy mixed marriages. They just don't let it bother them. Wouldn't you rather have your daughter married to a man with definite religious principles than with none at all?"

"Possibly," John agreed. "But that just makes it the lesser of two evils. However, the thing for both of you to do is to go into every aspect of the matter. Of course some couples make a go of it. Even the ones who do would probably be happier with a mate who held similar religious views. A lot of people marry what seems to be the only desirable person at the time. To me it's a wonder so many of them finally make a welded family."

As they ate supper conversation shifted to other things. Then the older couple went to spend the evening with friends and Faith had Neil to herself. If it had not been for the concern each felt about her parents' reaction, the evening would have been perfect.

That week Faith received a note from Neil's mother —a gracious, well-worded invitation to spend a week end with them and meet Neil's family. They were all very eager to know her, Mrs. Mackaig said, for Neil had painted a glowing picture. Faith's father felt she should accept. Her mother was less enthusiastic. She could see no possibility of a happy arrangement. The Catholic position was inflexible and, no matter how desirable the young man might be, no one was worth the sacrifice of a principle, according to her. Because Faith didn't see it now was not proof that she never would. It might be less painful to snap the affair off right then. Besides there were still a number of personable college seniors in the area—and there was no cure for heartache like the presence of another suitor.

But she helped Faith make a new dress for the trip and, though she said nothing about it, gave up the idea of getting a new pair of shoes so Faith could have some to match her outfit. The Mackaigs were no doubt well-fixed financially, and Margaret wanted her daughter to appear under no disadvantages of that sort.

Chapter 3

IN the previous year the town of Avalon had taken on a new look. A four-lane highway made a swerve on to Canaris Street, turning a residential avenue into a thoroughfare. Beyond the swerve the old houses were being sold for business places and professional offices. Beyond the business section on the road to Athens, there was a growing industrial section, and beyond this a series of housing projects. Avalon could never be a real city for it didn't have what it took to grow, Faith thought. But there were amazing signs of new cultures and new problems.

The Pentecostals had bought the old armory and rebuilt it into a church with a revolving electric sign which said "Jesus Saves" every other time it went around, with the hour of the service in between. The Christian Scientists were building, and there was even a synagogue in the offing. But on the hill, occupying one of the finest sites in town, there was a new Catholic church, called the Church of the Immaculate Conception. Vaguely Faith remembered seeing the foundation the fall before, but then she had thought nothing of it. Neil had asked about it, and if she had met the priest. But Faith was scarcely aware that such a person existed. Come to think of it, though, there were a number of

Catholic students in college, many of them from well-to-do homes. So all the people who had been going over to Athens to Mass could not have been of the working class. It must have been a wrong impression she had picked up somewhere. Neil was sure she had been given an unfortunate picture.

So the first day when she was out with the family car, she drove around it.

"Let's go inside," she suggested to the friends who were with her.

"What do you want to look inside a half-finished Catholic church for?" Edna Norton demanded. "There'll be nothing there yet. Once they get the images and altars in there's a lot to see. My father took me through St. Patrick's in New York and it was marvelous. I love to go there."

"Are you a Catholic, Edna?" Sally Morris asked.

"My dad is. And we children went to Catholic school till we got to the eighth grade. But my mother's Protestant and we're all mixed up. One of my brothers is Catholic, my sister sings in the Presbyterian choir at home, and I can't make up my mind."

This was the sort of situation Faith wanted to discuss. "Did it bother in your home, having two religions?" she asked.

"Not too much. At least it didn't bother me. My folks never talked religion around the house. Each one went to church, my mother alone and we kids with dad. Then my sister decided she wanted to go with mother, so she did. Why?"

"Faith's got a Catholic boy friend," explained Sally.

"That good-looking one who came over from Athens in the swell car last week?" Edna asked.

Faith felt a new wave of pride. "Yes," she said. "I met him in California when I went out to take care of Aunt Kate."

"Oh," groaned Pat O'Brien, "why couldn't I have seen him first? I'm in the market for a handsome Catholic with a car like his, and every date I've had this year has been a Protestant!"

"Are you Catholic?" Faith asked in surprise. She had known Pat more than a year but had never thought of the matter of religion. She had never considered the religious views of any of her acquaintances.

"With Patricia O'Brien for a name?" demanded Pat. "Did you think I was Jewish?"

Faith laughed "I'm glad I saw Neil first," she said, "But I'll ask if there are any more like him where he comes from. If he knows a good date for you, I'll have him bring one over."

"Do!" said Pat. "Where I live there are several lovely Catholic girls but not one respectable man the right age. And then they tell us over and over to marry within the Church!"

"We should have a mixer," suggested Sally. "In the Protestant group in my home town the girls have the brains and the boys are nitwits."

"Maybe there just aren't as many nice men as girls anywhere," Edna offered. But in the end they decided, judging from the number of fine-looking fellows on the streets, that the proportion was about the same. It was merely a matter of distribution.

They parked the car and went inside the church. It was almost completed but there were still no pews or kneeling benches. A huge crucifix rose above the altar and there were little booths on either side of the building. As Patricia explained about the church, Faith listened eagerly.

A priest came through the building, stopping a minute to speak hurriedly. Patricia called him "Father" and her tone was much more deferential than that of a Protestant young person speaking to a minister. Faith wondered if he would be the one from whom she would take instruction. He seemed very busy and soon left. Pat explained that he would have the responsibility for the building of the church, must say all Masses unless he had an assistant, hear the confessions, and make calls when people were dying. Most priests were terribly overworked, Pat said.

Faith left Pat and Edna at the dormitory and she and Sally rode around for a little while to talk. Sally was Faith's closest friend and her reactions would be interesting. She could understand from the standpoint of a young woman, which was impossible for any member of her own family, Faith reasoned.

"No one can blame you for falling for Neil, once they've seen him," Sally remarked, "but, if I were you, I'd want to know what his family is like and how strict he is before I plunged. Knowing you as I do, I bet you'll have a hard time knuckling in to the Catholic Church. Things Catholics take for granted gripe a Protestant terribly. You know Ted Neilson had been dating Pat some, but when he found how devout she was and what was involved, he broke it off. I imagine that's why she feels as she does."

"Would you marry a Catholic, Sally?"

"I'd hate to. Still, I wouldn't want to make a flat statement. It would depend on the man. And since right now there's a pre-theolog who looks mighty good to me, it's

24

hard to get a perspective. When you get down to brass tacks, it's the man that matters."

"That's exactly the way I feel," said Faith.

Neil's home is what ours would be if we had $8,000 to do it over and mother would have a decorator, Faith thought when she saw it. It, too, had been an old house with dated features, Neil explained, but they had removed the front porch, put in a Georgian doorway, painted the brick white, and added shutterdoors in a soft blue shade. The yard was immaculate, with a formal rose garden at the side. Inside the house the color scheme had been suggested by the dusky rose shades in the marble fireplace. This was picked up in the rich, plain drapes. Everything else was a soft, ice green, or beige, with accents of gold in a satin brocaded chair and a pillow on the couch. It was so perfectly appointed that Faith felt she was in the drawing-room of a very elegant castle, though she sensed that the treatment made the rooms seem larger than they were.

Cecelia Mackaig greeted her cordially. It could have been because the home was so much more elegant than her own, or just because she was visiting Neil, that Faith felt a timidity she had not known since childhood. Neil's mother spoke in a rich, well-modulated voice, and everything she said was correct. Here was a mother who would not need coaching, but she might be a trifle less approachable because of it. Her style was modern and chic. She knew what to wear for nature had not "confused" her and she was still a slender, well-built woman, who could pull her coal black hair back tight, wear dangling earrings, and draw her mouth to any shape she liked with lipstick. But she was not all superficiality,

Faith knew, for Neil had said she was a devout Catholic.

Neil had two elder married sisters, and one younger than himself, who was just back from a sisters' school in the East. She was a shy, pale girl who had been taught not to cross her knees, and she had none of her mother's glitter. Neil had said something about how Connie wanted to become a nun but her family, though glad to give one of their children to the Church, were not urging it as the girl was frail and they doubted if she could do the work of a teaching or nursing sister. Both she and Neil looked like their mother, so Faith decided Mrs. Mackaig was the dominant member of the pair.

When Mr. Mackaig came home she could see that exactness was an acquired habit with him. The Mackaigs had done a good job of training the lax member of their firm, and he fitted into the family scheme, though a trifle uncomfortably, looking occasionally at his wife for his cue.

The table was another aspect of perfection, but Faith could not quite enjoy the food as she would have elsewhere than in the home of a man whose family she wished to impress. She wished she had Neil's aplomb, for he had been at ease in her home under more difficult circumstances. She had no idea what was expected of her at the blessing, for everyone crossed themselves, and Mr. Mackaig began with, "In the Name of the Father, and the Son, and the Holy Ghost"—phraseology which Faith thought was reserved for the close of a prayer, not the beginning.

Then the conversation became general. Faith sensed a suppressed twinkle just behind Mr. Mackaig's eyes and decided at once that, if her father had co-operated, she and Steve could have forced greater conformity upon their mother, but the results might not have been entirely desirable. It was decided that she and Neil would go over to Dartmouth to Mass in the morning. The weather was gorgeous for an early drive, and they all wanted her to see the cathedral with its statuary.

The member of the family to whom Faith was most drawn was Neil's cousin. A year older than Faith, Molly Moriarity was Mr. Mackaig's niece and she had his warmth and humor. She worked in the library and lived at her uncle's. Faith was glad that the canon laws forbade marriage between persons of second degree consanguinity, or surely Neil would have taken to her. Molly helped Faith unpack, and dropped bits of informal information. She was another beside Neil who could answer questions. Molly explained that Faith must wear a hat to church, which Faith already knew from going with her father to St. Mary's. She would not be expected to kneel unless she chose, for Protestants often attended Catholic services and it was understood that they were onlookers.

"Don't worry," Molly consoled her. "Everyone understands and Neil would think anything you did was just perfect."

Except for the old missions in California and a quick look into the bizarrely ornate sanctuary of St. Aloysius years before, Faith could not remember ever being in a Catholic church. The cathedral was beautiful, though the altar seemed a little cluttered and the reredos was replete with symbolism. Neil let her into the pew first, then genuflected, pulled the kneeler down and dropped upon it, his eyes fixed on the crucifix at the front, his hands reverently folded. She had seen people genuflect

27

because there were always some High Church Episcopalians at St. Mary's, but many of the people knelt simply, and these always bowed their heads. She had never seen the Asperges and, without explanation, it had a heathenish aspect. Nor could she follow the movements of the priest and acolytes who seemed to be bobbing from one side of the altar to the other. Neil kept finding the place for her in the Missal, but her knowledge of Latin was insufficient to follow the rapid words. The *Sursum Corde* and *Agnus Dei* she could pick out, and one of the tunes sung in a response was like the one used in the Episcopal church when they knelt to sing, "Holy Father, We Adore Thee." She wondered if the people kneeling, then standing, then sitting, knew what was coming and if they understood the Latin words. Neil did, of course, for he was well educated. But she wondered about the rank and file. Even without an exact English translation the words probably became meaningful to them in some way.

But it was not the pageantry, or the novelty, or even the choir of little boys with their angelic faces above the the lace-trimmed surplices that impressed her most. It was the worshiping looks on the faces of the people. They really believed God was on that altar, not in a symbolic sense, as most Protestants did, but specifically in the Host. The Bread became the flesh of Christ at the instant the priest elevated the Host. Neil had explained it all. "Protestants had nothing like this," he said. "That was why they did not worship so ardently, so purely. When they revolted from the True Church back in the sixteenth century they had broken the Body of Christ, which was his Church, and they had left it on the altar." She did not believe all this but, if believing it gave the congregation such a look of adoration, there must be a fundamental truth lying behind it. If this was what made Neil what he was, how could she ask that he be separated from it? She had an impulse to kneel beside him, but felt that she must not. He was looking steadfastly at the crucifix, and he should not be thinking of her.

Driving back to his home for dinner, he asked how the Mass had seemed to her.

"It was beautiful in spots. I could even feel myself worshiping with you. But of course I couldn't understand it."

"It's worth learning about," said Neil. "Anything that will stand the test of time as the Catholic Church has, will bear study."

Faith shot him a merry glance. "I'm not to be proselyted, you said."

He laughed. "O.K. But I have a right to stick up for a good thing when I know it, haven't I?"

"I wish I knew more what was going on. Then I could understand better why the Reformers dumped so much overboard."

"That's what Catholics wonder. And when we see where it's got you . . ."

"How do you mean?"

"Well, the condition of Protestantism today. So divided. So many people who believe nothing and never go to church. The immorality and indecency . . ."

"Are we to blame for all that?" Faith asked edgily.

"Largely, Catholics think. You have so little to tie to. No great body of belief that is accepted by all of you and has lasted through the centuries. I don't mean that we think all Catholics are good or live up to the teachings of the Church. We have our share of renegades and apostates."

"What horrible names you call them! I'm ashamed of you, Neil," she said, laughing.

He seemed puzzled. "Maybe they are strong terms, but I've always heard them. And we feel people do take a loss who lose their faith. It's hard to explain, darling. Protestants think we're a scared, subservient people. They don't catch the feeling. It's so much more than the signs and rules and words and water. Even my family—and we're none of us mystics, unless Aunt Connie has a strain of it—feels the beauty that pervades it. Oh, Faith, I must make you see it enough so you won't break this thing off! I just can't lose you!"

This swept all her defenses away. It was one thing to argue when there was no issue involved. But when they skirted the possibility of a difference that would separate them, neither of them could face it. Neil had one conclusive argument. When they were up against the wall between them, he would overwhelm her with kisses and passionate declarations of love. She was his little Puritan, albeit a free thinker.

Mrs. Mackaig found a chance to talk with her a few minutes alone before Neil took her back to Avalon.

"We're so happy to have you come over, Faith, and hope you will come often. Neil is so fond of you and eager for you to understand the culture in which he has been reared. There are so many misconceptions about Irish people—caricatures of them as a roistering, unstable people. We are Irish, but not that type."

"I can see that easily," Faith agreed, laughing a little.

"Neil is certain he can never be happy without you and, of course, his family is interested in his happiness and welfare."

"Do you mind his marrying a Protestant?" Faith asked, determined despite her awe of Mrs. Mackaig to be as candid as Neil had been.

"Naturally we would have preferred a Catholic girl. But we are not narrow-minded and we have many non-Catholic friends. As you know, he would have to be married in the Church. Neither he nor any of us would feel he was married otherwise. But no one would trouble you about the practice of your religion."

"I haven't absolutely promised Neil," Faith felt compelled to say. "My mother, naturally, wants me married from my own home and in the Congregational Church. I know so few Catholics and much Catholic teaching seems very strange to me."

"No doubt you have never heard it well explained. The Protestant explanations don't express what we really feel. If my sister, who is a nun, were here, she could interpret it so beautifully."

"I'd love to talk with her," Faith said, then was instantly conscious that she had not told the truth, for she knew she would be awed at a nun, especially one who was related to Neil. They seemed such remote, unworldly creatures, with their snowwhite coifs and flowing robes.

Neil's mother is a wonderful woman, she thought, as she repacked her bag. But her face has a glitter, like sun on caked snow, and it doesn't look like her words sound. Neil looks like her without the glitter. And when he was worshiping this morning he had a beautiful expression. Many of the worshipers had it. Is it so

31

dramatic it does something to them all? It couldn't be a simulation of holy awe! That would be a wicked conclusion to draw. Even her mother would agree. Whole groups could not deceive themselves. The reverent position must help. Perhaps Protestants would look more like they were worshiping if they had their eyes glued on some one object of adoration.

Riding back when the cool waves of evening air were sucking fragrance from the long grasses, mingling it with the smell of dusty earth, Neil pressed his case more warmly. "Darling, I'll never be completely happy till you've given a definite promise and set the date. I love you so completely that I'll do everything in my power to offset this religious difficulty. How can I make you understand?"

They turned off the highway to stop the car and have a few more moments together.

"Oh, Neil," she almost moaned, "when I'm with you I want to marry you so much I can't even think straight. I'm afraid I'll promise, then regret it because of my family and my friends. I had no idea they felt so strongly about mixed marriages. It never occurred to me."

"But they have no objection except a prejudice against Catholicism, have they? What is it that makes Protestants dislike us so? I can understand how it was when Catholics were mostly immigrants, many of them ignorant. There was a social barrier. But that is past now. Our schools lead the nation and Catholics hold positions of honor in almost every state government and many in Washington. Our national loyalty is just where yours is. Don't you see how there's no foundation for all this animosity?"

She could not make him understand that the prejudice was against the Catholic marriage service and its guarantees, and she would not repeat the things Protestants said. She was ashamed of some of them herself. But she had heard so many statements since her friends knew she was interested in a Catholic man: Catholics were afraid of purgatory and hell; they could not think for themselves; they depended on the sacraments more than on righteous living; they could not be trusted in their representation of facts; the Catholic Church craved power rather than righteousness. But she could not believe all such things.

After they reached her home they remained in the car while again Neil presented his case. "Sweetheart, if I were not so sure that the gain would far outweigh the loss, I'd never have the courage to ask you to try it."

Finally she pushed him back a little, holding his face in her hands and eyeing him fondly. "There's just one reasonable argument for a Catholic ceremony as far as I'm concerned, in case you're interested."

"If you'll concede one, I'd love to hear it."

"It's Neil Mackaig. It's the way he kisses me, the kind of eyes he has, the way he sings, what he is, and the way my heart melts and runs all through me till I'm just nothing but one big response when I'm with him. If I do go to a priest and do all this for you, Neil Mackaig, it'll be the most overwhelming proof of love that a man ever had."

"I'll make it a million times worth your while, darling. It won't be a concession, once you see it right. And I might also hint that the reason I'm willing to scale down my own religious life and try to fit it to the pattern of a mixed marriage is because a little girl with heretical convictions comes between me and every other thought. I could hardly keep my mind on the Mass for praying that you would give me a definite Yes before the day was over."

Maybe that was what made the heavenly look when he was kneeling, she thought. Aloud she said, "I won't promise for sure, absolutely sure, Neil, but I'm nearer it than I've ever been before and I do think your home and family are lovely. But you must go. It will be daylight before you get to bed."

"I'll make up for it tomorrow night. Then I'll call you Tuesday evening for a long chat, then come back Thursday. I can get here by a little after seven, I think. Be ready with a promise, darling."

Chapter 4

WITH daylight and a practical Protestant world about her, Faith retraced some of her mental steps. The golden mysticism of a religious sphere beyond her ken had no staying quality against the directness of family logic. They were all interested in her visit and her reactions. Sally was even more probing than her family when they came from class together. Faith could talk more frankly with Sally for there was no personal emotion involved although Sally was more prejudiced than the McLaren family and fully as outspoken.

"I'm glad you had such a wonderful time," Sally said when Faith had given a glowing description of her visit. "Even so, Faith, I'd go slow. Why don't you read some books on it?"

"Neil's going to bring me some. I won't barge in without some study. But the Catholic service is beautiful, or would be if one understood it."

"They're master hands at romanticizing things. They have to be. If they didn't ring the changes on fear and romance as motives, they couldn't get people to bare their innermost thoughts in a confessional," Sally observed. "Still, some of our ministers say it's an escape and Protestantism would be better off if we had some sort of vent like they have. Do you suppose a lot of intermarriage would bring about changes in both groups?"

"Neil doesn't think anything would change the Catholic Church much."

"Will he admit that it is ever wrong?"

"I don't know," Faith hesitated." Catholics have been so hounded, and so in the minority, I suppose that's what makes them touchier than we are. I haven't tried to discuss all those points. We never have time."

"You know what Pat was saying the other day about your bringing a Catholic date around for her? It seems Ted Neilson was getting pretty serious with her and she really fell for him. Then, when he saw the antenuptial papers, he backed off. Said he couldn't take it. I'd do a little looking into it, Faith, to see how you feel. Ted's my second cousin and, if you'd like to see what they ask, I'll bring a copy over. He made several carbons when he had them so he'd have some to show people. A lot of folks won't believe anything like that till they see it."

"Neil will get me some when I want them," Faith said, stiffening a little. After all, it was her affair and Neil's.

"I don't mean to interfere," Sally apologized, "but Catholics aren't afraid to spill their opinions and they're likely to get the best of us. We've never been taught the answers as they have."

Harlan Torrance, an old friend who was studying for the ministry, was home for vacation and he made an opportunity to talk with Faith. "I know any protests I make about your marrying another man won't go over too big," he acknowledged, "because you'll know I am too prejudiced to think any man, whatever his religion, is good enough for you. But marrying a Catholic will bear some consideration. Always remember—they insist you study their religion, but just try to lure one of them into studying yours. There's where their belief in purgatory really shows up!"

"I'm sure Neil would listen to me if I explained my belief," Faith insisted. "He says we'll be just like my father and mother, and they argue all the time, and they're still in love. It's just that I can't explain what I believe as well as he explains his belief. The Catholics have something on us there, Harlan. They are taught as children to know what they believe. We aren't. I can see in a way why they all say those terrible things about Protestant education. I need to study on both sides of the question."

Harlan evidently felt it was little use to say more, for he changed the subject. Only once more did he refer to this topic when he asked Faith why he couldn't have been the one to sweep her heart away instead of Neil? Then everyone would have been satisfied.

But more of her friends were inclined to think difference of religion didn't matter. If you loved a man and thought his religion good enough for him, you would naturally think it good enough for your children. Some said that one religion was just as good as another, anyhow. It was just a person's interpretation of God and there was no use being narrow-minded about it.

But her mother's opposition remained positive. Margaret McLaren said she liked and respected Neil. He was an exemplary young man. But he was not a good marital bet for a Protestant girl who came from a home where people spoke their beliefs frankly.

So when Neil came back Thursday evening Faith said, "I'm not going to kiss you once till we've had a good, open-minded discussion. I lose my place in my thoughts once I touch you."

"Fire away," said Neil. "But there's nothing to keep me from kissing you. Even size is in my favor. And this was the night you were to say Yes."

"It can't be an unconditional Yes. Not just yet. What do the papers say that I have to sign, Neil?"

"I don't know that I ever saw any of the forms. But the gist of it is that you'll not oppose the practice of my religion and that you are willing for the children to be brought up Catholic."

"Sally's cousin, Ted Neilson, was planning to marry a lovely Catholic girl here in college, a Patricia O'Brien, but when he saw the papers, he backed out."

"Who told you this?"

"Sally Morris. She's my closest friend."

"Isn't she stepping out of the sphere of her own personal interests?" Neil demanded, with an edge to his voice. "If other people would leave us alone, we could work things out."

"People do seem interested, don't they?" Faith said. "But it's natural for my family to be concerned, just as yours is."

"I'll concede that," Neil agreed, "though my folks, in this case, are showing a lot more liberality than yours."

"Mine would be liberal if the marriage could be in our church. I doubt then if they would say anything against it. But then yours . . ."

"It isn't my family. It's my church. We've gone over this time and again, honey. Let's go over and see if we can find a priest around that new Catholic church that's being built. We might as well get down to brass tacks about this thing. The indecision is going to kill us both."

As they neared the church Neil remarked, "The more you study Catholicism and know what you're getting into, the more you'll like it. I'm not ashamed of my religion, but I still don't go for everything. I know there are tawdry aspects and there are priests who step over the bounds of their authority. Occasionally they put out stupid propaganda sheets that would sicken anyone. So you can see I don't swallow all the ballyhoo. But to me the Church has the Truth, and you can spell it with a capital letter if you like. I'd be sunk without the confessional. I can't say I like to go to confession and I think few people do. But it gives me a clean slate to start with and renews my courage. Without it I wouldn't be worth much, I'm afraid. If I felt less strongly, I'd give in to you, darling. Do believe it isn't hateful stubbornness, for it's a long way from that."

He parked the car in the open space near the church. Lumber was still piled about, the ground was hard-packed and bare. Beside the building was a small residence which Neil decided might be the priest's home. Faith stayed in the car while he went inside. He returned in a short time with some books and an explanation. After one look he had decided this was not the priest to give the instructions, he said. The man was overworked and not the person to spend the time Neil wanted spent. But he had a *Question and Answer Book* that explained most of the points customarily raised by Protestants, and a number of tracts. She could start with those and fire away at him when he was around. What he really wanted was for her to come to Athens and take instructions from a Father Endicott in Dartmouth, who was tops, a scholar and a man of culture and charm.

"Isn't it funny," she asked comfortably, sliding down in the seat and over nearer to him, "we're both so eager for the other to see the best of our religion and our families?"

"That's normal," said Neil. But Faith wished there were a way of loving that had less tension. "Let's go and have a good dinner out at that new place on the highway. I couldn't get away from the office on time so just caught a snack at a drive-in. If I'm to have the steak for which my mouth waters, I've got to get it chewed before midnight, for tomorrow's fish day at our house."

"Do you have to be as exact as that?" Faith asked. "I mean, must you watch the clock?"

"If we didn't, we'd get slipshod and the sacrifice would be meaningless. Some arbitrary regulations are necessary."

She was so tired when Neil said good night that she left the priest's book on the dining table. When she reached the kitchen the next morning her mother was sitting on the step stool, thumbing its pages.

"Where did you get this?" she demanded.

"Neil asked the priest over here at the new Catholic church for something to give me. I wanted to look at it last night but Neil insisted I'd have time to do that when he wasn't around. Why?"

"This would insult the intelligence of a literate eight-year-old, and must have been written with only the most ignorant Protestants in mind. Even the questions are foolishly simple. The Catholics can do better than this. They have some excellent philosophy if you want to dig into Thomas Aquinas. My objection is that they make him the ultimate. All theology ends with him, so to speak. Still he was a great thinker, and I'm sure he must twist in his grave at the sight of this."

"I'll tell Neil what you said, and I'm sure he'll bring something else," Faith said laughing.

But when she told her mother that he wanted her to go to Athens and take instructions at the cathedral in Dartmouth, Faith could see the disappointment and disapproval in her mother's face. Their home was turning into a battleground of Catholic-Protestant controversy, with Faith trying to defend the Catholics. Sometimes it was good-natured sparring, but at times the venom crept in. Faith could not see why her mother felt so strongly about signing papers saying her children could be reared in the Catholic faith.

"If it doesn't bother me in Neil, Mother, surely it won't bother me in my children."

"You may change your mind. You may sometime find that you do actually have a heritage worth transmitting—one that you haven't appreciated. More than that, such a concession makes your husband the preferred parent, and his family the preferred grandparents. Children almost always turn to the ones who hold similar religious beliefs. We'll be cut off from passing on our convictions. Have you thought of that?"

"Mother, nothing could throttle you!" Faith declared with doubtful admiration. "The Catholic Church, not you, should do the worrying. Besides, isn't that an un-Christian way to look at it? For a wife to be jealous of how much the children will think of their father, or the grandchildren of the other grandparents? It doesn't sound worthy of you, Mother!"

41

"It may be un-Christian," her mother conceded. "But, if so, the Catholic regulations inspiring it are in the same category. I've never claimed I possessed utter unselfishness though it doubtless is necessary for Christian perfection. But there's much more involved than just jealousy, even religious jealousy."

But, opposed as she was to Faith's going to Athens, Margaret McLaren stayed up into the night to help her daughter finish a new summer dress.

Faith was glad Neil took her over for the first conference with Father Endicott. He was so at ease himself and the priest was so gracious that her timidity wore off. She even asked a few unimportant questions. But with Neil there she did not want to say much.

"Keep in mind," Neil said on the way back, "many statements will be made flatly. The Church knows where it stands and has no hesitancy about stating it. But this doesn't necessarily mean that you believe it. It's my faith that's being preserved."

"I doubt if it needs any protection," she said, laughing a little uneasily. "It seems pretty well grounded to me."

"I'm Irish from way back, and we don't convert easily. Just don't give Father Endicott any occasion to think you're planning to proselyte. Ask questions if you like, but always with that charming innocence you use on me, and he'll think he has another heretic on her way back to the true faith."

"My mother would say this was dishonest," Faith protested. But Neil could see nothing wrong with it.

The second day he could not go with her. She could have taken his car and gone alone but Mrs. Mackaig offered her company and there was nothing to do but accept gracefully. She hated to appear ignorant before Neil's mother, so there was a short, stilted session. The next day Molly Moriarity went along and it was much better because Molly asked questions too. The lesson turned to the matter of approach to God. The priest elucidated the belief in the intercession of saints, the stored-up credits, and the utter mercy of God. Faith was almost bursting with questions to fire at Molly when they reached the car.

"Why didn't you ask Father Endicott?" Molly demanded. "That's what he's studied all these years for."

"I like your answers best," said Faith. "What I want to know is why you wander through all that maze of saints and angels and wind up with the Virgin Mary for your agent. You've no direct approach at all."

"It's not that bad," said Molly reassuringly. "We get a contact. More, I think, than you do with your I-can-find-Him-in-the-fields-and-woods-just-as-well theory. We have no intricate conventional network, but we think it is more pleasing to God than having people presumptuous enough to barge into his presence unannounced and flaunting their independence."

"Anyhow," Faith insisted, "even if it makes for a beautiful, courtly ceremony, I don't want to have to relay what I say through a courtier or lady-in-waiting."

"Just don't build up a prejudice about it," Molly advised in her pleasant, unrestrained way. "Always remember that Catholicism is much better than it appears to the naked Protestant eye."

After this Neil decided she would get more out of the experience if she went alone, so she would drop him at his office and drive his car. To her amazement,

43

the second day when alone, just as she rounded the corner of the cathedral to reach the offices in the rear, she came face to face with Brooks Marvin, whom she had known in ethics class in college. "Why, Brooks, what are you doing here?"

"Is the pot accusing the kettle of something?" he demanded. "I'm no doubt here for the same hellish reason you are. Who's feeding you this theological rot?"

"Oh, sh-sh!" begged Faith. "If someone should hear . . ."

"Maybe it would settle my mind. If I had known how bad it was, I'd never have started. But I'd do almost anything for Chris, and this pretty well proves it. I'm taking from a priest who's the prince of dogmatists."

"Father Endicott isn't like that. He's charming."

"Hand-picked, I'll bet. I've heard your boy-friend is well-heeled and that his family swings some weight in this area. Maybe you're getting preferential treatment."

"I hardly think that. But Neil did want me to come here."

"Trouble with me," Brooks went on, "I don't have the right comebacks and don't dare say what I think. I know these flatfooted statements are wrong, but they're hard to refute. They start from the assumption that God told them this and anyone who doesn't believe it is in a state of rebellion against God. No hint that the regulations have been garbled a bit from time to time as people saw fit. But if you think I'm going to keep my mouth shut forever, you're wrong. Some day I'll blow up and likely say all the wrong things."

The incident left Faith uncomfortable, more so because she must not repeat the conversation to Neil. If

44

they were to live happily together, they must stress the best of each other's religion. But the next day she asked Father Endicott some pointed questions about the dogmatic quality of Catholic teaching. He was ready with Bible quotations and historical proofs, some that seemed a bit far-fetched to Faith, but she reasoned that she was not trained to follow his line of thought. Then suddenly they were off the subject and she was being led delightfully along the path of the traditions of the Church and the time for her lesson was over before she realized it.

That evening when Neil was quizzing her she explained, "He thought I wasn't sufficiently impressed today, so he dipped into that international lore of superficial learning Catholics dote on displaying to the world. He used a lot of phrases I wasn't familiar with, tossed in some Latin, French, and a bit of Italian. Then he made a lot of references to Catholic literature. But I understood his tactics."

"You little heretic!" laughed Neil. "You're a worse sinner than I thought. What do you mean by superficial?"

"I mean things said over and over again till people believe them, whether they have a basis or not," Faith declared with sudden staunchness. "For instance that St. Thomas Aquinas is the greatest theologian of all time and all conclusions close with him. How can any thinking person believe that all of a certain line of thought was suddenly cut off with the death of one man? Even Christ said that people who worked in his name would do greater things than he had done."

Neil felt sure she had a wrong interpretation but he had no answer. He couldn't see why she hadn't asked the priest in the first place. "Maybe I need instruction, too," he admitted.

The other sessions went off smoothly and one night when they had gone for a ride, and the car was parked so they could see a shaft of moonlight hitting the tower of the cathedral, Faith told Neil that she would marry him and he might ask the priest to apply for the dispensation.

Whatever love he had lavished upon her before was now doubled. She wished that her own feeling were as positive, but behind her happiness was the shadow of her mother's grief and her father's doubt. Still she could not allow them to manage her life. Neil had kept this thought before her all the time. She loved and respected them, but her love was her own affair, even as theirs had belonged to them. If other people would keep out, he was positive they could make a go of it. Beyond the minimum demands of the Church, which neither he nor his family could help, everything would be done the way she wished. He would prove his love by this.

A few days later he brought her diamond. It was much more beautiful than any of her girl friends had been given. He had bought the best he could afford.

But an extended visit at the Mackaig home taught her much more about Catholicism than the instructions had done. It had been a venture into a different way of thinking, a different culture. There were other standards of conduct and even other aspects of morality. Things which were done at home without a thought might constitute a sin for a Catholic family. On the other hand they held a much less rigid attitude toward some moral issues than Faith's family. Neil's unconcern

46

when he lost twenty-five dollars gambling troubled Faith a little. But he laughed and told her it was a silly holdover from Puritan days. Protestants tried to make sins of such perfectly harmless things as gambling, moderate drinking, and innocent games, instead of stressing real sins like not going to church, flouting religious authority, or condoning divorce.

Not only was there a different morality, but there was a strange vernacular. The Mackaigs talked almost intimately of the saints, expecting no end of odd jobs from them and repaying the messenger service with candles and adoration. Purgatory was a region to be dreaded, evidently, more than hell—or at least it was more likely since none of the Mackaigs were mortal sinners. As a word it did not lend itself readily as an expletive, which might have accounted for the greater respect shown in its usage. Faith knew that the Mackaigs all seemed to figure on spending some time in this disagreeable region but transposing the concept of time into eternity seemed to puzzle the most erudite of Catholics. Even Father Endicott owned there was no basis for accurate measurements and the units of time were vague. There were indulgences to shorten the periods and masses for the dead helped, but it was all too complicated for explanation.

In this world of strange religious values people crossed themselves at unexpected times, said "God Bless You" when you sneezed, fasted before the Sacrament, abstained on Fridays and Ember days. They did penance. Certain things were mandatory that were matters of choice in the free world from which Faith had come. Here the sins were numbered and classified. Girls became brides of the Church, men took the Church as their bride. There were intricate and beautiful initiation ceremonies, often with inherited garments. There was music and poetry and art arising from the Church's fountain. One of the expressions that Faith liked best she heard on a day when Connie was in miserable pain and her mother was trying to ease and console her. "Offer your pain up to God, darling," Mrs. Mackaig suggested, and her face had none of the hard glitter, but looked like one of the pictures of the women saints, as she spoke. Faith could ask Neil about this one, and he explained that when one had a trouble or grievance too hard to bear alone, to remember the sufferings of Christ and how patiently he had endured, and then to offer up one's own troubles, even as he had offered himself as a sacrifice, was very helpful. "Don't you offer your troubles to God as a sacrifice?" he asked.

"I never heard it put that way. We'd say that we 'take them to the Lord in prayer' or we ask God to help us. We don't stress the matter of sacrifice so much."

Here and in other matters not specified by canon law they could talk freely. At times Neil even seemed interested in her viewpoint. She felt that she was one ahead of him when he became involved in transubstantiation and the mandatory fast that preceded Communion.

"It's a courtesy we owe to God," Neil insisted. "You can't ask so great a guest into your house without preparation. We can't see how Protestants can take God into their bodies with so little respect."

"Why, we don't take him into our bodies!" Faith retorted in amazement. "We wouldn't want him there. We take him into our hearts!"

48

"We take him to our hearts, too," Neil answered quickly.

Faith was particularly apprehensive when she heard that Neil's aunt, who had become a Reverend Mother, and the Bishop, might be invited to dinner. The elaborate Roman etiquette appalled her and she fled to Neil with a demand that he take her home before such a party could be staged.

"I'd be frightened to death," she protested, "more than with a Rear Admiral or a President of the United States."

"Just be your dear, natural self," Neil reassured her. "Don't worry. They all know you're a Protestant."

Catholics were very understanding at this point, or else they didn't expect much of Protestants generally. There was even an implication that God, himself, ignored in them sins for which the best of Catholics would sweat in purgatory, which, Faith thought, seemed unreasonable of him. But then the Catholic God seemed an unreasonable Creator in many ways—making arbitrary laws and with such dire results if they were not kept.

Toward the end of her visit Mrs. Mackaig invited her married daughters, with their families, to come and meet the girl their brother was to marry. Molly told Faith a number of interesting details about this part of the family.

"Celia's a lot like Neil," she explained, "Devout like he is, only more serious. You'll like her husband, Frank. He's a pill in his own way, but we're all fond of him. He's a non-Catholic, too. There'll be a houseful for they have three children."

"Do the others, Howard and Helena, have any children?"

"Sh . . . " laughed Molly. "That's a tender question. It's a moot point in the family whether they're flouting the Church's teaching on birth control, or whether they just haven't proved a productive combination. They've been married for three years with no visible evidences of the real purpose for which marriage was instituted. Aunt Cecelia is concerned for fear they are too worldly and thinks they may be falling away. Howard's a nominal Catholic. His mother was too but his father wasn't, so Catholicism was pretty well diluted as a religion before he inherited it, I presume."

Faith was glad for these identifying tidbits which helped place her prospective in-laws. Frank and Celia arrived first, their car about the vintage of the McLaren vehicle, and in something like the same shape. It was piled down with paraphernalia. The youngest child was ten months old and the equipment needed for it was comparable to that of four adults, so the father said. Then there was a child of three and one of five. Celia was exact and methodical like Neil, and handled her brood with an expert touch. Frank, her husband, was as unlike her as could be imagined. At once Faith loved him and, at the same time, wondered how Celia had happened to accept him. Frank was six feet four, raw-boned and grinning. His sheepish smile suggested that he had just put something over on someone, most likely his wife, but he seemed to be following her directions explicitly, though with quiet kidding. He would have fitted perfectly into the McLaren home and would have been understood, but he looked as out of place as a worn leather couch would have been in the Mackaigs' immaculate living room. The babies were adorable, well-trained small people, but Celia was much too busy with them for anyone really to know her.

Helena, the other married daughter, looked more like her mother than Celia did, except that the flash of glitter and chic that seemed only an over-dress on Mrs. Mackaig's face looked like the real thing on Helena. Of all the family, she appealed the least to Faith. Howard seemed interested in keeping the press in his trousers and not letting any of his nieces or nephews get him out of order. Faith felt that, with such an unfatherly attitude, perhaps it was just as well to have no children. But, of course, that wasn't what the priest had taught her. Howard and Helena had some friends to see and they spent most of the evening away, but Faith had an instinctive feeling that she could never have become acquainted with them at however close range. They had a protective patter of conversation to match the patina of worldliness which covered their personalities.

Though the most exact graciousness was bestowed on both couples, it was easy to see that the non-Catholic son-in-law was the favorite, and somehow, this was a comforting thought to Faith. They are more likely to feel I'm all right, since they are so fond of Frank, she thought.

Late in the afternoon the baby bit the end of its last nipple and Celia asked her husband to lay in a supply before the next feeding time. As Frank started for the car, he asked, "Any objection to my taking the family guest of honor along with me? I'll have mighty little chance to get acquainted."

It was exactly the chance Faith wanted. Frank was one of those people a stranger would approach on the street with perfect assurance and, in this case, he would be the man to answer questions the priest did not know, despite the clerical claims of the Roman Church.

"Well," said Frank, the minute they were in the car, "so you're over here learning how to be a safe spouse for a Catholic, I hear?"

"Yes," laughed Faith, feeling instantly at home with his banter. "Did you take instructions?"

"Did I? Can you imagine marrying Cele without it? I was all but an authority by the time I jumped the broomstick. And by now I can tell you a lot no priest knows or would advise."

"Has it . . . has the difference in belief . . . I mean, signing the papers, and all that . . . bothered you?"

"Not greatly. I don't let it. I naturally sit pretty easy in the saddle of life and, if the incense on the home altar gets too strong, and I'm in danger of being asphyxiated, so to speak, I sneak out till the air clears. Cele's a wonderful woman. I could have gone through ten states and not found her equal. So I string along and try not to cause her too much worry. I'm in a heck of a fix one way. My dad's a Methodist minister and my folks hate it so. I don't like that part. How about yours?"

"They are pretty apprehensive. That's one reason I was so glad when I heard you were a Protestant. I think it may comfort them."

"You'll work out a philosophy in time. I just keep my mother thinking that nothing will ever make me become a Catholic and at the same time keep Cele from utter despair. After all, it's a mean man that won't promise a woman like Cele anything she asks."

"Promise her anything?" Faith asked incredulously.

"Note, I said: promise. Nothing about fulfil. But I do want Cele happy and I'm blamed sure God is a lot more understanding than she's got him pictured in her own mind. So I'm in a better position to take chances than she is. I've even hoped that, if I should die before she did and she would call in a priest, as I'm sure she would, hoping I'd make a deathbed confession of my belief in the Church, I'd try to muster a sign of contrition, or something, just before I faded out of the picture."

"Why, Frank Halstead!" cried Faith, "What a wicked, blasphemous thought! And right at the door of eternity, too!"

"You're getting me wrong," Frank protested. "These things are absolutely meaningless to me. They mean a lot to my wife, who is all but a saint. And, if I arrived at heaven's gate with my arm still swinging with the sign of the cross, when I don't believe in signs any more than you do, and St. Peter accused me of dissimulation, I'd explain it something like this. That he left a will, so to speak, but didn't make the inheritance clear. So it was more his fault than mine about all this confusion. By the way, Steve McLaren, who was at State about six or seven years back, wouldn't happen to be your brother, would he?"

"He certainly is."

"I thought he might be. I knew if he was, you'd be used to my line. Steve and I hit it off well together." Frank must have caught an apprehensive look on her face, for he added, "Don't worry. You're marrying into one of the finest families in America. Neil's a prince in anyone's religion. He and Cele are the cream of the family. Connie's too young to tell about now and she has this nunnery bug in her head. Helena and Howard are pretty lax, I would guess. They'll try to jump on the band wagon around the last bend, I imagine, but that's about all. Of course they know the family will work hard on the purgatory business and they have the money to do it."

"Do they really pay for masses? Neil insists it isn't necessary. If you are poor . . ."

"That's a point I'm not too clear on. But Catholics resent it if you say much about the cost, so I'd lay low on that one. One thing I'm sure of. If you think there's anything a Catholic can do, and not get back into the Church—provided he'll spend the time and money—that's because you don't know mother Mackaig. But she's a pretty swell old girl at that."

Faith giggled. "The height of your disrespect, Frank, is in calling Mrs. Mackaig an old girl. It's worse than what you said about St. Peter."

"That's because she's a real person to you and, in your Protestant mind, St. Peter, as the keeper of the keys to the kingdom and standing by the golden gate, is unreal. You have a different conception of what it takes to reach heaven." It was the first time he had sounded serious. Faith found herself thinking—I'm just like the others, so much attracted to him that I hope he has the right conception of God and, of course, the right one is the one I have.

They had reached the corner drugstore, and Frank went in for the nipples. When he was back behind the wheel he took up the conversation again.

"I hope I haven't given you the wrong impression of this interfaith marriage business, Faith. It's a tricky matter and you can't face it with the rules that hold in other situations. Here's a family of good, devout people. No shamming or pretense, but a genuine effort to worship God and live decently with their fellowmen. But they're Catholics and Catholics have a phraseology that almost throws you for a loop at times. It makes them misunderstood, and sometimes hated. Often you can get a real bright one to interpret it and it makes sense. Molly's your best bet. She's sincere but it hasn't hit her as hard as it has the rest of the family. Neil's good, too. I think he's better at translating, as I call it, than Cele is. He's just as devout but, being a man, he's less emotional. The family won't heckle you too much. They'll try to slip a noose on you now and then but, with practice, you can get your neck out. They never intend anything but the best. And dad Mackaig's a prince."

"Do you go to Mass with Cele?"

"I used to, now and then. I use the kids for an excuse, mostly. Special occasions I tag along."

"Do you ever go to the Methodist Church?"

"I haven't gone there, either, lately. I don't know exactly why. But it's a nuisance to get to both services, so I tell myself that it doesn't matter. We've got a horrible old priest in our parish right now. Just lays 'em low. I can't see how they take it. But they're a disciplined group. Last time, after I heard him, I went right over to the Methodist Church to hear someone tell about the love of God in language I could understand. I had to get the taste of that priest out of my mouth. I sang 'How Firm a Foundation' and 'Blessed

Assurance' like I'd been a pillar in the church for years. But it did me good. There's something sort of simple and direct about the way the Methodists approach God, and I felt better for a week. I meant to start going again, but one thing and another came up and I didn't go back."

"Do you suppose you ever will?"

"Maybe. In a way, I'd be happier, I suppose. When Catholics stop going to confession and Mass, and get themselves excommunicated, they call it 'falling away.' Dad says Protestants don't fall away. They just disintegrate. Maybe the process of distintegration has set in with me. Anyhow, if I were you, I'd start right at the beginning going to your own church. Neil will respect you for it, and it might help in several ways. But I can tell you this, you won't find better Christians among any Protestants you know than the Mackaigs. Sometimes I think most of my problem has been that my wife's a better Christian than I am."

They were in front of the Mackaig home and Neil had just driven up and was coming toward the car, so Faith said hastily, "Thanks so much for asking me to go with you, Frank. I need to talk about these things with people who know. But I'm sure Neil and I can work it out, for he is so wonderful."

But revolving in the back of her mind all the week end was the thought that even the easygoing Frank had his problems. Here, again, was something she and Neil should discuss candidly, but when she tried to start the conversation, she could find no phrases to present her problem. So she decided it had better go undiscussed.

Two days later Neil took her back to Avalon.

Chapter 5

THERE is a low wall between us now, Faith thought. But there must be some hurdles for every couple. That was why people who lived together for many years grew to have such a deep understanding. One must not expect full understanding at first.

Since she had taken the instructions she really did feel better about it. It wasn't the priest, though he had done his part well. It was living with the Mackaigs for several weeks, venturing ever further and further into this world where one's love for God was described in poetic terms, and where soft music mellowed the harsh theology. Even abject obedience was dramatized, and the act of uncovering the innermost secrets of one's soul was laved with holy consolation. But she could not say these things to Neil, for he would not understand. Nor could she present her Protestant viewpoint, except in small doses. She must learn to do this tactfully but, in order to do so, she must know what she believed herself. Neil was sure that everything of value in religion had been tossed out by the Reformers—the little that was worth while in Protestantism was but the residue of Catholicism. She must study and be able to refute his charges.

She still pondered the matter of worship. Were Catholics—kneeling—their eyes on the crucifix—all actually thinking reverent, worshipful thoughts? Did a greater wave of adoration go up to God than when the Baptists at First and Lincoln Streets sang "Come, Thou Fount of Every Blessing," or the Presbyterians broke forth with, "The Lord is King, Lift Up Thy Voice."

The Catholics looked more worshipful, she thought, but perhaps they were better actors. She put the thought from her as unworthy. Besides, there was no telling in any congregation what proportion of the people caught the overtones of holy music beyond the clanging vibrations of their own production.

She was still troubled that her decision to marry Neil might cause a barrier between her and her family, so she worked harder than ever to present him and his beliefs in the best light, while trying to keep the family feeling on its customary, unreserved basis.

She had an overpowering desire to attend the Church of the Immaculate Conception and see if the Mass there affected her as it had the times she had gone with Neil. Very likely she would have to be married at this church since priests didn't seem to go to people's homes, not even to Catholic homes.

So one Sunday, a few weeks after coming back from Athens, she mentioned her desire, though not her reasons. To her delight her mother said, "I'll go along with you, if you'd like to have me. I used to browse around St. Patrick's when I was in New York and examine the images and study the symbolism. It's educational and even helpful to see how other people worship, though Catholic churches always seem cluttered to me. I couldn't commune regularly in such a spiritual mess. I need a straight road, so to speak. Still,

58

I know many great souls have found God through that maze."

This seemed quite a concession from her mother. Faith could not imagine her either as kowtowing to a bishop or imposing on the saints. She was a forthright and independent person, who would transact her business directly with God, and to him alone would she bow. He was the Trinity to her, but it was a Trinity so close as to be almost a unit, and about it her thinking was clear. Some of her ancestors had come to this country to establish a church without a bishop and a country without a king. Like them, she wanted neither, if it meant subservience. Still, she had married an Episcopalian and had often gone with him to Holy Communion, though she never went forward to take the Sacrament. She would have her Communion without the elements, and it was beyond the province of any priest or minister to bar her access to God. Yet she loved the *Book of Common Prayer* and used it devotionally.

When Margaret and her husband were near a Friends' meetinghouse they would go in together and sit quietly, waiting for the Spirit. They felt it came to them both from within and from without. Through the years it had hovered over their home. When they had moved to Avalon before Faith was born, they had adjusted to the Congregational Church. As the years had passed they had taken to responding to the Communion invitation because it said, "Come, not because you must, but because you may. Come, not to express an opinion, but to seek a Presence."

Faith and Steve had both been baptized as babies. Margaret thought the ordinance unnecessary, but it meant much to John. It was the way into the Christian church, in his thinking, and he wanted his children to be a part of it. They might need more sanctifying grace than their mother, he said, and might have to have it supplied from without, since only rare souls were born who could sit in the white light of God's presence and catch his Spirit without outward and visible means. Steve had been taken to Athens for baptism, but Faith had been presented to God in the Congregational Church, when she was much too young to remember anything about it.

In her early teens the pastor had a class before Easter. Since many of her friends were uniting with the church at that time and her parents were willing, she had joined too. But it was not a very meaningful service and she had always held a casual attitude toward it. There had been none of the time-tried phraseology of the Confirmation Service, none of the sense that the Holy Spirit had been bestowed by the laying on of hands in succession from the apostles.

"That wouldn't matter to me," her mother would always come back. "But there was no commitment, no challenge. Those young people didn't know anything had happened to them. I wish we had a minister here like some of the men at the service when I went out as a missionary teacher. We knew we were sticking our necks out. And from a Congregational shelter, too!" From such a background, Faith thought it would be interesting to attend Mass with her mother.

It proved a disappointing experience. Faith tried to analyze her own reactions. Perhaps she was disappointed because she wished so much to have it seem impressive to her mother. Certainly it was nothing like it had been in the cathedral in Dartmouth.

The choir chirped uncertainly and the priest's vestments were not glamorous, as they had been at the cathedral. The words were said so fast it sounded like a race against time. The priest looked worn and concerned. He had a number of intense interests and these he stressed without tact and in a raucous voice. He wanted his parishioners to dig down in their pockets and give more money. He wanted them to keep their dirty shoes off the kneelers. He wanted every Catholic child enrolled in the school which the sisters would be opening September twentieth. He wanted a lot more volunteer help to clean up the debris in the yard and plant shrubs and lay sidewalks. Even the Protestants in town showed more interest in their churches than his parish, he said. His tone indicated that he was comparing them to the greatest unit of sloth he knew. But he ended with a few words about holy Mother Church being the sole guardian of the truth. If you believed this (and it was indisputable) and fell away, you would go to hell. Yes, you would get there even quicker than the Protestants!

Faith was sick about the whole thing. It was so unlike the Mass at Dartmouth, with Neil worshiping beside her.

"Wasn't that awful?" she moaned as soon as they were in the car. "I did want you to see a beautiful Catholic service, Mother. Then we got into that!"

"Don't worry," said her mother. "I've seen some very effective ones. This priest is evidently overworked to the point of utter irritation."

It would have been easier if her mother had disagreed or been critical. When Neil came late in the week she told him about it in her most candid outburst so far, then was concerned for fear he might be hurt. But he was surprisingly sympathetic.

"I could have guessed it would be that way," he said. "The people of the parish could see the reason. But to outsiders it must have sounded bad."

"Neil, how can we have such a horrid person perform the marriage ceremony? And, if we can't be married in the sanctuary, where could we have it unless the priest will come to our home? His house isn't decent and the little chapel isn't finished, because I looked."

"What would you think of coming to Athens and being married in St. Aloysius? You've been there with me and, since it's my home parish, it would be easier to get the dispensation."

"I know I don't want it in this church here," Faith said. "But all my friends are here in Avalon, and mother will think it terrible to have it out of town."

"They could have a reception here, or a special party the night before, perhaps," Neil suggested hesitantly.

"I wouldn't want to wear my dress and veil before the real thing. Couldn't we have the minister marry us here, then have a second ceremony? I'm sure it's sometimes done that way."

"It's against the Church's teaching, honey. I'd be sinning with my eyes open, and you wouldn't want that. It would take no end of work to get me back into the Church."

"What unreasonable laws, Neil!" she burst out in her distress. "How can you believe in a Church that is so harsh and dictatorial?"

62

"It doesn't seem as harsh and dictatorial, as you call it, to me as it does to you, darling. In the first place, I know these laws were made for a good reason. Because I find them hard to obey now doesn't make them wrong. Besides, if I loved my Church and obeyed her only when it was easy, what would my loyalty be worth? Not much, would it?"

When he left he had extracted a promise that she would talk it over with her parents, though she knew that, in the end, Neil would win out, as he always did. She hated to have him guess how miserable the thing made her, and she deliberately put from her mind how much she knew it was costing her mother in suffering.

There could no longer be any happy planning. The old free, sparring way of talking to each other was gone. It was all factual now—just a polite effort to get things done with the least possible conversation.

One of the unhappy incidents took place when Neil brought the forms which her parents were to sign to obtain the dispensation. Neil said they were largely to produce proof that she had not been married formerly, but several of the questions were annoying. They had to be made out by a priest and answered under oath, just like a legal paper. This ruled Margaret out for she stated definitely that she would not take an oath. She would affirm, but that was all.

"Did you read these forms, John?" she demanded, displaying them on the table the next morning. "They ask if you are giving your consent for your daughter's marriage. Now are you?"

"Jumpin' Jehosephat!" said John, who was usually hard to ruffle, "don't the idiots know this is America?

Faith is of age and, whether or not I approve, there isn't a blasted thing I can do about it!"

"Oh, Mother," pleaded Faith. "Don't let father talk that way! If he goes to the priest with that attitude, he may queer the whole thing. At least, Daddy, you could say you thought Neil was a fine man and . . . and . . ."

"And equivocate and hedge. . ."

"But you do like him," Faith pleaded.

"Let me see those symbols of domination that the Catholic Church still swings over the heads of freeborn Protestants in this great land of ours," said Steve, reaching for the offending forms. "Don't worry, Sis. I'll go over and do some double-talking for you, if necessary. We can explain that mother, having been reared in a Quaker home, is opposed to taking an oath. I came instead. Let me look 'em over and see if there's anything in them that disqualifies me."

He read the forms aloud, annoyingly. Catholics weren't the only ones who knew how to make people uncomfortable, Faith thought resentfully. It seemed that, between the Roman Church and her own family, not a stone had been left unturned.

"What's this about whether you're a heretic or an infidel?" Steve demanded.

"I'm a heretic," said Faith wearily. "It just means that I'm a baptized Christian but outside the Catholic Church, which to them is the true religion. People who aren't baptized are infidels, no matter what they believe."

"You mean all our Quaker relatives are infidels?" probed Steve. "Hi, I'll have to get a letter off to Uncle Jack and Aunt Kate and tell them they are infidels so they can do something about it." He laughed in an effort to keep down the tension but the idea was not amusing to Faith. She was under such a strain that humor seemed a hollow thing.

"So people who don't believe that the use of water, or oil, or bread, or wine, or even words, are necessary for evidences of the Spirit, all are infidels to them," Margaret observed, as though she had not heard Steve's remarks. "What a strange attitude!"

"It's just a word—a technicality. Neil said so. Those words don't connote the same thing to them that they do to us. I'm sure they mean no insult," Faith explained.

"I wouldn't go that far," said her father. Then, seeing that she was almost in tears he relented a little. "Never mind, honey. I'll go over to the priest and dissemble and evade whatever is necessary to convince the Catholic Church that my daughter is fit to be a mate for one of its adherents. I feel like a purebred skunk doing it, but I'd feel still worse to let my daughter down. And you might tell Neil that this is the time when a Protestant needs to draw on the stored-up graces—when he gets in such a plight that he can't generate his own. Neil might do a bit of extra work with the saints for me in return for this."

"If I believed there were such a weird arrangement as a depository of credits, and its supply was inexhaustible, I wouldn't borrow so much as one teaspoon of favor!" said Margaret. "My soul is my own responsibility!"

"Since I have no religious scruples to interfere with my doing a Christian deed, I'll be happy to take oath on any side of any question that will make for good feeling," said Steve. "What do you want me to say about your ideas on birth control?"

"Just say that you know I'm eager to have a family and love children and that you don't know beyond that," Faith instructed.

"Just wipe from my mind that profound conversation we had about planned families . . . before you met Neil?"

"Steve, you don't have to remember everything I've said since I got out of high school," Faith protested.

"You surely don't aspire to have a baby every fifteen months to help swell the membership of the Catholic Church, do you?" asked her father.

"Oh, quit being so hateful, all of you!" Faith implored, and her voice sounded like a wail. "Neil doesn't want more children than we can take care of well any more than I do. Very few educated Catholics take those statements literally."

"How do they get around them?" asked her mother.

"Different ways. Neil said to tell you just to say you didn't know about points like that. Father Endicott told him that was the way to do."

"This form says you have to swear you've never been instructed," said Margaret. "And here is Faith relaying the very things you are to say to one priest from another priest, and all under oath!"

"Hand those obnoxious questionnaires back to me, Mother, before you burst a blood vessel," said Steve.

"I hate this more than any of you can guess," said Faith, "and I'd never do it for anyone but Neil. It's terrible to ask you when you all feel as you do. Neil hates it, too, though he doesn't see some of the implications that you do."

"Let's get the thing over with at once, while the instructions are fresh in our minds," Steve suggested.

66

Faith did not come downstairs to get the report when the men came back, but she could hear her father sputtering, so she leaned over the stair rail to catch every word.

"And after we got through perjuring ourselves . . . "

"You didn't swear on the Bible, Dad," Steve cut in. "He used a missal. For a Protestant, that would surely dilute the sin."

"Nothing in my own mind mitigates the fact that I lied. I said I didn't know what my daughter believes about birth control, and I know good and well that she's been taught that children are the gift of God, but, like any other blessing, they can be overdone. If she has a horde of little Catholics, beyond her strength to bear or look after, it won't be willingly, I'm sure."

"I doubt if Catholics hold to that any more than we do, Dad," Steve consoled. "Just note the families of the educated ones. Faith should be in good hands."

"Maybe she will," John conceded grudgingly. "I have a feeling that Neil is better than his beliefs. Anyhow, after the papers were all finished, the priest gave me a sour smile, and asked what I thought of these precautions. Imagine it! Finally I said it seemed strange to me that so many questions were asked and never once did they touch on whether or not my daughter was chaste, or intelligent, or had a good temper, or any of the spiritual graces, or would make a good wife for any man, Catholic or Protestant. Until this knot is tied I suppose I can't say the rest I had in mind but, once this outrageous ceremony is over, I may be compelled to go back and finish the discourse. If I do, the priest will be a surprised man. I doubt if he's used to what he'll hear."

Faith planned to work until nearly Christmas, then have the wedding a few days before. It would make a beautiful Christmas season. But Neil explained that it must be either before Advent, or after Christmas. Finally it was set for New Year's Day. She also had to give up the idea of a morning wedding because, without the Nuptial Mass, which they could not have in a mixed marriage, the ceremony could not be performed till one in the afternoon. At Thanksgiving Neil took her over to talk with his mother about the plans.

Mrs. Mackaig suggested that Faith come to Athens several days before the wedding so that every item would be perfect. Faith could see that most details would be handled without her direction, but there was no way this could be helped since she couldn't afford to guess about the regulations. It isn't really my wedding, in a way, she thought, because there's nothing I can do about it. She suggested that Sally, who arranged flowers beautifully, should do the decorating. But Mrs. Mackaig explained gently that no Protestant could stand before the altar, so a woman from one of the greenhouses was to do it. Faith had not meant to say anything to Neil about this but, when they were alone, she burst out with the story almost before she knew the words were coming.

"I'm sorry, honey. I'll be glad when this falderal is over and you're really mine. It's because Protestants don't believe that the Body of Christ is on the altar and they don't approach it with reverence. If Sally believed . . . "

"But, if that were the Body of Christ, and it had the healing qualities you claim for it, why wouldn't they scatter it on the streets, or just anywhere, to heal and help? Why let it cause dissension?"

"I never thought of that," Neil said solemnly. "But I'm sure it wouldn't be effective unless people made themselves ready to receive it."

"Maybe not," she said slowly, sorry for her outburst. She knew Neil was horrified at the suggestion.

After that she made few requests. She had asked to have just a few guests and that the wedding be kept simple, but she knew the guest list was long, for the Mackaigs had many friends and wanted to make an occasion of it. She wanted Neil's friend, Boyd Conner, to sing "Ich Liebe Dich," but it wasn't permitted in the church. There was no use to suggest "O Perfect Love, All Human Loves Excelling," though she loved it, because it was distinctly Protestant. But "The Lord's Prayer" was certainly suitable. When she found it, too, was banned because it closed with "For Thine is the kingdom, and the power, and the glory" she was even more hurt. What could be wrong about that? It was in the New Testament, which the priest quoted as authority when it pleased him. It was worship to God which did not deprecate the Catholic Church or offend in any way. Surely Catholics also believed that power and glory were attributes of God and that the kingdoms of the earth were his. But the priest was quite outspoken about it. This was the form of the Pater Noster which was in common use in Protestant churches and had come to connote Protestantism in Catholic minds. Authorities agreed that the words were a marginal gloss, interpolated by some copyist who had in mind words borrowed from the Greek liturgy, the priest explained. He made little effort to be gracious to a

Protestant bride and assumed she should know that anything that savored of Protestantism would not meet with his approval. He was certainly different from Father Endicott, who had gone all out to make her feel at home.

Both Neil and Mrs. Mackaig were there when the priest made his curt refusal and they were equally troubled and made every effort to soften the harshness of the rebuff, but their kindness and sympathy only made it harder to keep back the tears. Faith made no attempt to answer and declined to make further suggestions. I'll go through this horrid wedding for Neil, and only for him, she thought. After that she would have him, but he could go to his church and she would go to hers. She would keep away from Catholic regulations forever.

Mrs. Mackaig hovered over her as though she were an orphan, which she suddenly felt she was. Father Corrigan, Mrs. Mackaig explained, was a wonderful man, but he lacked certain social graces, and he could not realize how much details meant to a bride. He had worked so hard to build up the parish, having been one of the first priests in the area. In his early years he had suffered considerably at the hands of Protestants and the experience had seemed to make him exceptionally rigid. Mrs. Mackaig also agreed that "Ich Liebe Dich" would be sung at the reception in the home, if Faith wished it, though the other songs were not suitable for a wedding reception. Faith saw at once that Neil's mother actually did not know either selection but would not take chances with anything that skirted on Protestantism in a group that would be largely of the Catholic belief though she was very eager for Faith to be happy. She continued to consult the bride about details which made no difference, but Faith found it difficult to act natural. It's the priest's wedding or Mrs. Mackaig's, but not mine, she thought—I'm a puppet, pulled by strings.

Molly drew her aside. "Listen, sweet. Don't let all these people push you around. If you get in a tight spot, give me a wink. I can't do much about Church regulations, because they have us over a barrel there, but in other matters, I know some tricks. Aunt Cecelia likes this sort of thing and takes charge naturally."

"I suppose it doesn't really matter," said Faith, wearily. She wanted to cry. "I should have insisted on just getting it done quickly, since I couldn't have any of the say about it."

"I suppose we're conditioned to this—to regulations that seem so interfering to Protestants," Molly said in her pleasant, objective way. "Things that throw a Protestant into a tizzy, we take like the weather."

"It's because we're used to thinking it's our right," said Faith.

It always did her good to talk with Molly. Still she kept thinking of Anna Bickle's wedding and how they all helped decorate the church. The minister was there, directing, but laughing and helping. Just like anyone else, only they all felt he was the authority on etiquette. It had been fun to rehearse and there was no friction. If people disagreed, the last word belonged to Anna, because everyone said it was her day. Her mother was there, too, and so proud. I'm not having any day, Faith thought sadly, and mother isn't either. When she went to bed that night she cried.

She went home the next day, then Steve brought her

back for the final rehearsal. He was to be an usher. Coming over with him saved Neil from making the long trip twice. Steve was delighted to hear that his old friend, Frank Halstead, was to be Faith's brother-in-law, and he looked forward to renewing his friendship.

He was no sooner inside the door when he began noticing Molly, which gave Faith a new cause for apprehension. Molly was positively the most interesting young woman she knew, but Steve must not become attracted to her, or she to Steve. One more such affair would kill her mother.

She felt less an orphan with Steve in the room and he managed to be near a number of times when she wanted him. Her father would give her away, though protestingly, but Steve was acting in his place tonight. It was humiliating to have Steve see how many of her pet plans had been changed, but now it was a matter of living through the wedding. Then there would be a new start.

Steve began in his usual taunting way, asking in a whisper if Neil was going to wear the veil and carry the bouquet, since he had usurped so many of the prerogatives of the bride, but, when he saw that Faith was struggling with her own sensitiveness, he smiled and said, "Never mind, kid. A wedding is often something of a trial. But it'll be over at this time tomorrow, then everything will be swell. Neil's a fine guy and you don't want this to overshadow what he really is."

Steve had a way of striking at basic truths. He patted her hand as it rested on his arm. She must try to smile, for Neil was watching her anxiously, and she was sure he hated the affair almost as much as she did, for he was so quiet.

72

There was another discussion about witnesses because Sally, who was maid of honor, couldn't sign, being a Protestant, nor could any of Faith's family. Even Neil's best man was ineligible. So members of the Mackaig family had to be moved into place as inconspicuously as possible. Father Corrigan was out of sorts because so many heretics were in the wedding party, and in the sanctuary, too. He said something about not allowing it there if he had known, for the bishop would not approve. But Mrs. Mackaig offered to talk with the bishop and, evidently, the matter was straightened out, for nothing more was said.

Though Margaret McLaren wore a becoming new dress and was seated in the correct place for the bride's mother, and even stood in the receiving line as she should, she did not seem the mother of the bride, and Faith felt she was a remote person, not her own mother at all. It took more than location to sustain relationship, she decided. Her mother smiled but her face was drawn, and lacking its usual vivacity. Since the preponderance of the guests were friends and relatives of the groom, and even the ceremonial features were strange, Faith felt an outsider.

She appreciated the way Frank and Steve enjoyed each other and how they tried to make it the merry occasion a wedding should be. Molly and Sally tried hard, too. But having the pictures taken was a trial and her hand shook so when she started to cut the cake that Neil had to help her.

When he suggested that they make a rapid getaway she sensed as never before that, despite his conforming to all the wearisome regulations, he was a most understanding man. When the bouquet has been tossed to the waiting girls and the rice had been thrown, Neil swept her into the car. Farther away they would rip the decorations from it. He drove rapidly till they reached the top of the hill, where they could look back on the lighted city, saying little but managing to keep her hand under his on the steering wheel. Then he swung the car to the side of the road and slowed to a stop.

"From now on," he said, kissing her, "it'll be you and me against the world. I didn't like that fussy wedding a bit better than you did. But mother was so thrilled with it and somehow we let it get out of hand. I was so pulled every which way between trying to get the dispensation, appease the priest and coddle the bishop, and at the same time gratify mother! But let's forget it. Let's forget everything but each other. Oh, darling, what a lovely wife you are!"

Chapter 6

THEY walked again in the little enclosed garden where they had first felt close to each other. There were the hard paths, the acacias, the woody geraniums, now without blooms. The shrine was there but now, when Neil crossed himself, Faith understood the significance.

The bright California sun warmed them, bringing objects out in sharp relief. There was the old wall, more plainly seen now that some of the vegetation was gone, and it seemed a little higher. But one could still see over it in many places and survey the hills of waving grass at one side, and at the other, the blue Pacific. It was a dreamy garden, with the charm of age. Something in it said that seasons would come and go, but it would remain—a haven for lovers, a spot of shelter for the sorrowing.

Near the cloisters the vegetation had more moisture and was a deep, rich green. There were flowers here whose names and faces were new to Faith. There was still the wishing well and Neil dropped big bright coins in its watery depth, and wished that they would always stay near to each other.

"I'll always think of this as our garden, Neil," she whispered. "I hope they never take it away."

"I doubt if they will. One of the Brothers told me they might keep one of the buildings as a home for older priests. With the shift in population in this area, the school is needed several miles farther south."

They had come to California for their honeymoon. Uncle Jack and Aunt Kate took this time for a long-planned trip to Texas, and Faith and Neil lived in their cottage. It was two weeks of heaven and Faith's confidence in the ability of people to live and love together, regardless of creed, had come back. Once more they could talk frankly. Of course they must avoid the jutting rocks that rose up now and then as a barrier on this footway where they were searching for the flowers of grace. But they would allow nothing to mar their harmony.

By different paths their souls would seek God, but their hands would remain clasped, and the beauty of one trail should spill over and add to the beauty of the other.

It had to be so.

The little home was a dream house, a little too small for an expanding family, but it was planned for additions. Faith had never been so happy in her life. She chose color schemes, made drapes and pillows, did odd jobs of painting, and even planted a garden.

Neil was wonderful. She used the word a thousand times a month to describe her husband. He was interested and glad to give his opinion, but he didn't cramp her style. The budget, though not large, was adequate for their scale of living, and more than Faith had been accustomed to at home. Neil would take out what he needed for personal expenses, they would allow for savings and current bills, then the rest was hers. He never questioned her judgment.

"It's all yours," he would say. "If it buys one thing, it won't buy another. Juggle it to your heart's content, darling."

It took some scheming to manage a piano, but this was a must, for Faith wanted to play and have Neil sing. They made new friends through Neil's work and through a club which Faith joined. They found old acquaintances and cultivated them.

Brooks Marvin and Christine Fordham were now married and living eight blocks away. They were a good couple with whom to spend an evening and, if the conversation touched on religion, there was a fair balance. When Brooks made his near-blasphemous remarks, which must make Chris cringe, Neil was bright enough to set him in his place. Since Chris was so patient, and absolutely without comeback, even Faith often rejoiced to see Brooks flattened out. On the whole the friendship grew. Faith found herself interested in mixed couples. It gave one an idea what to expect and how to handle hard problems.

Patricia O'Brien had married Spud Mellow—a bad come-down from Ted Neilson, who had thrown her over because of the prenuptial promises. Spud would have been a trial, spasmodically at least, if all other things had been equal, but he had refused absolutely to have a Catholic ceremony, and Pat had finally persuaded herself that she could be happy without it. She was a girl who really needed a home, having always lived with relatives. Faith felt sorry for her, though Spud, with all his loud-mouthed statements and crude ways, was devoted and brought home a good pay check.

They had been married by a judge, since that was the lesser of two evils to Pat.

From the beginning, Faith took Frank's advice and started regular church attendance. Since Athens had no Congregational church, except a little one out in the suburbs, she began attending a neighborhood Presbyterian church. She could even walk if necessary. Neil seemed surprised when she made this decision.

"I thought you were a Congregationalist," he protested.

"I am. But I'd just as soon be a Presbyterian. It's all the same to me. They're a lot alike."

"They why don't they unite?"

"In some places they do. It's more the form of government. Some people like to have the congregation have the final word and that makes it a congregational form of government, whether it's Baptist, or what-have-you. With the Presbyterians, it's the presbytery that has the say. But we sing the same hymns and all that."

"Sounds like a terrible hodgepodge to me," Neil observed, "but it'll be less complicated than getting you clear out to a Congregational church. Will you have to be confirmed all over?"

"Heavens, no! My church in Avalon will send a letter at my request, commending me to the fellowship and care of this church, or something of the sort. It's all very simple."

Neil seemed puzzled but he approved of her attendance. Remembering the scornful remarks he made about the laxness of Protestant churchgoing, she was as faithful to her services as he was to his. Occasionally they had jolly arguments. Though well educated about his own church's teaching, he had wild ideas of Protestant beliefs, but he hated to own it. He kept insisting—perhaps to tease her—that Henry VIII was one of the reformers, and typical of those who split the church with heresy.

"You are always trying to make out that Henry was a reformer," she would sputter. "You know better than that! The reformers were people who sought a more direct way to God. What Henry seems to have wanted was a direct way to Anne Boleyn. Protestants consider him just as much of a skunk as Catholics do!"

"He was on your side, though," Neil would insist, sometimes with a mischievous glint in his eye.

"We don't want him, anyway. He's always getting more of both praise and blame for the Reformation than he should have. He got caught in a tangle with Catholic in-laws, a vacillating pope who couldn't come to a decision, and a country that was clamoring for a male heir. Add this to his way with women, and their way with him, and what have you?"

"We had a split church."

"I agree. But it doesn't make a reformer of Henry. The men who had been longing for Protestantism, and thinking through the new theology, were the ones who put the Reformation across in England."

Except to tease her, he showed but little interest in her side of the argument. After all, he knew what he believed. But he would cautiously admit that the church of the sixteenth century did need a housecleaning, though he thought those who wished to do so should have been more patient about it. No use going off the deep end. With a little more loyalty, it could have been settled without a split. Sometimes she thought he acted almost intentionally blind.

"It was a whole new idea, or collection of ideas," she

explained. "Some people felt the church should be supreme. Some that it should be fitted to national tendencies. Some believed in a gathered church, like the early Christians had. Great men suffered on both sides. Many of them must have had friends or relatives who disagreed with them. I suppose they just couldn't get their ideas across—just as I can't get mine."

She was sitting on the step stool in the kitchen, her blue apron with its yellow rickrack making a pretty color blob against the yellow wall. Neil was watching her, his eyes laughing. She knew he was scarcely paying attention to what she said.

"I suppose they got so concerned and wrought up they just couldn't help persecuting each other. And sometimes, Neil, when you're perverse, and won't admit that the Catholic Church is the tiniest bit wrong . . . why, I could almost persecute you!"

But he just threw back his head and laughed, then strode to the step stool and swung her off and around the kitchen several times, kissing her over and over again. "Damn!" he said softly. "What a heretic you are! What a cute heretic!"

"Will you have to confess that you called your wife a damned heretic, or would that be considered a point in your favor?" she teased, kissing him back again.

"I didn't call you a damned heretic, you little sinner. You know I didn't. I said you were a cute one. And I, personally, am glad we don't live back in those days, for one of us would have been in for a bad time."

"I'd have been on the wheel," said Faith. "And what a time it must have been for stomach ulcers."

Though the conversation ended happily, thanks to Neil's good humor, she felt a little conscience-stricken at her outburst. So the next Sunday she went to Mass with him, then on to the Presbyterian service. She was beginning to find the Mass helpful because it gave her time to think. When one understood the words and what the people believed, it did something, even for an onlooker. Too, it was a sally into Neil's spiritual homeland, and seemed to bring them closer together. Anything which welded their union was worth time and sacrifice. She read books on Catholicism, the lives of the saints, the poetry of Crashaw and Thompson and Chesterton. She tried to find why Cardinal Newman left the Anglican Church. Neil was moved at her efforts. He brought home Catholic music for her to learn, and suggested all manner of helps.

But, much as she loved this, she felt there should be some reciprocation. Her mother had said, "It will be difficult living with a man whose deepest loyalties demand that he turn a deaf ear to your opinion on many subjects. There is a closed door between Catholicism and Protestantism which Protestants, particularly Protestants in love, often refuse to see. But it is there. You will go with him, but he'll not go with you."

Faith was determined to prove her mother wrong. Protestants didn't go at the thing the right way. They either kept entirely still and let the Catholic have free run, or they adopted a challenging air, putting the Catholic on the defensive. They heckled Catholics, making fun of their most sincere practices, like the necessity of abstaining on Fridays and their belief in purgatory. She tried hard not to do these things, but she knew that Spud and Brooks were both thoughtlessly cruel, if not intentionally so.

She must get Neil at least to peek into her spiritual country, if only to give her a feeling of mutuality.

"I went to Mass with you last Sunday, Neil," she would plead. "If you would go to Mass first, couldn't you go with me one Sunday? How great a sin is it?"

"I probably wouldn't get more than a few extra hours in purgatory. But it's against the teaching of the Church to participate in false worship. Still, if you'll promise to use some of my life insurance to get me out . . ." He always joked about it.

But Faith forgot to be tactful. "What a crude expression, 'false worship'! With all this poetry of God, which you call the phraseology of the Catholic Church, why can't you find a more gracious way of describing the praises of people who don't use the same pattern you do?"

Neil looked surprised. "It isn't very gracious, is it?" he conceded slowly. "But it was coined under stress, I presume. And even poets use strong language when roused."

Finally one day he said he would go with her to church. There was to be a special minister and Faith was sure the sanctuary would be full. She would hate to have Neil see a small congregation on a bright spring morning, with not even the weather for an excuse, when he was used to four well-filled masses of a Sunday morning. She hoped there wouldn't be some whispering, elderly women or inattentive high school girls for, at best, the service would not seem very reverent to him.

As they reached their seats the choir was coming in, singing, "Joyful, Joyful, We Adore Thee," which should show Neil that Protestants really did worship with praise and adoration, and the congregation was joining in with better-than-average singing. There was a little confusion as hymnbooks were shared, but it was a friendly action and she would not have known it happened if Neil had not been beside her. For the middle hymn they sang "I Love to Tell the Story" and then there was even better congregational singing. Surely he could see how the people enjoyed worshiping together!

Then they read well on the responsive reading. She wondered how it would seem to him to have the congregation participating. But even on the Lord's Prayer he would not open his lips, for that would be a sin. How strange that Christians could not say "Our Father" together! The choir sang "Seek Ye the Lord" for an anthem, with an excellent tenor taking the solo. But still he's not as good as Neil, Faith thought. His voice doesn't have that appealing quality. Wouldn't it be lovely if we could sing in the choir together, when we both so love music?

The sermon was a written discourse on using one's time to the best advantage. It was not nearly so direct as the message by the regular minister usually was, and Faith was disappointed. She found herself wondering why the speaker didn't attack slothful living with a good right-hander, instead of approaching it so gently. Neil would be more convinced than ever that all Protestants had fuzzy concepts of God, an utter disregard for beauty, and were led by soft-spoken men who were afraid of losing their jobs if they told the unpleasant truth. She could feel that he was coldly unimpressed and she was almost as disappointed as she had been the day she and her mother had gone to Mass in Avalon. Trying to praise the Lord through another's eyes, especially if that other one were clothed in prejudice, was worse than going through a maze of saints, she thought.

The closing hymn was "Our God, Our Help in Ages Past." It was one the congregation loved and a favorite of Faith's, yet she found it hard to form the notes. The words meant nothing to Neil. They had no significance of long use or of comfort in sorrow. They had never been sung at a family funeral or before someone left on a journey.

People milled around in a friendly way when the service was over but she and Neil left silently. She did not feel like looking up friends to whom she could introduce him. Perhaps she didn't want him to go with her after all, for he had no way of reaching out beyond the confines of the stated repertoire for the poetry of God. It was in the Catholic Church, and there only, that he could respond.

They were almost home when he patted her hand and said, "Well, honey, why don't you ask me what I thought?"

"I can tell without asking, Neil. I know you so well I can feel your responses. And you didn't like it."

"It had its points. But, with all respect to my own Church, I must say I think she is in error to forbid our attendance at Protestant worship."

"Why?"

"It makes us think it's something more than it is. I'm sure Catholics couldn't be persuaded to go there any more regularly than Protestants do, if there wasn't a single obstacle in their paths."

"Why wouldn't they go?" Faith demanded, trying not to take offense.

"Nothing happens. You sing some community songs.

If you like them and know them, they are O.K. But nothing really takes place."

"Like what?"

"Like having Christ's Body before you. In a Catholic church you know that, at a certain time, the wafers will become the Body of God himself. It means something to be in a place like that."

Faith was silent. The distance between their conceptions of worship had suddenly widened again. But this time she must not say the wrong thing.

"Not everyone can believe that, Neil."

"We think they could if they would pray for the gift of faith. God would give it for the asking. You don't want it, do you?" He asked the question almost anxiously.

"Sometimes I wish I could, or rather, I wish that we believed alike. But I would have to twist my mind around something that seems superstitious to me, and I'd never be happy in an authoritarian church. I wouldn't want someone else doing my thinking for me."

"There's no force put on my thinking, honey. I was brought up this way but, in a sense, I chose my religion, too. At least, I could get out of it without bodily harm."

"But as long as you believe it . . ."

"As long as I believe it—and I pray every day that this will be until death—I cannot waver. My course is pretty well mapped out, and I know where I stand."

"Part of yours seems wonderful to me, Neil. There are lovely things in Catholicism that I wish the reformers hadn't tossed out. But don't you ever want to look over the wall—to try to get a new conception of God?"

"There's more in the Church than I can grasp. Why should I want to try a new field?"

"I wish," Faith said, "that you would try to see something good in my religion—as hard as I try to see it in yours."

"Anyway, sweetheart, I see something wonderfully nice in you. As for that service—why the man didn't even spice it up by telling you that you'd go to hell!"

"And you missed it?"

"I'm not used to it in every sermon and I could spare that part better than some of the others. Still, the way I heard it, old John Knox made some pretty harsh remarks now and then to Mary of Scots. Judging by your service today, the Presbyterian church has deteriorated considerably in the past four hundred years. Then that jig tune they sang in the middle," he continued, "sort of a catchy thing about loving to tell the story. My gosh, honey, Protestants care so little about telling the real story of sacrifice and redemption that they don't even bother to teach it to their children! In four hundred years they haven't pulled themselves together to do one effective thing!"

"Neil Mackaig, how can you believe that?" she cried, then knew one reason she was so terribly hurt was that there was an element of truth in what he said.

Neil had gone with her and had seen only the weak spots. The great hymns, the congregational participation, the minister's helpful prayer, all had fallen on closed ears.

"Don't get me wrong, honey. I don't feel individual Protestants are all that way. But in the main it's so. The other day I picked up a Salvation Army lassie when I was coming back from Avalon. She was hitchhiking over because she had no money . . ."

"Men shouldn't ask girls into their cars," Faith teased, in hope of deflecting the seriousness of the conversation. "It's as dangerous, or more so than . . ."

"Don't worry. It's not my practice. But I took a chance on the basis of that becoming blue bonnet she was wearing. I started to say that, however wildly heretical I think the Salvation Army is, its members do something! They make sacrifices, stand on street corners . . ."

"Are you suggesting that, as a proof of my Protestantism, I stand on a corner and beat a kettledrum?" Faith asked with wicked demureness.

"Young woman, your place is in the home! My home, to be exact!" But he was grinning. Sometimes she wished Neil did not have such an adorably infectious grin. It was such a barrier to argument, and was always between her and her best comebacks.

It was no use. He would either be facetious, or loving, or opposing. She had to take him as he was and let him worship his way, while she worshiped hers. Or perhaps she hadn't found the right approach. She would study and read, on both sides of the question. And she would not give up so soon, for there must be a way of breaking down the barrier.

At Thanksgiving time their first baby was born—a boy who had his father's dark hair and his mother's dark eyes. Neil was the proudest of fathers, and the grandparents on both sides joined in the rejoicing. Faith would have preferred the Methodist Deaconess Hospital which, though not quite as large as St. Aloysius, had the reputation of giving excellent care. But Neil wanted her to try the Catholic hospital.

"The family know more people there," he urged. "And, if you don't like it this time, you can go to the Deaconess Hospital for the next one. Because we both want a next."

There was no valid objection to the Catholic hospital. If he had been hateful or dictatorial she could have refused. But he was so skilful about it, and always so appreciative when she yielded. No matter how she resolved to remain firm the next time, she always weakened. She knew her people would have been more comfortable if she had gone to a Protestant hospital, though they said little.

The baby was named John Stephen, because Neil didn't want his child named for him. By pure accident the names of her father and brother were both saint's names, so there was no friction. Mrs. Mackaig brought over a family baptismal robe, and she wanted a party at the home afterward. Faith must not do one thing except bring herself and the precious baby, she said. Mrs. Mackaig wrote a note to the McLarens, begging them to come. It would mean much more to Faith, she said, if her people were there.

But somehow the day reminded Faith of the wedding which was never really hers. It belonged to the Mackaigs and the Roman Catholic Church.

The McLarens went, even Steve, because the baby was his namesake, but none of them felt at home. All through the ceremony Faith kept seeing the baptismal service in the Congregational Church, and she knew her mother was thinking of this, too. There parents brought their children forward and promised to bring them up "in the nurture and admonition of the Lord" and they were baptized by the ancient Christian formula. Or it might be modernized into a dedication service where the child was consecrated to God, and to the service of his truth. The choir might sing "All things come of Thee, O Lord, and of Thine own have we given Thee." It was always simple. It had been done that way with her and many others. Some stayed by the commitment of their parents. Some, like her, had wavered. Her mother must be thinking that too. It was hard to keep back the tears.

She was the more annoyed because the night before she had found an English translation of the Catholic service and knew that one project at hand was casting out the devils. She had thought about it in the night and tried to decide exactly what she believed. Strange that she did think of it, for she had never been interested in theology until she met Neil. Surely babies were born of the love of God. Casting out devils was a holdover from the time when people really feared demons. The idea of using spittle was obnoxious to her, though when the sacrament actually was administered, she scarcely knew it was being done. The priest placed his stole, symbol of his priestly office, over the baby to indicate that it had been received into the fold, and had touched its nose and ears with spittle. Faith guessed that this practice had come from Christ's use of clay and spittle to heal the blind man. It added to her annoyance that Father Corrigan was old and sickly looking, and she had taken a dislike to him as a result of the friction at her wedding.

Neil, on the other hand, was deeply moved. Faith had delved far enough into Catholic reasoning to know that he believed this sacrament was transforming his child into a potential saint. It could now be an inheritor of the heavenly kingdom. If he thought of the devils and the spittle at all, he would accept them as a part of the sacrament of sanctifying grace, and he would ask no questions, because this was the Church's way of doing things, and the Church was always right.

Mrs. Mackaig was very sweet with Margaret McLaren, which, in a way, was too bad, for she meant it all so well. Margaret could see in it only the sweetness of the victor who could afford to be gracious because she was winning. No matter how desperately sincere Neil's family were, that was the way it would affect the McLarens. In a sense, Faith reacted as her family did.

She was both hurt and touched that night after Neil had said his own prayers, when he leaned over the baby's crib, and she knew he was saying a prayer for the child, for his lips moved and he crossed himself twice. But she was thankful her child had such a wonderful father and, without visible evidence that she was praying, she sent a supplication after his, asking that in some way they might learn to pray together. No doubt Neil had asked that too.

Chapter 7

EIGHT months after little Stevie was born, Faith knew that there was to be another child. Still, they had wanted a family and, once the first years were over, it would be good to have them of an age to enjoy each other. But it was more difficult for her to do her work than it had been the first time, for she was not at all strong.

"We'll have to have a longer interval between the next two, Neil," she said, and he made no protest. But again he mentioned the Catholic hospital. Was there any good reason why she objected to it? Any lack of interest or care? Any interference in having a minister call if she asked for one?

It had not occurred to her to ask for a minister. As for interest and care, the sisters had been delightful, a bit possessive about claiming the child as a Catholic, in that the mother was not, but in every other way above criticism. There was no real reason for refusing to go back to St. Aloysius. All she said in answer to Neil's probing was that she felt more at ease in Protestant surroundings.

"You should be getting pretty used to Catholics by now, honey," he said. "If it makes too much difference, change over. But we all like Dr. Brown. He's been a friend of the family for years, and I'm sure he'd rather you went to St. Aloysius."

In the end she yielded, fuming inwardly because she let herself be persuaded. But when the time came for the baptism of the second child, she took a firmer stand. "I'd rather it was done very quietly, Neil, and without a party," she said. "Since none of my people can ever be godparents, or take any part, I know they'd rather not come."

She could see he was troubled. "Mother always wants to make a big thing of it," he said. "I doubt if we can make her understand."

He doesn't try, Faith thought. I'll tell her myself.

But it was as she had thought. Mrs. Mackaig was definitely hurt at the idea that she should not ask Faith's parents. Surely they would wish to see their lovely little granddaughter baptized.

"Would you want to see a grandchild of yours baptized in the Protestant church?" Faith demanded.

"Why . . . why, it would be against our Church's teaching for us to go, my dear. We wouldn't have any choice in the matter. Really the situations aren't analogous at all."

"In a sense they are to us," Faith persisted. "It's difficult for me to have my children baptized into the Catholic Church. It's much harder for my parents. They're not in sympathy with the wording of the ceremony. They feel shut out because they can't be godparents or have any part. Steve doesn't care, for he has no convictions. But I don't want them, and the less fuss the better."

It was her first spunky spell about anything of the sort and left her feeling as though she had committed a crime. But it would have been worse to make her mother more unhappy.

"What did you say to mother to cut her up so?" Neil asked a few days later. He had never taken Faith to task about anything but tonight he was concerned.

Faith repeated the conversation as faithfully as she could. "Your mother can't see it, Neil, but to my parents, such things seem just like rubbing it in."

"It's just unbelievable to us," Neil said slowly, after some time in thought. "It's unbelievable that good people—like your folks—don't want children given Christian baptism and Christian training. We can't get it."

"We like them baptized and given Christian training," Faith said, "but we like some say in how it's done."

So the second baptism was very simple and there was no party afterward. Celia was sick so none of her family came and, now that it wasn't forced on them Howard and Helena didn't come either. Faith knew that Mrs. Mackaig was brokenhearted, for she always wanted a family party at baptism time. But mixed with Faith's concern that there should have developed a strain, was a tiny bit of satisfaction that Mrs. Mackaig was getting a taste of the same pain that her parents suffered.

Yet when it was over she found herself regretting that she had taken a stand, regretting that Neil had been hurt. If they were to grow together, some way must be found to weld their religious interests, and this evidently was not the way to do it. She was quite sure that Molly and Mr. Mackaig caught some of her reasoning, but the others were baffled and unhappy.

One incident that aroused family conversation at that time was Mona Fletcher's conversion to Catholicism. Mona had married Allen Fletcher several years before

Faith had married into the Mackaig family, and Faith had become acquainted with her almost at once on moving to Athens. She and Allen were one of the mixed couples in whom Faith had an interest. Mona's people were strong Presbyterians with a history of missionary and religious work. But Mona had studied Catholicism and was now an ardent convert. She talked of little else and she seemed to be at the Mackaigs' each time Faith was there. At times she wondered if this was a design on the part of her in-laws to demonstrate the possibility of conversion and how happy new converts were. Mona talked of little except the priest, going to confession, and the number of potential converts she knew among Protestants.

Faith was almost at the point of checking to see if Mona were at Mackaigs' before visiting, for the conversations were becoming embarrassing. One day she made an excuse for leaving almost immediately. To her surprise Mrs. Mackaig barely suggested that she stay longer and Molly announced that she would like to ride with Faith as far as the library.

Out in the car Molly said, "I'm not going to the library, Faith. Mona sickens me so I can't listen to her any longer. We used to be friends but, since she's got this case of gagging conversion, I can take her just so long. She even annoys Aunt Cecelia now. I heard by the grapevine that one of the priests told her not to come to confession so often—that more time spent in living well and less in the confessional made for a better balanced life. I know she annoys you to tears."

"I feel she's trying to impress me," said Faith. "Lately any form of gloating gets on my nerves. I'm not as relaxed as I was before Margie was born."

"You're too sensitive, honey. If you're not in a hurry, let's ride round the block again. I'm not going back till Mona leaves."

"Come home with me. You can call up and tell them you're taking dinner with us."

"I'd love to. Faith, how is Steve? He hasn't written me since he went to Washington."

"He's fine. Molly, you're not in love with him, are you?" she asked anxiously.

"Shall I be honest? That brother of yours takes my breath away. I get to thinking that perhaps something will come of it, then he sort of veers off. He can't face the Catholic issue. Isn't that right?"

"He hasn't talked with me, Molly, but he might not let himself go if he thought he'd get entangled. And . . . and, Molly, you couldn't take his constant taunting. In time it would bother you. Catholics believe in the supernatural to a degree that Protestants call it superstition." She could talk freely with Molly.

"If Protestants understood our approach, these things wouldn't seem like superstition to them," Molly explained. "We don't attempt to place the supernatural in the same category as other ideas. There is where we're ahead. We simply say we have the gift of faith, and no further analysis is necessary. Actually, there are miracles around you all the time, if you would admit it."

"I admit there are miracles," Faith agreed. "Beautiful ones, like the love of God, the change of seasons, people healed beyond what medical science can do, and all that. But power in old bones, especially when you're not sure who they belonged to, the Virgin Mary flitting here and there, appearing to ignorant people behind anyone's barn! Molly, how can Catholics believe all this?"

"The Church doesn't sanction all the stories you hear. Only those that are investigated and that hold up are considered authentic. Even then lots of Catholics don't accept them. Most of us pick out the beautiful, the holy, or the miraculous and use what we can to increase our love for God. We need something beyond ourselves, we think. If I was sure I could get along without the sacraments . . ."

"Molly, there isn't anyone in the whole world I'd so love to have Steve marry. But to do it your way would kill my mother. And Steve's way might kill something in you!"

"That's what my Catholic relatives all say. But I'm not a strict Catholic, and wouldn't cause trouble over some aspects that seem important to Neil."

"Maybe that's why it does me good to talk with you. I don't feel you are casting a net to lure me into the Catholic Church, or feeling triumphant when someone goes over, as though it were a contest. There's no one I can discuss this religious mess with who soothes my nerves as you do, Molly," she added warmly.

"Well," said Molly, "I know if I were a Protestant it would irk me no end to have someone gloating over every conversion like a fisherman that has caught a wary trout."

Faith felt better for days after talking with Molly, but she was concerned that two such delightful people as Molly and Steve could not get together because of a difference in religion. She knew she must not encourage them for there seemed no way they could be entirely happy.

In her own home she tried to plan more activities where religious issues were not involved. They would never get anywhere using differences as a contest. She had been talked, or loved, into doing many a thing which went against the grain. It had been cushioned, gilded, and minimized, but it was still there. She had defended it herself till she knew all the arguments, yet the thought kept coming back that she had given up something precious, and under pressure. The priests might say she should never have done it. Then she would look at Neil and her irritation would melt away.

But she could not keep his stubbornness from rousing her at times. And when roused, she countered more often as the months passed by. Always Neil had to brace himself against her ideas or he would lose something that was precious to him. She resolved again and again not to say anything to hurt him, yet her own sense of being constantly overpowered, even lovingly overpowered, stirred up something in her. After each bout she promised herself to try harder to understand Neil's mind, his religious devotion, his holy awe. Then she would come up against an element of fear in him and, before she could recall the words, she would be trying to open his mind, only to find he had no desire to think through the things that seemed paramount to her. He was so satisfied with his own beliefs, so proud of his Church, that he left her deflated with his sweeping condemnations of Protestant variability. She decided she was trying to defend something for which she was not as well prepared as he. When the babies are older, I'll study more of the history and principles of Protestantism, she promised herself. I don't know well enough where I stand. But how could this be done without raising higher the wall that was beginning to come between them?

Then an answer came that was neither happy nor lasting, but it took their minds from the immediate problem.

Chapter 8

ONE night early in December, Neil was tossing Stevie up in the air to amuse him while Faith placed the dinner on the table. He turned on the radio but was giving it scant attention at first. Suddenly he called sharply, "Turn off that tap, Faith, and keep still!"

Since he never gave such an order or made any unreasonable demands, Faith was surprised into instant compliance. She went at once to his side to listen.

"My God!" he said solemnly. "They've bombed Pearl Harbor!"

They hugged the radio that night, each minute not consumed by caring for the babies.

"This will mean war," Neil said.

"And you will go?" Faith asked, frightened.

But she knew the answer. He had been in the N.R.O. T.C. He was intensely patriotic, just as he was ardently religious. But it was the following summer before he was called.

They had talked of what Faith would do but she had managed to avoid committing herself. The Mackaigs wanted her to rent her house and live with them. Two babies were too much for one woman, they said. They always had some assistance and they would love to help take care of the children. Faith could see at once that Neil considered this a perfect solution to the problem.

"Mother's got that big house, all the kid equipment you could use, a nice yard, and there'd be Molly and herself to help. Connie will be home vacations for a while though she's got such an advanced case of medievalism just now that she lives too imaginary an existence to be trusted. I'll be glad when she grows up."

"I know everything is lovely at your mother's, Neil, and they'd do anything for us, but the furniture is so exquisite and she has such valuable treasures. While the children are so small, I'd be holding my breath all the time for fear they'd break something."

"Mother loves the children a lot more than she does her treasures. Anyhow, she can put them away for the duration, as the art galleries do."

"My mother wants me to come there. She feels I have lived nearer your people since our marriage and now it is her turn. They have a big yard all fenced in and dad is always around to lend a hand."

She saw at once that Neil was opposed to this, though he did not say so. It's that the preponderance of power would be with Protestantism, she thought. He's afraid of it.

Back in her mind was another plan. She wrote her Aunt Kate asking if she might come to California, in case Neil was to be in the Southwest. So, when he came with the news that, after a few weeks he would be sent to Port Hueneme and was likely to be there for some months, she had a solution.

"I'm not going to either your mother's or mine," she announced, triumphantly. "I'm going to California, right on the coast, where my husband can spend his week-end leave with his family."

"But, darling, you can't. Much as I want you. Housing is . . ."

"Settled for us. Aunt Kate and Uncle Jack want me to bring the children and live with them. I'm the nearest to a daughter they have. Neither of them have a nerve in their bodies and anyhow the children can play outside. I'll be near my husband. We can walk in the old garden again."

"Why, you little darling! What a scheming wife I have. Now it will be much easier to go."

She found that if she made plans then told them to Neil, he was much less likely to try to overrule her than if she approached him hesitatingly. Besides he was swamped just now finishing up his own work. It wasn't likely that their automobile agency and garage would have much new business during a war. His father would have to train someone else to take his place for the duration.

"While you're in officer's training, Molly will stay with me and help pack and rent the house. Then I'll spend a week with my family when Steve's home on vacation. Molly may go over with me. Then I'll stay a few days with your folks before I leave for California."

She had planned it this way so the Mackaigs could not try to prolong her visit with them and shorten it with her mother. Neil did not seem to see through her mild conspiracy.

"Do you think Molly and Steve are still interested in each other?" he asked a little anxiously.

"I'm afraid of it. And, much as I love them both, they're simply not right for each other. Mother would . . ." She stopped and shook her head.

"Your mother's never become reconciled to me as a son-in-law, has she?" he asked a little wistfully. "I wish she didn't feel that way. I've tried."

"Neil, they all think you're just grand. But they'll always feel it was a one-sided arrangement. If Steve were to do the same, mother couldn't bear it. I doubt if he will, though. And, if he doesn't, Molly will suffer."

"Then why do you get them under each other's noses?"

"Steve asked mother to invite Molly and she wants to accept. I may go first so I can have a frank talk or two. I'll drive over to get in practice. If I'm to put this car over mountains and deserts . . ."

"I'm not sure you should," he began.

"Listen, big boy, I can drive a car as well as you can."

"Don't talk this uppity way to your lord and master," he said. "I won't stand for it." But underneath the nonsense there was feeling in his voice. Suddenly he whirled and caught her in his arms, kissing her as passionately as when she was a bride, and holding her tight. "Faith," he said, a little huskily, "I'd give my bottom dollar if you and I could see this religion business the same. It's the one and only basic disagreement. I do love you, sweetheart."

Then he went quickly out of the door.

She wanted to run after him, to insist there was some way it could be worked out. If only he would make sympathetic journeys into her world! But, if he would, she was not prepared to act as guide. If he is failing because of his closed mind, she thought, I am failing too because I have no clear chart. There was some truth to his accusations. Somewhere, her own witness had failed.

The days with her mother were like hours of play in a windswept field. The wedge which had come between them with her marriage and Stevie's baptism had lost its divisive power and there was more of the old free exchange. Faith was tired of being repressive with herself about her ideas. She even went so far as to tell her mother how she felt about Neil's people.

"It's not that they're disagreeable, Mother. But we don't speak a common language. I find mother Mackaig looking at me as if I had asked her something in a foreign tongue and she must appear polite and not let me guess she didn't catch on. It would make no end of trouble if I said what I thought. So I had to come home and toss some ideas on the breeze."

"It would be hard for me to live with people like that," Margaret sympathized. "I want my soul out where I can use it, so to speak."

"Trust mother," Steve put in. "She likes to hang her soul on the clothesline, where it will flap in the wind."

"There are those whose souls won't bear airing in public for lack of size," Faith said, not because she thought it but for the fun of expressing herself freely again.

"That's the truth," her father agreed. "Some souls don't make a showing because they haven't been cultivated. Your mother has strengthened hers by acting on her convictions. If I had one like hers, I wouldn't mind having it on the line, either. But even to me, life would seem pretty superficial if I had to stifle the thoughts nearest me all the time."

In a way that's what I have been doing with Neil, Faith thought. Somehow I must learn to be myself and still not to hurt him. Aloud she said, "You and mother disagree on so many things I wonder you've been able to keep your souls out in the open, as Mother says. You both say anything you wish—or at least I hope you don't think anything worse than you say."

Everyone laughed.

"We disagree," her father retorted, "but never absolutely. In soul we are together. I may need the sacraments and marvel that she is closer to God without them than I can get with them but, essentially, we walk the road together. If two can do that, difference of opinion is immaterial."

Once they got on a discussion of heaven and in what way the Protestant concept differed from the Catholic. "What do you think heaven is like, Mother?" Faith asked. "I need to clarify my thinking."

"Mercy, child, how would I know?" her mother demanded unsatisfactorily. "The Apostle Paul said that eye hadn't seen or ear heard that which God had prepared for those that loved him. I'd hate to put my insight above his."

"But you could still speculate," Steve suggested.

"I'll own I sometimes wonder though if the church triumphant is to form the core of the heavenly inhabitants? Will the men who have led the parade here be the ones in the front seats up there? Christ's statements were all about the inheriting qualities of meekness and humility. On that basis the women who wash the church dishes after a supper and do the menial tasks are going to rank above the ones who paraded in red hats."

"A few of the lowlier ones might even get ahead of some vainglorious Protestant leaders that I know," John put in.

It isn't the remarks they make, Faith thought, it's being able to make them when they please. She was glad she had come ahead of Molly for with a guest there would be some restraint, though Molly had gone as far as to say: "Now, Faith, above all, don't tell your mother to be careful what she says to me. That's part of your and Neil's difficulty. You tell your mother not to talk with him. He tells you to be careful what you say to his mother. Each of you is trying to guard and protect the Catholic belief. You do it too, even while you resent it. Remember, I'm not worried. If my religion won't stand up against the impact, I'll think of something else. Steve tells me I've never really met your mother when she was her natural self. He says she is a most uninhibited person. But at Aunt Cecelia's she's always in the wrong character, because Aunt Cecelia has the upper hand and, guiltily conscious of it, she's oversweet. Steve feels it cramps your mother's style. Let's be as we are."

Faith was apprehensive about a free exchange of ideas, much as she longed for it. Molly would be in the minority, so courtesy should be shown. But Molly led the way and the genial sparring of the McLaren family went on apace, with no noses out of joint. God should not be walled in, Molly announced, to the amazement of everyone; it was the antithesis of every Christian teaching.

To Faith it was a grand two weeks. She had Neil's letters, love letters as tender as any he had ever sent her. Molly and Steve took long tramps and came back tired, but relaxed. One evening Steve explained to Faith how things stood between them.

"I'm not signing any papers, Faith. I couldn't give up my right to free expression of my thoughts. Molly knows where I stand. She also knows I'm crazy about her—just not crazy enough to tie up my mind and my children's after me. I want her to take her time. If she can marry me and be perfectly comfortable about it, I'm hers, lock, stock, and barrel. She's one of the most fair-minded people in the world. But she's got this inheritance, and most people say a Catholic never quite gets over it. Much as I want her, I'd rather not marry her than to do it and not be able to make her happy. She must be perfectly sure and so must I before we jump. I've been studying this thing more than I let on and I know pretty well what I think. I'm certainly not an atheist. In some ways I stand closer to mother's point of view than you do, though for pure worship—and I do worship whether or not you believe it—I respond best to ritual. Anyhow, I'm not giving up my right to work out my own salvation as vocally as I please. Molly still has some thinking to do too. Thank the Lord, she has something to do it with. If I'm sent overseas, she'll have time to do quite a lot of meditating."

Even the week at Mackaigs' was delightful. The family agreed that, much as they would have liked to have the children with them, it was better for Faith to be near Neil as long as possible. Even when Mona came in several times Faith was not upset, for the relaxed, happy weeks at home had settled her nerves. Mona was certain one of her old friends, formerly an ardent Methodist, was about to turn Catholic. She tried to trap Faith into some concessions, but Mrs. Mackaig came to her rescue. After the caller was gone she apologized for her.

"Mona means well," she said. "But converts are sometimes overzealous and their ardor is wearing."

It was almost the harshest thing Faith had ever heard her say, for Neil's mother meticulously refrained from criticism. At the moment her chief concern was for Connie, who could not decide to enter the teaching order her mother preferred, but was determined to go into a discalceate, contemplative order, one of the most cloistered ones. She has a misplaced nostalgia, Faith thought. Connie's romance was entirely with the Church. She had never so much as cast her eyes in the direction of a young man.

Chapter 9

THE next two years were the happiest in Faith's married life. It was hard to leave the little house in Athens for she had spent much time and thought on it, but there was a restfulness to the California cottage, and living with Uncle Jack and Aunt Kate was a pleasure. There was always someone to help with the children, always a sunny yard where they could play. There was no strain about guarding her tongue because her Quaker relatives expected frankness, tempered by Christian charity. She began teaching Stevie a little prayer to be said at night and, when Neil knew it, he didn't object, but showed the child how to cross himself. They both smiled at his cute but awkward efforts.

"It isn't necessary," Neil admitted, "but he might as well learn. I can scarcely wait till he's old enough to take to Mass."

Faith felt badly about that one, remembering that she was not to take the children with her. But it was one of the few annoyances, and she said nothing. Later, when she took the children to the old garden, Neil was thrilled about it. "That garden symbolizes something to me, Faith," he said. It meant something to her too. The children could not understand it now, but later they would.

They reached California in the fall of 1942 where the months seemed to whiz by. There was a warring madness in the world, but in the little cottage there was peace.

One day early in the summer of 1943, a young woman who used crutches opened the wooden gate into the yard where Faith was playing with her children. She was well dressed and attractive, about Faith's age. Faith pulled up a chair and asked her to be seated.

"I'm Alice Reredon, Mrs. Paul Reredon." She put aside the crutches as she sat down. "I live up here on the hill just beyond the Methodist Church."

"And I am Faith Mackaig, Mrs. Neil Mackaig," Faith returned, "and these are my children, Stevie and Margie. We're very happy to have a caller this nice spring day."

"Isn't it lovely? I'm supposed to get out when I can. Now I'm looking up children for the vacation church school. All the Protestant churches go in together. We have a nursery department because there are so many babies. How old are your children?"

"Stevie is five and a half and Margie four. Would they be too young?"

"No. Margie could go in the nursery class and Stevie in the kindergarten. I have a little girl who is almost five and she will go. Would you mind telling me your church preference?"

"I was brought up in the Congregational church, but now I'm Presbyterian. My mother was a Quaker and my father an Episcopalian. Rather a mixture, isn't it?"

Alice laughed. "I think we're all getting that way now. My mother was Baptist and my father Lutheran, and now I'm Methodist because the church is close enough so I can walk. And Mr. Budlong is such a good minister. I've been helping in the church school on Sundays and now I'm trying to do this. Have you had any experience in teaching?"

"I always taught a church school class before I was married. That is, as soon as I was old enough."

"Would you mind if I sent Mr. Budlong down to call? It isn't my place to ask you, for I'm not on the religious education committee, but I know they need help. And it's all right for me to hint that you would —if you will."

Suddenly Faith wanted to do this. She loved working with little children and it would be an opportunity to compare her own with others. But what would Neil say? He was home so little she might be able to manage without asking, but she hated to do this. And she could not well teach without taking her own children.

"We'd be glad to have Mr. Budlong call. But my husband is a very strict Catholic and knows very little of Protestant teaching. He will be here on leave this week end and I can ask him what he thinks. He may object."

"Bring him over Saturday morning and let him see us in action. I'm sure he won't mind. We have a number of Catholic children and, at their age, it would be pretty difficult for us to indoctrinate them very strongly, even if we wanted to. Actually, this is a community project. Several of the churches furnish teachers and most of the children in the village come."

Faith promised to look into the matter. She wanted to know more about it herself before broaching the matter to her husband. But when she saw the pleasant little games they played, the children cutting out pic-

111

tures with blunt scissors or listening to stories, she could scarcely wait to say that she would help. Some interested man had made little benches, like pews, and in one corner of a large room these had been placed like a chapel, with screens that could be set up to make it a miniature sanctuary. A worship center had been made with a large copy of Tom Curr's "Follow Me," and an open Bible on a missal stand below it.

But someone was needed to play the piano and Faith found herself offering—just for the day, of course. Stevie was entranced. He was socially minded and loved both to hear stories and to sing. When the school was over, he was determined to stay. Faith promised to bring him back the next day. That was Friday.

Neil would be in late that night. For the first time Faith found herself dreading to ask his consent. She knew plenty of wives who sneaked about, trying to outwit their husbands about the use of the car, an extra afternoon out, or the purchase of an article the family could not afford, but nothing of the sort had happened to her. She had no idea how Neil would react. Besides, back of her dread, there was the feeling that she should not have to ask his consent to do something which was obviously good for the children, and which they enjoyed. Because she had no training in subtlety or supplication, she plunged in nervously. She could even feel her hand shaking.

"Why are you so disturbed about it?" he asked. "If you are sure it is good . . ."

"I am. But I wish you would drop by and watch tomorrow. And Stevie loves it so. If you saw for yourself you would feel better about it. There are at least six Catholic children in the group."

"I don't want this sort of thing to get a hold on the children," he said slowly, "but I can't actually see what harm this could do. And, if you want to play for them. What are the songs like?"

"There are a few religious ones—songs about God's love for little children. Just what is within their comprehension. Then there are little games and nonsense songs. Stevie just loves to sing."

"I'll take a look," he conceded.

She knew he was apprehensive but could not bear to refuse her. The next day, though a bit disapproving of the worship center, he granted that the stories were well told and said that it was no concession on his part to state that the pianist had a way about teaching children to sing.

"Go ahead, honey. But, remember. You have to keep this thing in bounds."

What bounds could there be but the understanding of a child's mind? She threw her arms around his neck, telling him how pleased she was that he didn't care.

Before the vacation school was over Faith had a regular job playing in the kindergarten department of the church school. She felt a little sneaky about taking the children, for Neil's knowledge of Protestant procedure was too hazy for him to realize that this was the main Protestant training ground. He was having less leave all the time and was now seldom home on Sunday. If he came, she told Mr. Budlong that she could not be at church school. On these days she went to Mass with Neil, then they took the children for a picnic on the beach, which Stevie considered the only thing nicer to do with one's time than to go to church school. This program avoided tension and did a great deal for Stevie, who was a forward, determined child who needed companionship. But always Faith had a sense of divided loyalty.

In the fall Neil was transferred to San Diego and now it was possible for him to be home only very occasionally. Faith saved her gas and drove down when possible to spend time with him there. Sometimes she took the children. One Saturday, while waiting for him, she drove to St. Joseph's Cathedral so Stevie and Margie could see the picture of Christ and the children. Stevie was much impressed and tried to tell his father about it. Even Margie jabbered enthusiastically.

"What's this you took them to see?" Neil asked as they drove away from the ferry.

"It's a picture at the Catholic Cathedral. You should go yourself sometime when you're in town. It's very effective. The children saw a picture of Christ and the children at the Methodist Church above the children's worship center, and they have always remembered it." In a way it salved her conscience to say this. She was deliberately reminding him that the children had other religious experiences than those prescribed by his church. She was relieved that he did not seem disturbed. Perhaps he was thinking of something else.

In January of 1945 he was sent overseas. Faith talked of going back to Athens and Neil felt that it might be the best thing to do. Still, there was a possibility he might not be gone long and she would want to be in California if he came back. If she went East, there would come up the matter of living either with her own family or with Neil's. Whichever decision was made, someone would be dissatisfied.

When, shortly after he had left, she found that she was again pregnant, her mind was fully made up. By staying in California she could choose her own hospital without suggestions from anyone. Also she could have the child baptized by a Protestant minister. She knew that this method, though not approved, was acceptable to the Catholic Church and would prevent a child from going to limbo, wherever that mythological place might be. She could not endure the Catholic ceremony without Neil's presence. If he wanted to have anything further done on his return, he could do so.

Another point in favor of remaining in California was the school. There was no parochial school in the little village where they lived. The nearest sisters' school was in connection with St. Anne's, where Neil went to Mass when he had week-end leave. But it was overcrowded and uninviting. It was easy to say that her gas allowance was insufficient to take the children back and forth. The public school was a new, attractive building with sunny windows. The children were happy there and doing well. She sent regular reports to Neil of their progress, and he seemed satisfied and did not ask her to make any changes in her plans.

Mrs. Mackaig seemed more disturbed. It was evident she did not trust public instruction. Faith was graciously reassuring for it was easy to be gracious at a distance. She told Mrs. Mackaig how well they were doing and helped them write little letters of their own.

But from the sixth month of her pregnancy she was apprehensive that something was wrong. She did not feel as she had when carrying her other children. She had more pains and was often dizzy. It was difficult to get the medical care she needed, for doctors were scarce and overworked. There was a community hospital in one of the villages fifteen miles down the coast. Alice had taken treatments here and one day she went with Faith and arranged for Faith to go there when her time came. There was little use asking for a private room for these were always filled by patients in serious condition.

Neil's mother wrote anxiously, urging Faith to come back to Athens where she could have better care, but Faith always countered with the argument that she hated to leave the coast while there was a possibility of Neil's return. She had been able to get part-time help and her mother was planning to come to California. With what her Uncle Jack and Aunt Kate could do, they were all in good hands. She explained about the hospital. It was small but efficient. She knew the Mackaigs would feel better if she were in a Catholic institution but for once she would go where she liked. She wrote Neil her plans but letters were so irregular that she had no answer.

By August she was so miserable she wrote her mother to be ready to come at any time, suggesting that she call Mrs. Mackaig and explain the situation, for letter-writing had become such a task. The next week when she went to the hospital for an examination, she stopped to talk with the minister of the Community Church and ask if he would come over and baptize her child in case there was the slightest danger that it would not live. She explained that Mr. Budlong would do it, only it was a long drive for something that had no meaning for her and was being done solely because of her husband and his people. If the baby proved to be healthy and strong, they would wait to have it baptized till her husband returned from overseas. The minister shared her unconcern about the sacrament for its own sake but he appreciated her desire to make her husband and his family comfortable.

Then she drove slowly home, trying to cushion the bumps. She longed for Neil. The other times he had been with her; without him the pain and anxiety was much harder to bear. She hoped he wouldn't mind too much her having a Protestant baptism, in case it was necessary. As he had said so little about taking the children to vacation church school, he might be growing more liberal.

Three hours after she reached home her labor began. Uncle Jack drove her back to the hospital, though he couldn't see too well and couldn't miss the bumps. Before leaving the house she wired her mother to come at once, and sent the children to Alice Reredon's to play until dusk. This would give Aunt Kate a little respite. Alice, on crutches, could do more than many women who strode rapidly.

Faith tried to think what was needed but the pains were coming too fast for clear thought. Either she had miscalculated or the baby was arriving prematurely. By the time she reached the hospital she could scarcely speak. Even through the anesthetic she could feel the searing pain, not all the time, but coming in waves. Sometimes she seemed out on the ocean, being borne along on the crests, up, then down. She tried to speak, to find someone she knew, but the dizzy, gyrating room spun till she could not find a familiar face. There were only white splotches bobbing around. She heard herself moan, but when she tried to form the moans into words, her lips would not move.

Finally the pains subsided. Then there was no sense of time. She slept or woke, but there was little difference. Sometimes there was a pain and a nurse gave her a hypodermic. Sometimes they put a thermometer in her mouth. But she remembered nothing. Once a man, who looked like Steve, stood by the bed, but she could not speak.

Hours later she remembered. There was to be a baby. It seemed a long time ago. She had never been so sick before. Her head was sunk in the pillows and wouldn't move. But she must ask about the baby.

Then she heard low, angry voices in the next room. They didn't want her to hear but some of the words reached her—terrifying words, for they said the baby was in limbo and it was her fault. She was frightened and began to shiver.

Then some time later she was in a strange, shady region with an opaque light and queer, egg-shaped forms floating about. Then the forms became babies and she was searching for one that must be hers. She couldn't tell which was hers, and people said there was no way to get it back out. But she had to do this before Neil came. He mustn't know that she let this happen to their baby. Then sometimes Neil was beside her, but he was angry, like the voices in the next room. Then he would be gone again and she would try alone to find it . . .

A nurse came and put something in her arm and the bed stopped shaking. She was quiet and went to sleep. But the dream recurred. She was sure her mother and Steve were near, though she could not talk with them. If only they would keep the horrid dream away!

Then once when she woke several people were standing about the bed. One of them was a man in a Geneva robe, and he spoke in a very gentle voice:

"When thou passest through the waters, I will be with thee, and through the rivers, they shall not overflow thee . . . O God, our finite minds cannot fathom Thy ways, but we trust Thy love and feel underneath us Thine everlasting arms. Sustain this mother with the knowledge that her little one is with Thee, the Light Eternal . . . and that, as Thy Son, our Saviour, gathered the little ones to Him and held them in His arms, Thou hast, for Thine own good reasons, taken this child back to Thee . . ."

So they had got the baby out of limbo. It was in heaven now, and she could rest. Then the minister was praying again:

"O God, in whose hands are all the deep places of the earth. Thou who art round about us and within, heal with Thy tender love the hearts and bodies of these, Thy servants, that they may both seek after Thee, and find Thee, in whom is rest and peace forevermore. Let not your heart be troubled. Neither let it be afraid . . .

"The Lord bless thee and keep thee. The Lord lift up His countenance upon thee, and give thee peace . . ."

And with that she went to sleep.

It was a slow process getting back to health, trying to untangle the thing that had happened to her. Little by little she pieced it together. Her mother, as soon as she got the telegram, had called Neil's mother to say that she was leaving at once for California. She had been fortunate enough to get a flight. Mrs. Mackaig, in turn, had called the priest at St. Anne's, long distance, to alert him about what was happening. She was concerned for fear her daughter-in-law might make no provision for her child's baptism and the family felt it might be an abnormal birth. Faith had no way of knowing exactly what Mrs. Mackaig had said but she was certain no expense would be spared and the priest would know that Neil had attended Mass at St. Anne's when in that area.

According to Steve's account, which was not couched in the most reverent terms, the priest was off giving some sinner a boost into heaven. There was a shortage of spiritual ministration just as there was a shortage in butter and nylons, and Steve insisted that the man was in no way to blame for not getting there. It was hours after the baby's death before his housekeeper relayed the message to him.

Usually the priest had trusted the devotion of Nurse Patty Coyle, who said openly that she took no chances that the little dears would live forever in the shades when she could save them in the name of the Trinity with a few drops of holy water and a few seconds' time. Especially the puny ones. Of course, if she was sure the parents were Protestant and would raise a fuss if they found out, she did it secretly, or consulted a priest. But few families cared, even if they did know. Mrs. Mackaig had corresponded earlier with the priest and he had promised to talk with Nurse Coyle and they would both keep a weather eye out for the Mackaig baby to make its appearance. Unfortunately it came the very day the nurse's brother arrived from Europe and she had the day off.

The priest and Steve had exchanged some bitter statements. The priest felt he had failed a good Catholic family when they had put their confidence in him, or so Steve interpreted it. He held the Protestant relatives responsible since promises had been made that Mrs. Mackaig's children were to be reared as Catholics. He even hinted that it could be spite work, since it was known that they objected strenuously to Catholic sacraments.

Faith found herself frightened about Neil's and his family's reactions, and even somewhat fearful of the priest. But Steve had no inhibitions about telling a Catholic clergyman his opinions. He said that he came of solid Protestant stock and couldn't be bullied by any notions of priestly control of the gates to heaven. Besides, Steve had no emotions involved, as his sister had. He felt that he gave Father Hammel as good as he got, suggesting that, since God had provided such an intricate way of getting innocent babies back to his presence, it was careless of him to predicate it on such an unstable foundation as a nurse's hours on duty. Even worse, Steve had challenged the priest to find anywhere in the Scriptures that innocent babies were to be punished for sins they couldn't commit. Only celibate men could have thought that one up, Steve suggested, but it had proved a wonderful device for getting people baptized, willy-nilly, into the Catholic Church, and had swelled its rolls by no one could estimate how many million adherents since the idea's conception.

Faith knew that none of these statements would make for smooth sailing when she must once more live near the Mackaig family, though undoubtedly Steve's firm stand kept the priest from trying to talk directly with her. The minister of the Community Church in the village came to see her and Mr. Budlong drove over and she found them both comforting. Trained in dealing with people of other beliefs and schooled more in

Christian patience than Steve was, they both understood more fully her position. Mr. Budlong even went so far as to call on the Catholic priest with the hope of explaining the situation. The gesture did little good, for Steve's words had been totally blasphemous from Father Hammel's viewpoint. Faith felt that at least an effort had been made. So far she had not been able to write her husband. Her mother wrote both Neil and Mrs. Mackaig, telling of Faith's serious condition and the baby's sudden birth and almost as sudden death. It had died in its crib within an hour after birth, while concern was felt for the mother's life, she said. She had flown out the minute she heard that Faith had left for the hospital and Steve had come down from San Francisco where he was stationed, arriving before his mother did. Margaret had said nothing of the child's dying unbaptized, for she did not know what to say. Actually neither she nor Steve had thought of it till it was too late. If Faith had been conscious, she would have remembered. Under less of a strain, any of them might have done something. When they talked with the minister of the Community Church about a prayer at the hospital and again at the grave, he remembered the young woman who had asked him to baptize her child, and he was sorry he had not known in time to fulfil her wishes.

Steve had to return to his base but her mother stayed on, taking care of the children and nursing Faith back to health. It was a hard road for her mental condition made recovery slow. She was haunted by a sense of guilt in doing something that would worry Neil and might cause friction with his family. Molly wrote her a sweet letter that helped. She was evidently disturbed about what Steve had said to the priest, which he must have told her himself, but she felt it was to be expected in his state of mind. Faith was amazed that Molly seemed as little concerned as she was about the baby's fate and planned to ask Molly as soon as she was able to write.

Mrs. Mackaig wrote, suggesting that the children be sent back to Athens, or she would come for them, so they could be entered in a parochial school. She was sure this would be her son's desire. She laid strong emphasis on the excellent sisters' school near their home. In her state of health Faith at once interpreted the letter as a statement of the family's loss of confidence in her and their desire to get the children's training into their own hands.

Margaret answered the letter as courteously as possible, explaining Faith's difficulty in regaining her strength and that it would be much more difficult for her if she were separated from her children. Now that the war was over Neil might return at any minute, and she did want them all to be together. The children were doing well in public school and were too small for doctrinal teachings to make much difference. Both Faith and Margaret knew this was contrary to the Catholic philosophy of education, but they put it in anyhow.

Faith prayed that Neil would understand about the baby. Surely he was too intelligent to believe in a limbo.

Then came the long-awaited letter from him, but it was written before he had heard from her mother. He was in a hospital and had been through a harrowing experience. He was so eager to hear from her but no mail had reached him in over a month. Just as he was in one hospital long enough for it to catch up with him, he would be transferred again. He hoped she would cable, or have her mother do so, the minute the baby came. He must know how it was and how she was doing. He prayed for her every day, he said. The thought of his reaction, once he knew, shot terror to her heart. Here was an act, to her a superstition, to him a sacrament. How could they ever come to see alike?

With his love sustaining her, she had been able to endure its practice. She could adjust the reasoning of St. Paul to her own situation. He had said that, since idols were not gods, meat offered to them was not harmful to the strong of faith. She did not believe in the devils which the priest exorcised so she could ignore that part. But when it was not done, Neil might find it more difficult to adjust his thinking.

The last paragraph of his letter, though tender and loving, shot a new fear into her already anxious heart: "My darling," he wrote, "if you could have seen our chaplains under fire, with absolutely no thought for themselves, hearing the confessions of the dying, working side by side with the medical corps, giving the Sacrament where there was terror on every side, going wherever they were needed, to Catholic and non-Catholic alike, you would know why we appreciate our clergy as we do. I doubt if there is any greater bravery to be written into the annals of American history than the sacrifice of Catholic priests. This whole experience has done something for me. If there was ever a time when I sinned by questioning my Church, that time has gone. I was sure death was but moments off when a priest placed a crucifix in my hands. He may have seen my St. Christopher or my identification tag, or he may have taken a chance. I couldn't speak and things were pretty blurred, but I held the crucifix to my lips and tried to make a sign of contrition. The priest was all but mowed down, but he stuck right with me and even started the prayers for the dying. Then another blast came. I woke up in the sickbay with a pharmacist's mate working over me. The priest was not to be found. I tried to check up but, since I didn't know his name, I'm not sure. Likely he's another of the great souls who died at his post. When I think how God intrusted salvation to the Church, and how nobly that Church has ministered to her friends and even her enemies in every time of need, I say another prayer that you may grow to believe that such faith is the greatest gift we can bequeath our children, and that your resentment will melt away in the very beauty of God himself, which the Church offers you. If you had been at death's door, as I was, and had felt the tenderness of her ministrations, you would feel as I do, I am sure."

She let the letter drop in her lap. She had been at death's door, even as he had. A man in a plain black gown had prayed, "Thou, who art round about us, and within . . ." and there had been neither crucifix nor oil, nor even holy water, but there had been communion and health and peace. This was something no words could explain to Neil, for what the minister said connoted nothing to him. And he would not even listen to her tell it.

She spent hours trying to write him to explain why the child died unbaptized—that she was unconscious and there was no one there. But, no matter what her explanation, he would feel she should have gone to Mercy Hospital in San Diego or the Queen of Angels Hospital in Los Angeles. He would not accept her excuse that she would not have had time to reach either

of these places after labor set in since she had arranged
beforehand to go to the little Community Hospital and
with the minister there for her baby's baptism. She
tried to explain how ill she had been but that she was
slowly regaining her strength. She wished they could be
together through their months of convalescence. Wasn't
it strange that two people, neither of whom had suffered a day's serious illness before, should both be near
death at the same time? She was glad he had had a
priest near in his hour of need, then she tried to explain
that she, too, had had the ministrations of her church
and she quoted some of the words the minister of the
Community Church had said and the helpful support
of Mr. Budlong, who had called regularly and brought
her books. She rewrote this part of the letter four times
and finally sent it off in a form that did not satisfy her.
There was no use trying to explain that Protestants
were likely to think their souls must go unadorned and
unannounced into the presence of God. To Neil Protestant worship seemed stark; its simplicity connoted
poverty of ideas. Even death, to him, was dramatized—
beautifully dramatized. But she could not say this. As
for the chaplains, if there had been Protestant men side
by side with the Catholics, he would not have seen them.

She waited nervously for the letter which would be
an answer to hers. At last it came from a hospital in the
New Hebrides. Of course he was dismayed at what had
happened but now they would have to make the best of
it. He would see what could be done. For the first time
he expressed concern about the children's schooling,
and said he was anxious to be discharged so they could
get back to Athens and a better way of living. He expressed concern at her illness and hoped she was im-

proving. He felt so far from them all and longed for home. But it might not be long now.

She read the letter many times, trying to fathom his meaning. It seemed to her that he was more concerned because the baby had died unbaptized than because she had been so near death. Perhaps, if he had been with her, he would have considered having the baby baptized as his first concern and saving her life as secondary. It was an ugly thought and might have no basis. But it had seeped into her thinking and she could not eradicate it. Could it be she had lost some of Neil's love by this incident? The thing was unthinkable. Far better for him to be violently angry than that. As she worried, her progress toward health was retarded.

As soon as she could drive the car she went back to see the minister of the Community Church near the hospital to thank him for his services. Alice Reredon had told her that he had come with Mr. Budlong to see the children's chapel at the Methodist Church and had wished there could be something of the sort in his own fast-growing church, but he was so overworked that he had no time to raise funds for extra projects and what was on hand was needed for the new education building and a better sanctuary, which was difficult to get because of war restrictions. He did not recognize her until she told him who she was, for she looked neither like the healthy woman she had been before the baby's birth nor the woman she had been in the hospital. But he seemed pleased that she had returned to say that his ministrations had confirmed her faith and helped toward her recovery. Then she made a shy suggestion that she would like to contribute money for some little pews for a children's chapel, a Bible bound in red to open on a stand, and a picture of Jesus and the children for above the table. It was to be in memory of the child she had lost and in appreciation for the comfort he had given her.

But grateful as he was and much as she wanted to make the contribution, she felt a little sneaky about it. In a sense, she was giving Neil's money. At least he brought in the pay check. She had never given as much to her church as he gave to his. In addition to his regular pledge which was larger than hers, he gave to the collection for the use of the pew and many extras. He would certainly not approve of this gift.

But she had some money saved and it could be done without his knowledge. If it seemed wise, she would tell him later. Cele gave liberally to the Catholic Church out of Frank's pay check and Frank did not approve of Catholic expenditures, so it seemed fair to balance this.

But a perfect marriage was predicated on absolute understanding between man and wife. Frank knew what Cele was doing and let it slide, regardless of his own or his family's feelings. But she trembled at the thought of the storm that would follow if she took the reins in her hands as Neil's sister did. Somewhere there was weakness in her tactics. Only time could tell whether or not she was doing right.

Chapter 10

IN late November Neil reached San Francisco. Two weeks later he had his discharge. A taxi brought him, unannounced, to the gate of the yard where Faith was playing with the children. Even through their first embraces Faith could sense a strain. Neil was thin and nervous, not at all like his easygoing self.

The papers were full of admonitions to accept the changes and idiosyncrasies of returning men with tact and calm. But Faith was far from strong herself, and Neil insisted they must start East at once so they could spend Christmas with his parents. If he thought of this as a difficult undertaking for her, he did not mention it.

Margaret McLaren had returned home as soon as she knew Neil would be arriving. The cottage would have been overcrowded had she stayed, and both women felt it would be easier for the family to adjust without her presence.

From the first there was a tension never known before. It went beyond the matter of a difference of religious belief. Much was nerves, just nerves. She could tell Neil was making an effort to be patient with the children. Much as he loved them and wanted to be with them again, they now annoyed him. They had reached the chattering, nonsensical age when they loved the repetition of rhymes, singing silly songs, tussling, chasing each other around the house, arguing, racing for the telephone or to answer the doorbell. Almost everything they did was annoying, yet they were actually delightful, responsive children when one was not imprisoned with them in a small space. Aunt Kate and Uncle Jack were people of calm tempers and serene convictions. There was a whole California beach and miles of grass-covered hills. If the children had wished to yell, throw things, run pellmell, or any of the other normal activities of childhood, the opportunity was there. They had many friends in the little neighborhood. If they wandered too far from home, the various mothers relayed their yoo-hoos up the hillside to call them back.

Now here they were in the back seat of a packed car, and on the way to the home of a grandmother who had exquisite taste in household furnishings, and whose personal etiquette harked back to a disciplined sisters' school in the East, where she had not been allowed to cross her legs. What would the Mackaigs think of their grandchildren? How could these children fit into the precise pattern of Mackaig living?

"I don't see how your mother will endure these hoodlums in the winter when they can't get outside," Faith almost moaned. "I didn't realize how noisy they were, they were outside so much."

"They are sort of out of hand, aren't they?" Neil agreed. "It may be good for them to live in a more restrained atmosphere."

"Children need a father," Faith observed, hoping he would feel she was agreeing with him, though she was not so sure the restraint would be beneficial.

She was sure he did not approve of the way she had handled his family while he was gone. Yet other people thought she had a talent along this line. Two days before Neil had arrived Alice Reredon had asked her up to discuss her own problem. Alice's Rachel was just between Margie and Stevie in age and had played so much with them they considered her as a sister.

"I need to ask you something before you go, Faith. And you'll need a chance to think it over. You know my trouble with my leg is worse than it appears. If having it amputated would have kept the disease from spreading, I'd have gone through with that. But it's all through my system. I've known it for some time and I'm sure that's why the doctors were reluctant to do any cutting. I was in Los Angeles for another check-up last week. They give me a year, perhaps a little longer. Or it could be six months. I have to make some plans for Rachel and I wanted to talk with you."

"Oh, Alice, is it that bad? I had hoped . . ."

"I know. So did I, at least at first. Now I'm beginning to accept it."

"Alice, you are one of the finest people I have ever known—so courageous and so useful with your limited strength. I can never thank you enough for what you've done for me. And if I can do anything about Rachel . . ."

"I've wondered if you would take her yourself, Faith. I know you've been concerned because you knew that, when your husband returned, he would take the children to the Catholic Church, as you had agreed. If you had Rachel to go with you, perhaps it would not be so lonely. She is Protestant and she's a very adjustable child. More than that, she loves you dearly."

"But what about Paul? How will he feel?"

"Paul isn't Rachel's father. She is the child of my first marriage. Paul is good to her and fond of her, but he's in the regular Navy and will make it his career. He'll be all over the world and will have no way of taking care of Rachel. He has no relatives close enough to come home to them. When I'm gone I hope he'll marry again just to have a home port. But I want to leave Rachel with someone she can tie to. If . . ."

"I'd love to have her, Alice. Unless my husband objects, I'll certainly take her. I'm sure he'll be willing for he has always wanted me to be happy."

"It would be such a relief to me. Please talk with him as soon as you are settled. I'd like to have Rachel think she is going on a visit before I get to looking too bad or when I can no longer make a good home for her. It would be easier for both of us."

"Alice, how can you be so sweet and cheerful in the face of such a fate?"

"At first I couldn't. Losing Jim was the hardest. We were just lost in each other. He died in 1940 and I was married to Paul only a few months before I met you. I had no idea then that there was anything serious the matter with me. Just thought it was something in my leg and I didn't even go to a doctor. Of course I wouldn't have married Paul if I had known. But he's been good. And he'll get over this. I've worked out a philosophy. I suppose everyone does. This life has been a sort of washout for me, in a way. So I'm sure there is something better. Some new start. I needed this training for it. I look at it as a discipline I had to have. Jim was a wonderful person and now I think of his death as just having gotten a few jumps ahead of me. I picture him where he has a fuller opportunity and can do some of the things he couldn't do here. He was an orphan and thwarted so often. Don't you think of heaven as a new opportunity with some of our earthly limitations gone, and us on a straighter path to God? It may not be orthodox but I feel we'll still have to grow some. Maybe this is my version of purgatory, but it's different from the Catholic notion because I think I can do something for myself and they teach that it's a place where you're dependent on other people to do for you."

"Maybe Protestants do have a sort of purgatory in their thinking," Faith agreed. She was glad Alice had such a firm hope and, if it could be worked out, she wanted Rachel.

She thought of this conversation as they drove east, but this was no time to mention it to Neil.

In the motel the last night before they reached Athens, Neil found a chance to say after the children were asleep, "I suggested to mother that we simply don't discuss the matter of your losing a baby. I'm trying to get my poise back, and you need yours. The less we say about it the better."

"Neil, I'm so sorry you all feel as you do. It's hard to lose a child, but when you have the sort of faith to sustain you—and my faith does that—it . . . it's easier."

"Let's let it drop," he said stiffly. "I wouldn't be able to get your reasoning or see how you could excuse yourself. However, it might be a comfort to you to know we all blame ourselves as well. I should have written Father Hammel. Or mother should have gone out to be near."

A terrible answer came to Faith's lips, but she closed them tightly. They were too close to this, and to other tragedies, to think well. She must keep her head. She would go and talk with some priest about it—with some priest who had a tender heart. Surely someone could tell her what to do to regain Neil's love. But now she was too miserable to talk. When she thought he was asleep, the tears came and a sob shook her whole body.

Neil reached for her hand.

"Faith," he said, "you mustn't cry like that. You'll tear yourself apart."

"I'm torn apart now," she moaned. "I was nearly dead, but you didn't care!"

"Listen, darling," he pleaded, "that isn't so. I did care terribly, when I heard it. But, by the time I knew, you were on the road to recovery. But the other thing . . . well, it was irrevocable."

"I don't see how you can believe a loving God would do such a horrible thing. Doesn't it . . ."

"I don't have to see in order to love and obey, Faith. It isn't for my puny mind to decide what I think God wants. He has already told his Church. He provided one way of salvation. It's my place to see those rites are provided for my children."

His nerves, like hers, were on edge. If they could live with some semblance of calmness for a few months, things might work out. She would try so hard. Then, if he still felt the same . . . But the thought would start another spasm of sobs, so she put it forcibly out of her mind and tried to remember where she had packed different household items three years before.

The holidays went off better than she believed possible. She warned the children that they must be quiet because, in the North, people were shut in during the winter and they couldn't endure such a din. She confided her fears to Neil's father and he became her ally in keeping them in bounds. At the first show of confusion he suggested a ride to see the city with its lighted trees, banked with snow. They had talked about snow all the way from California and wanted to get their hands in it.

Faith found a chance when alone with them to warn them not to mention going to the Methodist Church school. Their father knew it because he had been asked about it, she explained, so they would not think she had deceived him. But their grandmother was a strict Catholic and they were to be Catholics, too. It would hurt their grandmother if she knew they had been inside a Protestant church.

When they asked questions she told them to wait till they were alone. And they mustn't worry their daddy, who wasn't well yet. This was the truth. But she could see a new phase in their development ahead and wondered what she could say that would be loyal to her own viewpoint, yet still loyal to her promises to Neil. Right or wrong, they were promises.

She should have known that her children would be the questioning kind. Well, as soon as he was able, she would send them to Neil and let him give the answers he wished.

If possible Mrs. Mackaig was more gracious and gentle than ever, but it only made Faith feel worse because she had allowed their grandchild to die unbaptized. She felt they could not trust her as they once had done. Though she had often felt rebellious at the submissive part she was forced to play, still the outward relations had been mostly gracious. It might be that the Mackaig family did not enjoy being in the position of forcing their own way all the time, though she was sure there were times when Mrs. Mackaig had felt trium-

135

phant. But even triumph can go sour. It has already for Neil, she thought. I must not make him feel this more than I can help, or he will lose his love for me.

Neil ruled that the children were too young to go to midnight Mass on Christmas Eve, but the rest of the family went. Faith would have enjoyed attending the earlier services at the Presbyterian Church but she gave this up so they could all be together. It was an emotional strain to attend Mass with Neil and, when the choir sang "Jesu, Bambino," it was difficult to control herself. Neil seemed to sense her difficulty and moved very close to her, for which she was thankful, though he showed no other sign of noticing except the look in his eyes.

"Do we have to go to the sisters' school?" Stevie demanded, when he found that was the plan.

"Your daddy wants you to go there," Faith answered.

"It's an excellent school," their grandmother put in "You will have much better teachers than you had in public school."

Faith was apprehensive about putting Stevie in a school he didn't wish to attend but to have so much as expressed a doubt would have precipitated a family crisis, so she watched her words carefully.

To her great delight Margie came home exultant. The little nun who taught the second grade was, according to Margie, the prettiest, sweetest teacher in the world and knew more than anyone. Margie was her devoted slave and wanted to take her a gift every day. Neil was delighted and, because the child's reactions eased the strain, Faith also rejoiced. Stevie was less pleased with his teacher. She was all right, he said grudgingly, but school was no fun. Not nice as it had been in California. Sometimes Neil tried to reassure the boy but on other days he was impatient. "You do your part and everything will go well," he said. "You'll grow to like it."

The difficulty was not with the teachers but with the priest. Father Corrigan was an older man who had missed developing the gentler Christian graces. He knew his dogma, but not his boys, and he used corporal punishment. When Margie heard of a case she came home frightened almost to illness. Stevie seemed more stubborn than fearful, but Faith lived in terror of the day when he would openly rebel. She had promised herself that she would not hold her husband over their children as a policeman, yet once when Stevie spoke with disrespect of Father Corrigan she said before she thought, "You mustn't let daddy hear you speak that way of a priest. Catholics are supposed to treat them with respect."

Stevie remembered the genial Mr. Budlong in California. At least two thirds of the adults in his congregation had called him "Bill." "I'm going to be a Protesttant when I grow up," he said. "Then you can call the minister by his first name and joke with him. I've never seen a priest as nice as Mr. Budlong."

Faith was at a loss for an answer. If she warned the boy not to say such things before his father it would give the youngster a warped idea of Neil and, possibly, of the priest as well. Yet, if Stevie made any such remarks to his father, Neil would either jump on the boy, or feel that she was stirring her son to rebellion. She decided to say nothing, help the boy with his harder studies, and minimize the disagreeable features as much as possible. "When daddy is really well again, we'll talk more with him about it," she would say. "But we must not worry him now."

One day in the spring Stevie came home crying and said that he would never go back to school. The priest had whipped one boy and had even slapped a little girl. Faith was utterly sick about it. Even Margie was pale and said that, if it wasn't for Sister Angela, she'd go right back to California to school.

Faith decided that she must talk to her husband. He looked concerned and said, "I'm sorry Stevie's so unhappy. We should never have let him start to public school in the first place. He evidently has had no discipline and needs it, however hard it is for either you or me to see him get it. Maybe we can find a good Catholic boarding school for him in a few years. He would likely adjust more happily if he didn't feel your sympathy at home. Boys often work on their mothers that way. He must guess you do not approve of parochial schools."

"I've said nothing against them, Neil, and Margie certainly loves Sister Angela."

"You don't always have to put in words how you feel for children to understand. Stevie must know your feelings. Likely much better than you guess."

But something had to be done. Evidently there was no chance of talking it out with Neil for he placed the blame squarely at her door and, in his present physical condition, argument would only add to misunderstanding. She lay awake that night and finally decided to go directly to Father Corrigan. She had heard Brooks Marvin remark once that if you stated you were a Protestant and said it with your chin out, they might get the idea you were a trouble-maker and would walk more softly.

He agreed it didn't make one popular in a Catholic community, but it did get results. Chris belonged in the St. Aloysius parish and their children had started to the parochial school but now were going to the public one nearer home.

Faith timed herself to reach the school after the children had gone home, hoping to catch Father Corrigan before he was busy with other matters. She did not want Stevie to know her plans and waited on the far side of the building till the last boy had left the yard. So it happened that she was in front of the rectory when an ambulance pulled up and someone was carried down on a stretcher. It seemed an inopportune time to knock but she was determined to go through with her plan. She had worked herself to the point of making some very firm statements to the priest and hated to lose the determination her anger had generated. But the icy crust that had been forming around her heart melted at the very sight of the young priest who answered her knock.

"I came to talk with Father Corrigan about my son," she began, "but seeing this ambulance, perhaps I should not come in. Has anything serious happened?"

"Please come in," invited the priest. He had a delightful smile, like Neil's had been before the war, and his pale brown hair curled on his head. "I am Father Donovan and I was sent to take charge of the school while Father Corrigan is in the hospital. He has ulcers but he's refused to do a thing for them till it became an emergency. I'd be glad to talk with you about your son, Mrs. . ."

"Mrs. Mackaig. Mrs. Neil Mackaig. My son, Stevie, is in the third grade, but he's very unhappy." She did not say why, but she felt sure that Father Donovan knew. Before she left she had told him that the children had been contented in public school in California, but she managed to say a word of praise for Sister Angela. She was frankly positive about her own Protestantism. The young priest simply said, "Let me see what I can do with Steve, Mrs. Mackaig. Don't try to sell me to him, please. Just let me work things out. I was a kid myself not too long ago. A regular brat. So I can remember how I reacted."

"You don't look like you had been a brat," Faith said, smiling appreciatively.

All the way home she found herself thanking God for the miracle that had happened. She prayed that Stevie would love the new priest, and that the glory of his new ministry would not be worn thin with overwork and authoritarianism and listening to people's sins, but that his sense of humor and health, and his love of God and all things beautiful would follow him through the years. She even prayed for poor old Father Corrigan, who had so soured because of his inner difficulties, or had developed digestive troubles because he was so sour with little children. She asked that God would give him a good rest and improve his disposition and find him a place where he could serve the Lord without blighting the lives of small children.

She wished she dared tell Neil about the change but she was afraid he would guess why she had gone to the school and disapprove of it; so she acted as though she did not know what had happened and let him tell the news to the children, who rejoiced openly. She knew Neil was relieved too. He was normally indulgent, and he must be fully as eager to have the children happy at school as she was. It was just that his plans must be achieved within the framework of the Catholic Church.

Whether her prayers helped or not, Stevie changed his tune almost instantly. Father Donovan became his hero He even tackled his catechism with determination, because Father Donovan knew the best stories, could coach the best ball, sing the best songs, and find the grandest spots to take the boys on hikes.

It all added up to a happier home life, and there were moments now when she felt that she and Neil might find the way back to their old understanding again.

During the war Molly took a job in a library in New York City and now she was back for a visit. She spent several days with Faith and, when alone, they talked freely. Steve's work kept him in New York part of the time and he and Molly were seeing more and more of each other. Molly could scarcely put a sentence together without mentioning him.

Faith listened with great interest then said, a little mischievously, "You know I'm always interested in the status of this affair, Molly. I think you should make a definite statement before you leave."

"That is the hard thing to do, Faith. Steve makes no reservations about his feeling for me. And I'm simply crazy about him. But he insists that, if we can't be married on the open basis that your mother and father have, our present friendship is better. He feels you and Neil are missing something. Perhaps I shouldn't have said that, honey," she added anxiously.

"He's right," Faith acknowledged. "It didn't bother me much till Neil came back from overseas. If we hadn't lost the baby the way we did, things might have stayed the same."

"I was so sorry about that, Faith. And I'm sure Steve's remarks didn't help your family relationships. He was terribly steamed up when he got back."

"You don't think, Molly, that God is so terrible he would punish a baby for not being baptized when it couldn't help it, do you?"

"Of course not. That isn't Catholic teaching, anyhow. A Catholic can think anything almost that he wants to about limbo except that it's neither heaven nor hell. I imagine a good many of them worry the doctrine around till it doesn't bother them too much."

"But it's still a punishment, in a way," Faith insisted. "It is being deprived of something considered valuable through an accident. Either it is bad, or they shouldn't make a fuss about it."

"You have something there. After Steve told me, I got to reading everything I could find about it, which is largely nothing. It's mostly strong tradition. Anyhow, you weren't to blame and no one should victimize you. What did the Mackaigs say?"

"Nothing. That's what makes it so hard. If we could talk, we might get over the tenseness. I used to say Catholics and Protestants could discuss religion if they'd listen to each other and try to be fair. But now I've quit trying. I go to church alone. Neil takes the children with him. It's lonely for me but my only other choice is to stop going as Frank has, and that isn't good either."

"Maybe Steve's right that this thing has to be settled before there are complications. He doesn't rush me and . . . and I don't know just what to do. I'm used to the sacraments but if I could decide the Episcopal claims for the apostolic succession were authentic, perhaps. . . Anyhow, I'm not so smugly sure one side has

142

all the answers as I once was. I've been reading a lot. That's both helpful and upsetting."

"I think so much of both you and Steve, and I do want you both to be happy. If getting married would accomplish this, I'd urge it!"

"Listen, darling! It won't take any urging to get me to marry your brother once I get my own mind settled. The great thing about our relationship now is that we can say anything we think to each other. Once people get on the defensive . . ."

"How right you are!"

"Faith, do you suppose it's partly because Neil hasn't been able to pull himself together after his war experience? Even to me he seems different—as though he just had to make something come out right."

"I think he does feel that way," Faith agreed slowly.

Chapter II

FAITH read her letter from Alice Reredon several times, trying to think how she would present to Neil the matter of taking Rachel. She had hinted before, but had hesitated about pressing for a decision. Now Alice was losing ground rapidly and felt it was time Rachel should be sent away. If Faith could take the child, both she and Paul would be relieved. She added that Paul was certain he had known an officer—a Neil Mackaig—who had been under fire with him. He was much interested because the Mackaig he had known was badly wounded and he had thought him dead. Paul remembered him as a conscientious officer and a good Catholic. Alice also said that her letters would be very few from now on, but she had an excellent nurse, and there was plenty of money from her family for medical expenses and for Rachel's education. She hoped Faith would answer soon, for time was running out.

Faith laid the problem before Neil that night, telling him what a well-adjusted child Rachel was and how fond they all were of her. She emphasized her admiration for Alice and the friendship that had sprung up between them. Neil seemed doubtful till the matter of Paul came up and Faith relayed his message. She could see this might have a bearing on whether or not Neil would give consent.

"In a way it's up to you, Faith," he said surprisingly. "It will add to your work and responsibility more than to mine. You say she gets on well with our youngsters and they love her. But what about school?"

"I'm sure she'll want to go where they do. They love it now that Father Donovan is in charge."

"In that case I can't see where there would be friction. Do as you like. I'm fond of children and hoped we would have another eventually, when you are strong enough."

He knew she was still taking precautions to avoid another pregancy, but perhaps he thought it natural since it was little more than a year since she had lost her baby. A fleeting thought came to her that another one might help to heal the breach between them, but there was also danger of widening it.

The next day she wired Alice to send Rachel whenever she wished, then followed it with a long, cordial letter. The children wrote too, urging Rachel to hurry up and visit them in time to play in the snow.

When Rachel came she slipped as easily into living in her new home as a kitten would have crawled into a warm bed. She had her mother's enviable disposition. She was a bit dubious about going to Catholic school but, since Margie and Stevie pronounced it good, she was willing to try. Soon she was singing the praises of Father Donovan as loudly as they did. She was a little frightened of the nuns' habits at first, and concerned that she would do the wrong thing. But in a few weeks she was saying "Our Blessed Mother" and making the sign of the cross, and she asked if it would be all right for a Protestant to have a crucifix like the one Margie had.

"Yes, Protestants can have a crucifix if they wish," Faith assured her.

"Why don't they use them right along?" asked the child.

Faith hazarded that Protestants felt that the empty cross, which signified both Christ's dying and that he had risen again and conquered death, was more significant to them than the symbol only of his dying. She could see that the child was puzzled.

A few days later Rachel came to Faith and said, "I guess I'll have a plain cross instead of the crucifix. I saw a lovely one in the book store and, when I get enough saved, you can buy it for me." But she loved the little statue of the Virgin Mary which Neil got for her and, to outward appearances, showed it the same reverence the others did.

Early in January word came that Aunt Kate was ill, so Margaret McLaren went out to take care of her. Faith was glad her mother would be near enough to see Alice, though the latter was failing rapidly and, by the end of February, was kept under opiates. Just before Easter she died.

Faith had a long letter from her mother. The hard part was telling Rachel, who would not take the news casually. Faith spent the evening with the child in her room. After they were in their night clothes, Stevie and Margie came in to listen. Stevie lay on the rug, pulling his robe about his ankles. The girls sat on the bed.

"Will they bury my mother?" Rachel probed.

"They'll bury her body, honey. But the lovely part of your mother, her mind and personality, will live on."

"Is that part up in heaven now?" Rachel asked.

"No one knows for sure, darling. But people who love God as your mother did will go to live with him some way. Perhaps your mother already has a new, well body, and can do anything she likes in her new home."

"Won't she go to purgatory?" Stevie asked, much concerned, for they remembered their Aunt Alice, as they had called her, very well.

"Protestants don't think there is exactly the same sort of purgatory Catholics do," Faith said, trying to choose her words carefully. "Perhaps we'll not get right into the presence of God at the first moment. We may have to grow a while. But we think we'll go to a place where we'll have an opportunity to do things we've wanted to do here on earth and for some reason or another couldn't get them done. Maybe we didn't have a chance. We think there will be no sick bodies when we leave this earth and we can be with people we love. And no one will be hungry or thirsty or too cold or too hot. We should be happy that your mother has gone to such a beautiful place and that now she isn't in pain any more."

"I'm glad about that part," said Rachel solemnly. "But I can't help missing her when I think I won't see her again."

The subject was so near the children's hearts that they told it at school the next day and one of the nuns who overheard told them about purgatory. It was a place, she said, where even good people were put so they could be purified and made ready to see God. But they couldn't help themselves and they couldn't get out unless people here on earth helped them, which, the nun said, the children could do by praying and priests

148

could do by praying and saying masses. Rachel was disturbed at this and Faith could see the havoc worked in the child's thinking by the two interpretations.

"Don't worry, honey," she consoled her, "your mother didn't believe in a purgatory like that. In any case, your daddy Paul is a Catholic and he will have some masses said if it's necessary."

From the first Rachel went to church school with Faith, who had assumed the responsibility for a class. Then the child often stayed for the church service as well. It added something to the worship for Faith to have Rachel with her and tempered the loneliness she felt when her own children went with their father. Sometimes they compared notes. As most of the conversations came when Neil was gone, he did not realize that they took place. Faith prayed that he would never know of them for fear he would oppose such a free exchange of viewpoints. It was inevitable that the time would come when he would object to some phase of Rachel's Protestantism. He was eager, almost grasping, for evidences that Steve and Margie were absorbing the rigid religious training to which they were subjected. In order to humor him and always with the hope that she might win back some of the confidence he had once appeared to have in her, Faith would relay remarks which she felt might be of comfort. Even as she did so there was a division in her own mind which troubled her, but for which there seemed no clear-cut solution.

One day a little playmate from a Christian Science family hurt his hand and Faith, without thinking, put antiseptic on it and bandaged it carefully. The little boy's older sister was somewhat concerned at this medical treatment and protested. "We don't use medicine

when we are hurt," she had said. "We trust in God."
Margie, small as she was, had caught an unpleasant implication, so she returned, "We trust in God, too. But
we believe in helping him along a little."

Neil laughed appreciatively when she told him.
"They're quick, aren't they?" he said proudly. "Given
the right training, they're sure to come through with a
strong conviction."

Faith made no reply. Neil saw one aspect clearly, but
there was something he could not appreciate and she
had no idea how to approach the matter. With each rebuff the wall between them seemed to grow higher. It
was true that Margie received religious instruction with
appreciation. She and Rachel held long conversations.
Rachel was the older and Margie could not always hold
her own, but she had an excellent understanding for a
child her age.

Except for his devotion to Father Donovan, Steve
disliked the whole thing. He said little in his father's
presence, doing his complaining to his mother.

On matters of abstaining, since she did the meal planning, it was comparatively easy to avoid issues. There
was never meat for anyone on Fridays or Ember days.
She even hid or disposed of leftovers so that the matter
could not be discussed. Always she made a special dessert so that the meal would seem good.

When Rachel first came, Faith suggested that, since
the family did not eat meat and so many people were
starving, that they also eliminate expensive fish, and use
the money as a sacrificial offering for hungry people.

But Neil did not approve.

"You'll just confuse the issue to them," he said. "Give
the money if you like and teach the children to give to

others. I'm all for it. But to tell them they are putting aside Friday for that purpose would just mix them up. The Church teaches Catholics not to eat meat on Friday. They are to remember that on Friday Christ suffered for them, and they in return, give up something for him. They do this because it is a Church law. This is what they are taught at school and hear at Church. Why throw another idea in?"

Such decrees left Faith unhappy for days. Neil did not wish to make her miserable, but he was jealous of every prerogative of the Church. There must be no personal interpretation or explanation. As usual, the easiest way out was to say the least. But it was not the way a wound healed the fastest. And it added to Faith's resentment about her children's training.

When nothing unpleasant happened for a time, she took new hope that someday they would be happy again, as they had been before the war. Then always something, perhaps entirely outside themselves, occurred to produce irritation. Once it was a day spent with Neil's family. His father had been ailing for some time and was unable to be about. It was hard to find someone to come in so Mrs. Mackaig could have a chance to rest or leave the house. Faith offered to go over to relieve her. She was fond of her father-in-law and never felt that he was pressuring her.

As Mrs. Mackaig left the house, she asked Faith to pay the driver when he came with things she had left at the cleaners. The bill was in the desk and the money with it, she explained. When Faith went for the money she saw, directly beneath the cleaning bill a statement from the parish church for fifteen dollars for masses said the previous month for an unbaptized child. She did not look at the date but decided later that they must be old bills for, surely anything done would have been long before this, since the Mackaigs were not pressed for funds. It could have been an accident that they were left where she could see them, or it could have been done purposely. She wished she could talk the matter out with Neil but he had asked her not to speak of it and this would surely not be the time to open the subject. But the very necessity of silence added to her annoyance and distress.

A few days later when she went again to give Mrs. Mackaig a little respite, Neil's Aunt Connie, who was a Reverend Mother, was there. Faith was always ill at ease for she had never grown accustomed to the etiquette of addressing religious aristocracy. Now that she felt a hidden vein of disapproval in her husband's family, she was even more shy and self-conscious than ever. Mr. Mackaig asked her to go to the library for a book he wanted. To reach this room she had to go down a long hall. It opened just behind the living-room and she was scarcely inside when she heard the two sisters talking in low tones. Her instinct was to get the book as quickly as possible and retrace her steps, moving quietly so it would be unnecessary for her to speak. She was sure neither of the women could see her and, from their words, she knew they were not aware of her presence.

"She is undoubtedly a restless, unhappy woman, as we all are until we give up our own wills to God and are willing to obey his laws," the Reverend Mother was saying.

"For years I hoped she would decide to come into the Church. I am sure she was on the verge. We have tried not to push her. It has been difficult for Neil for he was so very fond of her. But since her child was lost, she has been on the defensive. Defensive Protestantism is an unlovely thing, no matter how charitably we try to regard it."

"They have nothing to hold to," the Reverend Mother continued. "If there ever was any cause for revolt it has long since passed. They are trying to hold together the shreds of a heresy. Perhaps she senses this and longs for the stability of the true Church—especially when she sees how comfortable and happy you all are. She is a bright woman and cannot help seeing these things. Have you thought of a novena?"

"I suggested it to Neil but I think she's hardly ready for that, yet. She keeps the letter of the law. I have no doubt that she does better than many Protestants at keeping their vows. But one cannot help knowing she is resentful. And her very attitude will undermine the most excellent teaching."

They were moving away now and Faith stepped farther into the corner of the library to make sure she could not be seen. As the murmured voices grew more faint she caught the words "It may be that a novena . . ." then the door closed. Fearing they might return she stood motionless till they had time to reach the street, then she picked up the book and slipped upstairs the back way.

Though perturbed, she joked with Mr. Mackaig and went out of her way to show him that she was glad to be there. He's such a dear, she thought. Neil used to be like him in some ways. Since he was feeling much better, she made an excuse to leave a few minutes before time for his wife's return.

The habit of hiding her feelings was growing steadily. She knew this was unhealthy, yet she either chose the wrong time to talk with her husband, or there was no right time.

There were only two days left in the school year. As soon as vacation came she decided to take the children and go to her mother's for a week. They had not seen each other since her mother returned from California. Faith had an intense longing for the frank conversations in her own home, and its lack of tension. If Neil would only relax and laugh as he used to! If constantly divided loyalty can split a personality, I wonder how long mine can stay intact, she thought.

Neil did not object to her trip to Avalon. Like his father, he was inclined to allow others freedom to do as they pleased. It was just in this matter of religion that he had become so difficult. She would try to keep this out of her mind and enjoy the drive over. The children were gleeful at being out of school and having a chance for a new place to play. They worried a little because there was a rumor that Father Donovan might not be back and the fifth grade teacher was very strict, but there was a long vacation ahead and soon they forgot to talk of school.

When alone with her mother, Faith sputtered about the conversation she had overheard, particularly the mention of a novena. Her mother was amazingly calm about it. "I wouldn't let it trouble me, if I were you," she said, "God is assailed all the time by people who are determined to finagle him into converting someone to their particular belief. I'm sure he'll know how to handle it."

"I thought you believed God changed people's minds—sometimes, at least—when others prayed for them, if they were sufficiently fervent and importunate. Don't you?"

"I believe in asking God to reveal himself to people. Since none of us can possibly have a perfect understanding of him, it seems a little presumptuous that we insist he reveal just what we like to think he is ourselves. Besides, since we think there are different roads to him, we can't expect everyone else to trot along the path we happen to like. All Protestants should fear is that Catholics will live their faith better and pray more purely."

"It annoys me to have them say that defensive Protestantism is an unlovely thing but, Mother, it's the truth. I can't seem to find a way to take the offensive, and I'd be afraid to if I could."

"Any defensive is ugly. It's easier to see that than to know what to do. Certainly, though, if we pray for guidance, some course of action will be revealed."

The conversation was interrupted by a letter from Steve, who was back in New York. He and Molly had at last settled their problems and were planning to be married. An Episcopal minister, who was an ardent student of the apostolic succession, had convinced Molly that Episcopal orders were valid and their sacraments would have the same potency as Catholic ones. Steve was indifferent on that point but he accepted a transmission of spiritual grace and found worship in his father's church helpful. They had attended confirmation classes for adults and now were planning to go into the Episcopal fold together. They had set the wedding date for June thirtieth and would be married in the Little Church Around the Corner. Steve urged his parents to come for the wedding. It would be no use to ask Molly's relatives, except a few upstate cousins who were already Protestant.

"I'm glad for them," Faith rejoiced. "But what will this do to Neil and his family? They're so fond of Molly and they'll feel worse than ever now. They've worried for fear of this for years. You know Molly's never been so staunch as the rest of them. But it may draw fire from me and Molly will get the novena instead."

She said nothing about the matter when she returned to Athens and finally Neil was forced to bring it up. She was sure he had known for several days but, like her, he hated to talk about it. He was very brief.

"I doubt if she'll be happy," he said, "fine as Steve is. But I never knew a Catholic who left the Church to be genuinely comfortable outside of it. Usually it's easier to throw the whole thing overboard than to go into another church. But she's taken plenty of time. We'll have to admit that."

Then the subject was dropped.

Another matter that would not bear direct scrutiny was the problem of Rachel. Faith enjoyed her and found her a great consolation for the loss of having her own children share her interests. But definite situations arose from having a Protestant child in the home with two Catholic children which made Neil apprehensive. He felt they would be more firm in their faith if there were not opportunities for making comparisons. Now it was becoming necessary either to tell the children not to discuss religion at all, or to mute Rachel at every turn. Neither method was desirable. A free exchange with frank statements from both parents and puzzling questions discussed rationally might be stimulating. But Neil would not allow this.

The week following their return from Avalon, Rachel came home from church school thrilled at the prospect of vacation school. Margie immediately clamored to be allowed to go too. Some Catholic children in the neighborhood would attend and the teaching would be about the life of Christ, the advance folder said. Faith had to answer, "You'll have to talk with daddy about it, dear. Of course I'd love to have you go, but he may feel differently."

She could see Neil was disturbed by the request. "I would like to say Yes, Margie," he said slowly, "but it is hard to be a good Catholic and listen to the teachings of other churches. God wants us to worship the way he directed, which is the way the Church teaches. To listen to something else will just confuse you. You have your music and you can go to the park. I'm sure you'll have plenty to keep you busy."

Like most children she did the greater part of her fussing to her mother when her father was out of earshot. After a few days Rachel felt so sorry about it that she offered to give up the school. Faith, rebelling inwardly, went over to tell Mr. Dickerson, the minister, the reason. When she returned she heard Margie sputtering to her father about a Jehovah's Witness who had wanted to leave some papers with her.

"What shall I say when folks come to the door like that?" she was asking.

"Just tell them this is a good Catholic family and we're not interested. If I'm around, call me," Neil directed.

So they were a Catholic family? Was Neil trying to deceive himself? There were two adult members and only one was Catholic. Stevie was working with a mechanical toy, but he looked up to watch her. Neil should know that such statements as he had just made hurt, unless it could be that the nomenclature of Catholicism was so strong in his thinking that the words slipped out unintentionally. If so, he should qualify it. But she was still so raw from the incident of the novena, the defensive Protestantism, and Rachel's giving up something she loved, that she could not completely hide her feelings, so she turned and went slowly upstairs. In a minute Stevie followed her. She went to her dressing table and pretended to be fixing her hair in order to have her back toward him. But he understood and came over and put his arms about her.

"Mother," he said, "don't feel so bad. When I grow up I'm going to be a Protestant, so you'll have someone on your side."

So the children sensed the situation. She found a brief, unholy joy in the boy's reaction. "You'll have to decide your religion on some better foundation than that, Stevie," she said, squeezing him hard against her. "Your daddy loves the Catholic Church so dearly that he can't see how people can love God without doing it through the Church. He would feel terrible if he heard what you said, for he has tried so hard to make you love the Catholic Church, too."

"I don't, though. I like to sing in the choir when Father Donovan leads it. And I don't mind school if I have a good teacher. But I hated that horrible catechism and I didn't want to be confirmed last year. I just had to or daddy would have been sore. And Father Donovan wanted me to, and I like him. But when I'm twenty-one I'm going to be a Protestant. I liked Mr. Budlong awful well and I know it's easier to be a Protestant than a Catholic. Everyone says so."

"I'm not so sure of that," Faith said.

Neil was coming up the stairs. Stevie turned away and went to his own room. No further comment was made about the incident, but she could sense Neil's anxiety. He was trying so hard to make his children Catholic. Margie fitted into the pattern naturally. She loved the stories of the saints and asked her grandmother to tell them. She was fascinated with handling a rosary or a statue. She lived in a romantic world peopled with saints and angels, where great music was sung and great art produced. She saw little that was wrong in anyone. For two years she had been under the spell of Sister Angela, who could make the most arduous task a sacrifice offered for the glory of God; and who had a skilful way of skipping around points that annoyed small minds. "Their thinking will open up so they can grasp this easily later on," Sister Angela would say. "Why push them now?" There was never any problem getting Margie to attend Mass. She was ready every Sunday to skip out to the car with her father, her hand in his. Neil was closer to Margie, even as Faith understood Stevie better.

In her own way Rachel was just as responsive to Protestant teaching as Margie to the Catholic. She was still at the age when children like to go to church. Rachel and Margie carried on endless conversations, comparing the things they had learned, but none of these ever took place when Neil was home. With that sixth sense of children in such matters, they knew enough to be silent then. Faith thought that if he could hear them, without a block in his mind, it might help him to overcome his fear of Rachel's influence, for she was sure it was fear. Except you become as little children, she quoted to herself, you cannot enter the kingdom of God.

Once she heard Margie saying, "And when the priest starts or stops something, he faces the crucifix and we all stand and cross ourselves and he says 'In the name of the Father and the Son and of the Holy Ghost.' Daddy showed me how it looked in Latin because I'm going to study Latin next year. It's here." The child thumbed through the missal till she found the words, "And it sounds about like this, *'In Nomine Patris, et Filii, et Spiritu Sancti.'* If I were a boy, I'd be a priest when I grow up. Maybe I'll be a nun like great-aunt Connie, who is a Reverend Mother. Only I wouldn't want to be a closed-up nun. I'd want to be on the loose." The child was serious and Rachel shared her mood. Neither of them smiled.

"Won't Latin be terribly hard to learn?" Rachel asked. "I'd rather study a language people talk. Only priests talk Latin."

"I just love it," Margie insisted rapturously, taking up the missal. *"In Nomine Patris, et Filii, et Spiritu Sancti.'* Aren't they beautiful words? Do you have any beautiful words you say over and over in the Presbyterian Church?"

"Yes, we have beautiful ones, too," Rachel said, "but we don't say them in Latin. And sometimes the people talk, too. And when the choir comes in we sing. Sometimes it's 'Holy, Holy, Holy, Lord God Almighty. All Thy works shall praise Thy name in earth and sky and sea!' Don't you think those are beautiful? I like it where

160

it says 'earth and sky and sea' because it makes me think of the hill where we used to play in California and you could see the earth and sky and sea all at one time."

"Those are lovely words," Margie agreed. "What else does the minister say?"

"He doesn't always say the same thing," Rachel explained, evidently trying to remember. "Sometimes he prays and he says, 'O God from whom all holy desires and all good counsels do proceed,' but I'm not sure what holy desires are."

"Oh, I know that one," said Margie, delighted to display more wisdom, "Sister Angela told us. They are things it is good to want because they please God. And it's all right to have them in the Catholic Church, too. In fact," she speculated seriously, "I believe you're supposed to."

Rachel continued, "And at the end of the sermon Mr. Dickerson says, 'these words which we have said with our lips may we believe in our hearts and practice in our lives, through Jesus Christ, our Lord, Amen.' That means you're not to pretend but really go out and act like Christians."

Faith was amazed. Mr. Dickerson did often use these words in his closing prayer. Somehow they had lodged in Rachel's mind. She prayed that some course would be revealed to her and that Neil would come to see there must be a give and take.

The little girls were an answer to her prayers because their sweet interpretations were without contention. Under the spell of their influence she hurried about several Sunday mornings and went to Mass before going to her church school class and the service which followed.

The months went by with less friction than usual. The Mackaigs spent the summer at an Atlantic shore resort. Steve and Molly honeymooned in Europe, fortunately, since their presence would have added to the strain. At times Faith thought Neil's family sensed her inward rebellion and tried to avoid irritations. They were good people, except that they must hold the upper hand religiously because they believed it was what God wanted them to do. They were neither the first, nor the only religious group to hold this view. It was so often more a matter of struggle for power than of obedience to a still, small voice. They thought God told them something because they so much wanted him to. There had been Presbyterians and Episcopalians, Congregationalists and Lutherans, and all manner of other Christians who had missed the overtones of God's voice in trying to make others hearken to what they felt were the fundamentals. Individually, Protestants could be as cantankerous in their contentions about God's will as any Catholic, but they did not have the machinery for enforcing their wishes. Most Protestants would have felt such compulsion wrong, even if it had been in their power to use it. She had fallen into the Catholic machinery years before when she voluntarily surrendered her rights and responsibilities, Faith mused. But at what point should one stand up for "the freedom with which Christ hath set us free" that Mr. Dickerson was always talking about? To Neil such freedom was barren nonsense, because there was only one great freedom, and that was freedom to serve God as he had commanded.

But when Faith heard that Father Corrigan had been sent to a sanitarium for convalescent priests, and that Father Donovan would be in charge of the school the coming year, she sang a *Te Deum* of her own and decided another crisis had been passed. When she saw the young priest digging around the shrubbery that bordered the schoolyard a few days later, she stopped to chat.

"I'm so glad you're to be with us another year, Father Donovan," she said warmly. "Stevie loves you and I feel you are doing a great deal for him. If the prayers of a heretic have any efficacy, I'm doing all for you I can." She could laugh with him and he would understand.

"I've an idea they may do more good than those which are solicited, since yours come so spontaneously," he returned.

So the year that Stevie was in the fifth grade passed uneventfully. Faith and Rachel went regularly to the Presbyterian Church and now Rachel was singing in the junior choir. Margie was confirmed and Rachel watched with mild envy when she put on her lovely white dress and the veil that made her look like a child bride. But she clung loyally to the Protestant church, her church school class, and the choir. Neil watched carefully to see that no unguarded statement of hers suggested her beliefs, and Rachel was quick to discern what could and could not be said in his presence. Margie was almost as careful, and Stevie was fast developing a reticence that troubled his mother. There would never be the free-for-all discussions which the McLaren family had known and which had cemented a bond even across strong differences of opinion.

Before Thanksgiving, John McLaren died. Neil was in New York at the time and Faith called him, hoping he would fly back for the funeral. He expressed his deep sympathy but said it would be impossible to be there. He sent flowers and did all the gracious, correct things, but Faith wanted him with her when her father was laid to rest. It must be that he did not want to attend even a Protestant funeral, she thought. Yet almost any Catholic would do that.

She took the children without consulting him, knowing that they would catch the meaning when the choir sang:

For all the Saints, who from their labors rest,
Who Thee by faith before the world confessed,
Thy name, O Jesus, be forever bless'd,
    Alleluia.
Thou wast their rock, their Fortress, and their Might:
Thou, Lord, their Captain in the well-fought fight;
Thou, in the darkness drear, the one true Light.
    Alleluia.
O blest communion, fellowship divine!
We feebly struggle, they in glory shine;
Yet all are one in Thee, for all are Thine.
    Alleluia!

The bishop of the Episcopal diocese was there, wearing a rochet and chimer, the Methodist minister, a doctor of divinity, wore a robe with purple bands, then came the Congregational minister in a plain Geneva gown over his business suit, followed by the Baptist minister who had a prejudice against clerical garb which he called "monkey clothes." The congregation thought they were all dressed appropriately, for every man expressed his own opinion on an unimportant matter. Besides it was a service designed, not for correctness, but

to pay homage to a man who had been loved by everyone and who now had gone.

The children were much impressed by the service
and talked steadily of it. They were more concerned
about heaven and what it was like than when Rachel's
mother had died and they asked questions which Faith
found hard to answer.

"Are you and grandma sure grandpa is in heaven?"
asked Margie.

"We're very sure, darling," her mother comforted
her. "No one has been there, but we know God is good
and he has something beautiful for people who love
him."

After a long time the child asked timidly, "Would it
be wicked to have Father Donovan say a Mass for grandpa, when he wasn't a Catholic?"

"Why, n-no, honey. It isn't wicked."

"I think they give the priest some money," Margie
speculated, "because it takes his time and he's so busy.
But I have some in my piggy bank."

"You can have what I've got," Rachel offered.

"I'll give you what you need," Faith said. "You talk
with Father Donovan about it. I'm sure he'll understand." And I'll talk with him too, bless her darling
heart, Faith thought.

"I'd feel lots better if we had some masses, Mother,"
Margie said. "You know there could be a slip up about
this thing." She was so sweetly serious that Faith caught
her in her arms just as the child burst out, "O Mother,
I just couldn't bear it to have grandpa disappointed!"

Faith told Neil about it when he returned and he
seemed pleased in the way he had been those first years
of their married life.

Steve and Molly came for the funeral and it was good seeing them again. She was relieved that Neil was away for this first visit as it removed all strain. Molly went to the Mackaigs but only for a short time. The matter of her change of religion was not discussed. Once again the innermost thoughts of people's lives had to be concealed, Faith thought, when a spiritual nearness would have helped so much in crossing the hard places.

Chapter 12

FAITH and her mother had planned to take the children to California when summer came, and all live together in the cottage. Any form of movement was better for Margaret McLaren than brooding on her husband's passing. Uncle Jack had rented the cottage for the winter and was living in a home for elderly people. He had friends there and the excellent care he needed because of his increasing infirmity. Unfortunately, he passed away before they had started for the coast. When Faith called Neil at his office to give him the sad news, she did not suggest that he go with her to help with final arrangements and settle up the property. She did not even think of it.

The cottage, the car, and several thousand dollars were to go to Faith. There was some money for Margie and Stevie. But there was also a great loneliness. With her father and Uncle Jack gone and Neil no longer close, except physically, she had only Steve to whom she could turn for masculine help.

Each day she prayed that something might open up to bring Neil and her close together again. Or was it "again"? They had started with the wrong premise—a premise that gave him certain priorities. She had been so convinced that she would not resent these advantages yet, after a time, she had. In a sense Neil had a justifiable complaint against her. She had been unable to keep her promises, in spirit, at least.

As they were driving back with the car that now was hers, Faith remarked to her mother, "I sometimes wonder if I'm more abysmally stupid than most people or if God is slow in answering my prayers. When people want to get along together and to make a Christian home, as both Neil and I do, wouldn't you think there would be some opening, some incident. . . ."

"I'm sure it isn't God," Margaret insisted emphatically. "He gives his people brains and, if they ask humbly, he gives them grace. But there's pride on every side, and misunderstanding. I've tried to console myself with thinking that these family frictions are part of the plan for bringing religious groups together."

"I hope someone benefits from them," Faith said pessimistically.

"Remember, there are always future generations. People who get themselves and their children involved in such spiritual conflicts may be the ones who are moving Christians faster toward unity. I didn't want you to marry Neil because of this very thing but, now that you have, I feel sure God will help you find a solution. So don't give up."

Faith analyzed her own and, as nearly as she could, Neil's attitude, struggling to avoid every occasion for conflict. She knew this strain was part of the difficulty, but she couldn't get away from it. And she trembled for Stevie. The boy was advanced for his age and he was just entering that period when youngsters must argue and dispute every issue. The matter of religion would certainly come to the front and, where parents could not stand together, they were at a distinct disadvantage. The lack of an open family forum was sure to show itself.

When she returned home it began to be noised about that Father Corrigan, who had been in the sanitarium, was much better and was insisting on the resumption of his duties at St. Aloysius, and that Father Donovan was to leave. Stevie at once announced that he would not go back to the parish school. He had heard that the sister who taught the sixth grade was too strict and, besides, the boys who went to public school had lots more fun. But his remarks were made only to his mother.

"Why don't you tell daddy how you feel?" Faith asked. "If he understood, perhaps he'd be willing for you to go to public school."

"Don't you have any of the say over me?" Steve demanded combatively. "Why don't you tell daddy that you want me to go to public school? He'd have to listen to you."

Unfortunately, he would not, Faith thought with a sickening conviction. But she promised the boy to try. That night she sidled up to the subject as warily as possible.

"Neil, Stevie is so opposed to going back to the parish school now that he's heard Father Donovan is going to leave. He's apprehensive about Sister Veronica for she is said to be very strict. He would be off to a bad start from the first. And he's at such a touchy age."

"We're not sure yet that Father Donovan will leave," Neil countered, "and Stevie's ideas of Sister Veronica are built on hearsay. He may find he likes her better than he thinks. If we minimize his fears, he'll get in a better state of mind. He may think you are in sympathy with him and that is why he keeps nagging you. He says very little to me about it. Boys often assume that their mothers are easy marks. I wouldn't worry about it. You just make him worse."

. She had an impulse to tell him how the child had taunted her with having no voice in the matter but again, as she had done hundreds of times before, she closed her mouth.

The next week she and Rachel both decided to go to Mass before attending church. The priest read a letter from the bishop of the diocese, ordering that all Catholic children be sent to parish schools whenever one was available. There was a paragraph of comparison between the education offered by the Church and that which the public schools offered, with all points in favor of the former. Faith wished that she had not brought Rachel because the child's quick ears took it all in. So did Stevie's, but he was sullen, rather than curious.

On the way home Rachel said, "Our school in California wasn't like the bishop said. Maybe he hasn't been in all the public schools. I like public school."

"The bishop has possibly had more chance to see an all over picture than you have had," Neil observed stiffly. "His position and age might have something to do with his judgment." Neil was seldom curt with the children but his tone stated plainly that the last word had been said, so Faith immediately changed the subject. She could see that not only Rachel but Stevie took it as a rebuke. In addition to the children's feelings, her own resentment returned. She could as well have lived in the middle of the nineteenth century for all the say-so she had on this important subject. And all because years ago she had signed a statement to which her husband and his family held her rigidly.

Rachel and Margie, both in the fifth grade, mourned their separation from Sister Angela, who so far had been promoted along with them. Their new teacher, Sister Maria, was a plodding, middle-aged woman with a clear conscience and little imagination. At no time had it ever been claimed that the Grace of God was bestowed evenly upon his creatures, even when they had been equally exposed to opportunities. No matter how often Sister Maria had knelt to receive the Eucharist, she had not acquired the devoted, yet joyous, love for God first and little children next, which permeated Sister Angela. So it was a sad comedown for them to sit through the dreary discipline of things that had to be learned instead of darting about happily picking up no end of interesting facts with Sister Angela. The little girls moped and struggled with their studies and the lilt went out of Margie's voice when she read at home and Rachel kept whispering that, if Margie could only go, too, she would want to attend public school, even if Uncle Neil didn't think it was any good.

But it was with Stevie that there was the most trouble. His teacher was an irritable nun who seemed to have never committed a mortal sin, but had never cultivated the gentler virtues either. Sister Veronica believed that, by the time a child reached the sixth grade it needed discipline more than coddling, and discipline she was prepared to give. She was a better teacher than the fifth grade sister for she knew her subject matter. On days when her bunion was not troublesome and it was neither hot nor chilly, and when everything went comfortably along, the children learned well. Unpredictability here made the trouble.

Where Father Donovan stayed no school could be an utter failure. With all his multitudinous duties he had a way of popping in and out so that a sulky child or an annoyed teacher hesitated to show any nastiness. He could pick out a trouble like a good fisherman spots a trout. He had a way of laying a gentle hand on a restless child and passing on some of his grace. If I could believe in stored-up favors, Faith would think when she watched him, it would be in seeing what he can do. Sometimes she thought of taking her problem with Neil to him, but he and Neil were friends and she could not well offer it as a theoretical case, for he would know at once, with his uncanny way of seeing people's difficulties. Besides, he was so near their age that his wisdom could not be great, despite the boast that the priests had all the answers.

When news came that he was to be transferred the first of October and Father Corrigan would be back, wails arose on every side. Faith heard ardent Catholic mothers wondering what the bishop could mean to return an old, ulcer-eaten man to a post that had been filled by one like Father Donovan. But others said that the parish was Father Corrigan's and he had built it out of nothing, coming when there had been but a handful of Catholics in a small town. Now Athens was well on its way toward being a city with several parishes, and he was entitled to the largest if he wanted it. Truly he had labored and other men had entered into his labors. He could scarcely be demoted unless guilty of malfeasance, which, of course, he never would be.

Among those who mourned Father Donovan's leaving, no one did so more audibly than Stevie. He could not say what he thought of Father Corrigan in his father's presence but he could shout his praises of Father Donovan and so, by implication, condemn the older priest. Neil was far too astute not to know what was happening but he was powerless against his son's strategy. As soon as Father Corrigan was back Stevie talked of how he hated school. He did not mention going to public school but, again, the implication was there.

Neil chafed under the dilemma. He loved to have his family happy and now he had been jockeyed into the position of being the parent who was to blame for his boy's unhappiness at the very moment when he was most eager to establish and keep rapport between them. Because Faith refused to support his arguments, he blamed her for inciting the youngster to rebellion. Again it was a blame with few words attached, but it was there just the same.

One morning late in October Frank Halstead rang the doorbell. In answer to her invitation he came in, settling himself leisurely in a big chair. "Where's Neil?" he asked.

"He had to go to Dartmouth on business and may stay over. In addition he's on some sort of committee for the Holy Name Society and that may take more time. Could I help you?"

"In this case you're better than Neil. I can sputter openly to you. Confession might be good for my soul but this isn't one to make to a Catholic."

"What's your trouble?" Faith asked. She liked to talk with Frank and seldom had an opportunity.

"Candidly, I feel like a polecat. That's not the approved formula inside the booth, but I'm sure it could often be said with more sincerity than the old blah-blah they've been using for centuries. Bet the priests would like a variety themselves."

"Isn't it supposed that there's quite a variation between the account a saint gives of himself and the confession of a hardened sinner?" Faith asked, laughing and beginning to feel relaxed as she always did with Frank. "But why are you in such an unregenerated state?"

"Well, here I sit talking with a charming sister-in-law about my troubles when my wife really needs my strong right arm at home. My son needs me too, but in this fracas I can't give either of them a lift. It happens that this is the slack season in my business and our offices are being painted. I could just as well give a bit of moral support in handling my son but, instead, I ducked bravely out. I refuse to ram a lot of ideas I don't believe down a small boy's throat so I left it to her and the priest. Kind of hard on the kid as well as on her, but he takes after me and he's sort of inventive when it comes to worming his way out. May be a good experience for him and, if I'm not there, I can't be accused of anything by anybody. I may have to be out of town quite a bit this week but I was going by your place and it looked comfortable, so I thought I'd check the possibility of killing a few hours here."

"Frank, you're a . . ." Faith began, laughing.

"I admit it," he agreed. "But what are you going to do when you're married to as fine a woman as Cele is and every instinct of your being is against her beliefs? She's got on pretty well with our two oldest kids. They're more like the Mackaigs and slipped into the groove, went to parochial school without complaint, never heard anything but what they were taught there, swallowed everything unquestioningly and made good, ordinary Catholic kids. Potential saints, to Cele, of course. But the Church says raise a family and it stands to reason she couldn't go along and have all of them Mackaigs, no matter how dominant that strain is. Tony took after me. He's fire to try Cele's soul, no doubt. Not bad compared with what I was at his age but a real worry to his mother. She's determined he has to sing in a boys' choir they're starting, and he must learn to be an acolyte or altar boy or whatever it is. The others went through the paces without a hitch. But Tony's something else."

"I hope Neil doesn't insist on Stevie's assisting Father Corrigan," Faith interrupted apprehensively. "He'd do anything, no matter how he disliked it, when we had Father Donovan here. But now he's terribly rebellious."

"Trouble with us, Faith, is that our kids are not our kids. I put myself in the role of secondary parent when I wrote my John Henry on that antenuptial contract. From then on I've had to keep still or raise a row. It would kill Cele if she knew how I feel. So I've diapered babies and taken the bones out of fish on Fridays, helped 'em dress and given 'em rides on the merry-go-round. But my kids haven't the faintest notion what I think on any important subject because I might get tangled up with a religious issue. I know some mixed families work out a better plan. But not us. It's partly Cele. She wouldn't go to a show the Church disapproves of. She wouldn't hold an opinion contrary to its teaching on a political issue, and she swallows their propaganda hook,

175

line, and sinker. I love her and flunkey for her. But I've become one of the Protestants my dad is always preaching about. He says we haven't stood up to be counted for so long that our knees would buckle if we tried. You should hear the old boy lay his congregation out now and then. I imagine that knowing the little I got from mother's estate has slipped into the coffers of the Roman Church has got him down. It hasn't done too much for my self-respect, either, but it was in the general fund before I knew it so it went for Catholic education and pew collections. I should have kept it separate."

"Then maybe what I did cancelled it out," Faith said, feeling better to make a confession. "I'd saved quite a little of the allotment the government sent me during the war. Uncle Jack wouldn't let me pay rent and part of Neil's salary went on most of the time in addition to what he got in the Navy. So we weren't too pressed. When the baby died the minister of the Community Church in the village was so good. I owed my recovery to him for he renewed my faith in a good God. I was too weak to think for myself. Afterward I gave him some money to furnish a tiny children's chapel. I did it in memory of a baby that could not be buried in a Catholic cemetery. You can guess how Neil would feel about that if he should find out."

Frank gave a low whistle. "That is something. If Neil knew, he'd think you had used his money to spread heresy."

"I know I can trust you not to mention this, Frank."

"Who would I be to get anyone else in bad? I haven't started to tell you all about Tony. On top of refusing to sing and all that, he's taken on a bosom pal who is unspeakable. The kid uses statements I wouldn't repeat to an old-time teamster. One of our neighbors left town in a hurry and put their place in the hands of a broker for renting, or we'd never have got this family in a good, middle-class, Irish Catholic neighborhood. If being anti-Catholic makes a Protestant, they are in the lead. This brat that's Tony's age is bigger than he is but only about half as quick. He's the only kid in the neighborhood that goes to public school and he'll make a caricature piece for good Catholics for years, a sample of Protestant education. He knew some lore about Catholics in general and the Irish in particular and he started in. Then he got more personal. If Tony couldn't give back as good as he got, it wasn't because he didn't try. At first it was 'My dog can lick your dog,' then it got to be 'My dad can lick your dad,' then they got to 'My church can lick your church.' They fought all over the place. Cele's been almost crazy. Tried to keep Tony shut up in the house but a tied dog couldn't be crosser. Finally the kids had one brawl so violent it seemed to clear the atmosphere. I'm not sure who got licked, but Tony's face was a mess for days. Up to then, understand, he had been fighting in the Catholic cause and, much as Cele deplored it, at least he was on the side of righteousness."

Faith snuggled down in a comfortable chair and listened appreciatively.

"Then it seems, " he went on, "that Tony told the kid I was a Protestant, so they made up. The next fight was between most of the boys in the fifth grade at St. Regis and against Tony and that brat. See where that puts Tony? And where I stand? I'd be willing to help my kid out if there was a thing I could do. But even acting as though I know there is a feud would make it worse for him, and would get the whole family on edge. Of course I'll get him the bicycle he wants for his birthday. I'll make it a surprise so Cele can't object on the grounds that he doesn't deserve it. Just come home with it some night." Then he finished with a sigh, "In a neighborhood where most of the people believe that civilization through the dark ages was saved by the Irish and that all worthwhile culture stems from them, see what I mean?"

"Yes," said Faith. "But isn't there any way you can talk this over with Cele?"

"Listen, Faith! When I was first married I used to try to edge up to Cele with an idea. Went all around Robin Hood's barn to present it so as not to upset her. It never worked. Now I've given up. She thinks God gave her the gift of faith. Maybe he did. But, if so, she's got such a shaky grasp of it that she's afraid to take chances on having it undergo examination. Thinks freedom of thought lands you where I am and, at that, she might have a point."

There was no use asking Frank's advice about her problem. He knew but one way to handle his—to sneak away. She had done some of this, but it was almost as unsatisfactory as fighting.

She decided to talk with as many friends as she could find who had contracted mixed marriages, and learn how they had handled their situations. She had not seen Pat Mellow for months, but one day when they met while shopping, she said, "Pat, come on up and have lunch with me today. My family are away."

"I haven't done a thing like that in months and I'd love to," Pat agreed. "Nothing cheers me up like a confab with an old friend."

Once at the table the conversation fell easily into the groove she had planned. "I've wondered how you and Spud would make out religiously," she began. "Spud is so unbelieving and you were always so devout."

"Everyone wondered," Pat acknowledged. "I might as well confess that it did bother us. In fact, I just couldn't settle down and be happy. After I had that heart attack and death seemed closer, I knew I'd be miserable every minute outside the Church. We have a wonderful priest in our parish and I talked with him. I told him I'd promised Spud the children could go to any church they liked and there would be no pressure about a parish school. Spud had promised that I could go to Mass though we both knew I couldn't take the Sacrament because I was married outside the Church. I knew Spud thought I should stay by my deal and I really did mean to. But, Faith, maybe you know by now—a Catholic just can't go against the Church and be comfortable about it. We all crawl back, just as Protestants say we do. At least most of us. I suppose some don't care or are converted to other religions. But they're mighty few."

"What did the priest say when you told him you wanted to break your promise to your husband?" Faith's question was one she had thought of more than once.

"He said it was a wrong promise in the first place, because it was against God's laws, and so it was more wrong to keep it than to break it. It was like swearing you would serve the devil instead of God. I told him I had no idea how Spud would react—that he might even pick up and leave me rather than do it. But the priest said I'd have to try before I could have absolution, because as long as I was living in sin there was no use saying I was sorry. Maybe you think that was easy—tell ing Spud, I mean. I knew he'd rant and rave and I didn't mind that so much for I'm used to it, and he doesn't mean most of it. But I was honestly afraid he'd walk out. He's been a good husband, Faith. Well, I waited a while, getting up my courage. Then one day I blurted it all out. I told him a man took a chance when he married a Catholic without a Church ceremony, and I was sorry I had failed him. But I just couldn't take it any longer."

"What did he say?"

"You know Spud. At first he said I could do anything I liked, but I'd given my word and, if I had any honor, I'd keep it. He wouldn't do a thing about it. Then, when he saw I really did mean it and that I'd get a job and pull out and take the children before I'd go on any longer, he finally said he would. He told the priest he didn't believe one word of Catholicism and he thought it a one-sided, unfair proposition, and all that. But he insisted I was a good wife and he didn't want to break up his home and finally he gave in and had the priest marry us."

"Did that take care of your difficulties?" Faith asked.

"It certainly made things a lot better. It wasn't as if Spud had any convictions of his own—he actually doesn't believe anything. It was just prejudice with him. But I couldn't be the same without the Church. I know I'm a different woman, and I think Spud senses it and is glad. You can understand because you know how unhappy Neil would be. You couldn't live with him. He'd be a different man. Still, there must be some things about the Catholic way that are hard for you. Any fair-minded Catholic should see that. So I've wondered how you re-act and if it's bothered you at all. Everyone feels you got such a wonderful man and you two are suited to each other in every way except religion."

"I didn't realize it would be hard for a mother to have her children brought up in a different religion," Faith said. "Maybe it would be just as hard for a father. It would for Neil. But Stevie isn't happy in parochial school. And Neil suspects me of influencing him."

"He would. Men are like that. Spud insists on the public schools so I haven't said much. But I'm going to start Becky Sue to parochial school next year. I've finally got him to say it's all right. One thing about Spud, noisy as he is, he'll argue things through. I'd rather have him that way than one of these close-mouthed men you can't talk with. Our oldest boy is like Spud and refuses to go to Mass any more. But the others like to go and I think he'd rather they did than not. He must see it helps train character."

Patricia's method of solving her problem was no more fitted to Faith's case than Frank's had been. To have threatened Neil would only have widened the gap. Neil was grappling with a deep-seated principle. He might be wrong, but he was intensely sincere. If by some means the block could be removed from his mind and he would try to see her position, they might talk again. Then she would remember that they had never had an honest coversation on the matter of religion. There were facetious ones, which ended in kisses, or sharper ones that left a minor sting, but there had never been a clear-cut facing of the basic differences between them.

On her part she had learned much that was reward-ing. The Mass was no longer a series of meaningless motions carried on by a man in a rich robe to impress an audience. The delicate wafer of Christ, which was to keep bodies and souls unto everlasting life, was no longer superstition to her, as it was to many Protestants, for she knew that back in the days of the early Church the thought had become part of the warp and woof of the thinking of men who were trying to make real a thing of the spirit to ignorant and groping sinners. The Protestants could sing, "O Thou, within us and above, close to us in the Christ we love," but there were some who needed the tangible, whose souls cried out for the concrete, and for them this Body was given.

She had seen what the Catholic Church at its best could do for little children, as with Margie's love for the beautiful words she must scarcely comprehend, or the holy awe on her face as she listened to stories of the saints.

"We have all sinned and come far short of the glory of God," Mr. Dickerson read from the Bible, and Faith bowed her head in penitence, knowing that, much worse than being a heretic, she and Neil had both sinned as schismatics, for heretics violate only the faith, and they had violated the law of love. The worst of it was that neither of them knew any confession formula, any penance which might atone for their sin, or set them back on the way toward God. Both continued to go to church, both had the sacraments, both were considered exemplary people by their neighbors. They were even suggested as a couple who had made mixed marriage work—by people who did not know them well.

Yet with Father Corrigan back in charge of the school, and Stevie breathing rebellion with every breath, Faith felt she was living on a pile of explosives. The terrible fear of hurting Neil had dulled with the years. She had been hurt too often herself. She was more concerned now for the children, though her dislike of a brawl was just as great. But one could not make as many concessions as she had made, bitter concessions, and hold the one to whom they were made as an idol. It was the price she paid for refusal to yield her entire will to Neil's. And she knew his love for her had blunted, also.

In October there was a school parade representing the founding of the first Catholic mission in the area, near the spot on which the school stood. The sisters in charge had dug back into the early years of the Church and inserted some saints and heroes, finishing with the later ones and honoring Father Corrigan, the pioneer of the present parish, who was newly back on his job.

Stevie was a rebellious St. Augustine, who was openly sulky, to the disgust of his mother and the anger of his father. But no one could trounce a boy for his attitude, so the sixth grade sister and Father Corrigan could only wait for a more definite act of disobedience.

The little girls, however, went in whole-heartedly. Now that they no longer had Sister Angela, school had become so drab that they welcomed anything which gave play to their imaginations. Because Margie was so pretty she was chosen for Queen Isabella, though she wanted to be a discalced nun and walk demurely with downcast eyes. Faith was relieved to have her a queen, and well-shod, for the ground was getting cold. She assured Margie that to be a queen and receive Christopher Columbus was a desirable part. Rachel was St. Teresa of Avila. The whole neighborhood turned out to see the parade and pageantry. The Presbyterians who lived near the school seemed fully as appreciative as the Catholics.

Two weeks later there was another parade, which had a less happy aftermath. The Protestant churches of the city had planned a rally with a children's parade which would culminate in a pageant on the steps of the Messiah Lutheran Church, to be held on Reformation Sunday. The good-looking young Lutheran minister was dashing, even with rabat and clerical collar, and he had a sense of rhythm and a way with children that made him as popular with the Protestant youngsters as Father Donovan had been with the Catholics. He had a booming Luther League from which he could draw for speaking parts, then he worked in children from all participating Protestant churches.

Along with a zeal to do honor to the man who had nailed the theses to a church door some hundreds of years ago in Germany, the Reverend Mr. Cassel enjoyed drama, liked to prove that Protestantism was again on the march, and that there was more unity than was sometimes thought. As co-worker, he had the director of Christian education from the flourishing Baptist Church, who shared his enthusiasm.

Rachel was chosen for Catherine von Bora. The costume which had done for St. Teresa of Avila needed only a little working over to do for Catherine von Bora, since the onlookers would not be critical about the details of nuns' habits in the sixteenth century. But Rachel's fun in being in the pageant was less because Margie could not take part.

"I'm sure they'd let her march, too, if I ask." Rachel said. "And the girl that's being Anne Hutchinson may not be there."

"Oh, Mother, couldn't I please do it?" pleaded Margie.

"Honey, I'd just love to have you, but I know daddy wouldn't like it."

"I s'pose not," Margie sighed. "That's what comes of being a Catholic. And some of the people I just couldn't be, could I? I even hate to have Rachel do Catherine von Bora when she was such a wicked woman."

"How do you know she was wicked?" Stevie demanded. He specialized in being a thorn in everybody's flesh.

"Cause she was a nun and she married a wicked man."

"Protestants don't think Martin Luther was a wicked man," Faith explained, suddenly determined to state her case. "We think he was a brave man who said what he thought was right when he might be tortured, or even put to death. He believed some things in the Church should be changed so he tried to talk to the pope about it." Then, seeing the troubled look on Margie's face she added, "You mustn't worry about these things, honey. Catholics and Protestants think differently. When you are older you can study it from both sides."

"Don't worry about me, Margie," Rachel said, "I read a story about Catherine von Bora in my church school paper and she was a good woman. Only you aren't supposed to think so when you are a Catholic."

"Anyhow, I don't think daddy would like it if he knew." Margie was worried.

Faith wondered why she had not thought of this before. They had talked a little of Rachel's part but no name had been mentioned and it had not seemed an important matter. Now she was sure that Neil would not like it.

"We'd better hurry," she said to Rachel. "Throw your coat around you and I'll drive you down to where the line is forming."

"Could I go along, Mother?" asked Margie.

"I can't see why not. Then I can bring you back to our corner and go back to the pageant at the Lutheran Church if I want to. Be a good boy, Stevie," she called.

Neil had gone to his office for the Sunday paper which he had accidentally left on his desk. If they hurried, they could be away before he returned. She hated this maneuvering, but it would avoid friction.

She had not thought of the parade as being of much importance, and was amazed to see so many children lined up from the various church schools. The Baptist Boys' Band led with "Onward, Christian Soldiers" and the historical characters fell into line, skipping nimbly through the pages of history, albeit somewhat erratically, because there were so many of them and no denomination, particularly none with organizations in Athens, could be omitted. Wycliffe led, holding an open Bible, and after him were Luther and Catherine von Bora, then John Calvin with a long white beard. Then there was John Knox, heckling Mary of Scots, and Pilgrims— the men in broad-brimmed hats and women in gray chambray and white aprons. Then came Anne Hutchinson and Roger Williams, and William Penn, because he had stood for so much and must be included, though there was no Friends' meetinghouse in town. Then came John Wesley, riding a white horse, and Alexander Campbell.

Though there were many unhappy histories of mutual persecution, they were all sorry for this and walked hand in hand today. So no one was amazed when a Puritan maiden slipped out of line and helped hitch up Roger Williams' galluses when they broke, though in history she might have helped drive the agitator for soul freedom from her colony. Though a Baptist and a Luth-

186

eran had planned the program, it was fair to all. Protestants knew they borrowed from each other's liturgies and sang each other's hymns and learned new things about God from each other. Though they liked different names for things and different ways of being governed, that was no sign that one was better than another.

When the band had finished "Onward, Christian Soldiers" and was swinging into "The Son of God Goes Forth to War," Faith started the car slowly. If she could drive around the block she could let Margie run home, then come back to the church. She must see it all. Little chills were running up and down her spine as she saw the numbers marching. She needed this for she had been so long on the defensive.

"Mother," pleaded Margie, "let me go, too! I want to see the funny Protestant saints. It won't hurt me!"

It seemed a silly thing to refuse. There would be Catholics all through the crowd, some sullen, some critical, but many just looking on with friendly curiosity and enjoying their neighbors' children as the Protestants had enjoyed St. Teresa and St. Ignatius Loyola and the other Catholic saints two weeks before.

"All right, honey. Daddy will surely understand that you would want to see Rachel."

By luck someone in a parking place backed out just as Faith was in a position to take it, giving them a view from the car. The Pilgrim marchers had reached the church yard, singing:

O God, beneath Thy guiding hand
Our exiled fathers crossed the sea,
And when they trod the wintry strand
With prayer and psalm they worshiped Thee

"Mother, let's get out and stand closer so we can see," Margie begged. Neil would never be caught at a Protestant rally, so Faith took the little girl's hand and they crowded in with the others. Faith sang as she walked:

> Laws, freedom, truth, and faith in God
> Came with these exiles o'er the waves. . .

"Do you know all the words, Mother, so you can sing whatever song they sing?"

"Nearly all of them, darling. I've known them all my life."

Though out of sequence, "A Mighty Fortress is Our God" had been left till all had reached the church yard so they could sing with the organ—the largest in town. Now it pealed forth with *"Ein Feste Burg"* and, with the Lutheran minister to lead and the Baptist band hitting as many of the notes as it could, the whole congregation sang the great Reformation hymn.

Then the Methodist minister displaced a pilgrim as he made his way to the platform that had been built at the church steps. He also stepped on Anne Hutchinson's toes which, he stated openly, would have been according to history, if he had been a Congregationalist. This made everyone laugh. Anne was a Protestant St. Teresa, he said. Then he asked them all to join in the Apostles' Creed, following a sentence he wished to repeat from a form of service in *The Methodist Hymnal*: "Where the Spirit of the Lord is, there is the one true Church, Apostolic and Universal, whose Holy Faith let us now reverently and sincerely declare."

With a booming voice he led out and the Episcopalians and Lutherans and Methodists spoke right along with him; but only some of the Presbyterians knew it and the Baptists and Congregationalists (who were building a new church at the edge of town) could only hit the high spots. There was some confusion about the descending into hell, but everyone, even the most non-liturgical, felt the Spirit working in their memories and came out strongly with:

"I believe in the Holy Ghost; the holy catholic Church; the communion of saints; the forgiveness of sins; the resurrection of the body, and the life everlasting."

Margie kept whispering, "Can I say it, too, Mother? Can I say it, too?"

The minister of the Christian Church preached a few minutes. He reminded the people that they had a great heritage, a heritage of struggle for freedom, but that that freedom, however precious, could be kept only with eternal vigilance. There were too many Protestants who thought of the modern meaning of the word as one who objected, forgetting that the original meaning was one who witnessed. If people ceased to witness, their faith began to fail. Now some, who had not prized their faith, had neither witness to make nor faith to lose. Their precious possession had gone by default.

Margie's quick eyes took in everything as the minister talked. She would not understand the words but she must guess that the people were stirred. Mr. Dickerson read prayers from the *Book of Common Prayer*, because no minister was supposed to use the liturgy from his own denomination. First he read, "O God, by whom the meek are guided in judgment, and light riseth up in darkness for the godly, grant us in all our doubts

and uncertainties the grace to ask what thou wouldst
have us do; that the Spirit of wisdom may save us from
false choices; that in thy light we may see light, and in
thy straight path may not stumble; through Jesus Christ.
our Lord."

As a last prayer he read, "O God, who art the author
of peace and lover of concord, in knowledge of whom
standeth our eternal life, whose service is perfect freedom . . ." At the end of each prayer some of the people
said, "Amen." Then they all said "Our Father" together, slower than in a Rosary, and some said "debts"
and some said "trespasses" because, of course, it was
their sins that the Protestants could not agree about.
Then, at the last, they used the great phrases which
made it their "Lord's Prayer," and came out with a ring
on "For thine is the kingdom, and the power and the
glory, forever and ever. Amen."

Faith felt the tears in her eyes and, looking down at
her little daughter's face, saw the wondering expression
as people prayed standing, their heads bowed, the men
holding their hats in their hands. A few knelt, but this
was all right, too, for Protestants knew you could pray
in any position. It was the spirit of man which reached
out for God.

After that they sang more songs, the band, the organ,
and the junior choirs from all the churches leading in
"The Church's One Foundation Is Jesus Christ, Her
Lord," and "Holy, Holy, Holy." The service went off
well, seeing there had been but little rehearsing, and
such a wide spread in the ideas of how much should be
planned and at what point liturgy and spontaneity
could part company. The little acolyte from the Episcopal church was almost too small for the cross he had

to carry, but a bigger, unliturgical Disciple of Christ from the back row slipped through and gave him a hand, so that, when the organ swept into Festal Song and the audience was singing

"Rise up, O men of God!
Have done with lesser things;
Give heart and soul and mind and strength
To serve the King of kings!"

he could be ready to help hoist the cross up, shining and straight for the verse

"Lift high the cross of Christ!
Tread where His feet have trod;
As brothers of the Son of Man,
Rise up, O men of God!"

Many would have liked to stay longer to sing, for the most stately hymns now had a clarion ring and they could hear the echoes going down the little gulleys to the river, but the Pilgrims were wiggling, Martin Luther was getting out of hand, and the safetypin holding Roger Williams' galluses had sprung open again and even his cape could not conceal the difficulty. They closed with "Old Hundredth" which all knew well. Faith got through the "Praise God from whom all blessings flow," but when she came to "Praise Him, all creatures here below" and she thought of the divisive ways of praising God, and the barriers in the path of one's communion with him, a lump formed in her throat. When she thought of her father and Uncle Jack above in the "heavenly host" it became too large to manage and the last triumphal note had to end without her.

The Episcopal rector said the benediction, then the people, after a minute's hush, broke ranks and parents went to find their children. Catherine von Bora had seen Faith and Margie all the time, delighted that they were in the front circle. She bounded forward at a pace unlikely in an ex-nun of the sixteenth century. People round about were saying what a thrilling service it had been and how well Mr. Cassell and Miss Brighton had done with it, and there were whispers that the Baptist-trained director of Christian education would fit well into the role of Lutheran pastor's wife, with just a bit of coaching.

Margie plied her mother with questions and made wondering comments about an experience more remarkable to her than to anyone there. "Mother, they said 'I believe in the holy catholic Church,' but they don't, do they? They hate the Catholic Church, so why did they say it?" Then, in a moment, "But, Mother, they do have beautiful words, just like we have, only different. And why don't they cross themselves? And, Mother, what is a mighty fortress . . . and when they descended into hell, why didn't they go down on their knees?"

Just then Faith heard a commotion in one of the big elms above her head and, looking up, saw three or four boys, among them Stevie. A surge of joy came over her that he had been there, too. In his sullen, bitter mood he would not be receptive and he would not gain from the experience what Margie had, with her keener spiritual insights, but he would know that his mother's religion was a great, marching force, also, and perhaps he would respect this.

Then, as she waved to him and turned back to her car, she came face to face with her husband. Neil had been standing a little behind them, but where he could easily see. She had no idea how long he had stood there.

A few years before she would have been ill with fear of hurting him, or with the prospect of a quarrel. But that time was past. She was startled, but not dismayed. Most of her concern was for Margie. Casually she explained that she had driven down to bring Rachel and that she would take the girls home. She did not mention Stevie. Unless his father saw him and demanded that the boy go with him, it would be better for him to come back with his friends, for it was within easy walking distance.

Between her answers to Margie's questions, she tried to think what she would say when Neil opened the subject. "By the 'holy catholic Church' we mean all the Christian churches everywhere, dear. 'Catholic' to us means something that takes in everyone. You belong to the Roman Catholic Church . . . ." I've had this heritage all the time, Faith pondered, and didn't realize how proud I was of it. "Yes, darling, we do put more to the 'Our Father' than you do. We think they are beautiful words."

"And, Mother, I asked Sister Angela why it was false worship, and she said it wasn't because the other people weren't true, but because God gave the Church a better set of words to use to praise him. She said we knew Protestants sometimes meant to worship God in the right way. These people today did mean to do it right, didn't they?"

Bless Sister Angela! "Yes, honey, they think they are worshiping the best way, the way that God wants them to, just as the Catholics think they have the better way."

"Then why don't they talk with each other about it?" Margie went on.

All Faith could think to say was, "I wish, dear that they would. And I pray that sometime they will."

"I'll pray for your intention, too, Mother," Margie offered. She had learned a new phrase and was eager to use it.

Neil did not come home directly. Faith was glad, for the children were eager to discuss the afternoon's experiences. Even Stevie and his friends joined in with their appreciation as Faith served cookies and punch. She had no idea where Neil had gone but she suspected he was at his mother's. It was not till after the children had gone to bed and she was reading by her bedroom light, that she heard his step in the downstairs hall.

Chapter 13

NEIL stood behind the big green easy chair. He fingered the books on the side table, but without nervous motion, for he disliked a show of disintegration of any type. He was still the best-looking man Faith knew, though much of the spirituality was gone from his face. That is what his marriage has cost him, Faith thought.

Her heart was beating rapidly and she dreaded the hour ahead but she had no intention of weakening. The experience of the afternoon had put stamina into her spirit. She would say some of the things she should have said long ago.

"How is it you took Margie to a Protestant rally when you know that is forbidden?" he asked with cool evenness.

"In the first place you left the Sunday paper in your office and I had no idea it was a thing of such consequence. In the second, she would have had to stay alone at home when everyone in the neighborhood was gone—most of them to watch the parade. You made no provision to entertain her in order to offset it and I had to take Rachel up where they were to form in line."

"Is it more important that you should look after someone else's child than that you should keep your promises about your own?"

Even six months before she would have hedged, would have apologized for having Rachel, and would have tried in some way to mollify him. Now she said steadily, "I made a wicked promise, Neil. I have known it for a long time. I think you know it, too. I had a great religious heritage, but I was very deeply in love. In face of that love I minimized it. I'm glad I tried to learn about your religion for it has taught me much. You have steadily refused to look into mine. It was good for Margie to see what she saw today. As for Stevie, he didn't ask leave and I did not know he was there till just a minute before I saw you. It was as much your responsibility as mine to know his whereabouts. But I'm glad they both saw it."

"Do you mean that from now on you plan to break your marriage vows openly, as you have already done covertly?"

"I haven't broken the antenuptial promises in letter. Just in spirit," she retorted.

"How about the precautions you take to avoid having another child? You have gone to such lengths that I feel mutually guilty. There's much more than spirit to that!"

This was the truth and she acknowledged it. "I don't want another child, Neil. They are children of my body but not of my soul—I am hushed up for fear I'll say something to give a wrong conception of the Church. I have no say-so about their schooling. . . ."

"Except for the past few months our parish school has been excellent. One of the best in town, and you know it!" he said sharply.

"I've never denied that, Neil. But some of the time it has been most unsatisfactory. My complaint is that I am a mother, yet I have no right to help decide what is best for my children's welfare. And that's just one of the things. You wheedled me into saying that, if our children were to be left to the care of relatives, they must go to your family, no matter what the situation or how much better equipped my family happened to be to care for them. Now this looks morally wrong to me, even if they should go to relatives of yours who would satisfy me in other respects."

"Those were sacred promises, made before God," Neil said sternly. "There is no way they may be abrogated or ignored. Your refusal to co-operate involves me."

"I'm sorry for that part, Neil. And all the rest, too. But the God I worship hasn't set any ogre to watch my marital life. Besides, I'm sure he doesn't want the earth replenished with people who quarrel and fight about him. I think he'd rather we all died off quickly!"

He scarcely seemed to hear her. He was trying to find a way of presenting his case. "Sometimes," he said, at length, "I'm convinced the whole trouble has hinged on your losing that baby in California. When I gave my first reluctant consent to your taking the children to the Protestant vacation school, I had no idea how far you would go. Evidently the experience made you determined to take the children out of Catholic influence and you used my absence overseas as an opportunity. It all fits into a pattern and it's one of the best examples I know of the person who steps out of the path of righteousness for just a step, then the rest of the way goes downhill so fast she cannot catch herself."

"I don't understand you," she said in amazement.

"You knew we all wanted you to go to a Catholic

hospital and that it was your duty to do it. There a child would have been given Christian baptism, even before birth, if necessary. . . ."

"If I had planned to go to a Catholic hospital, I couldn't have reached one in time. It was all I could do to get to the Community Hospital."

"I know that. But, if you had done any of the right things, this wouldn't have come between us."

"But I didn't want to go to a Catholic hospital. Remember, I protested it before. I had heard that in some cases the mother is sacrificed to save the life of the child —even a deformed child. It was my life, after all."

"You were probably overconcerned . . ."

"Except for my children, I'd be utterly unconcerned now," she said. "I had no idea, Neil, how indifferent you were to my suffering, or even to whether or not I lived. Evidently both our marriage vows have been kept in letter rather than spirit."

"Faith, that is not the truth! I was crazy about you. I could be yet if we had any points of contact. But you are so resentful of my religion. My Church and my children's belief are paramount issues with me. It's been very difficult for me to have Rachel here. She's a nice little girl and under normal conditions I could be very fond of her. But I see you taking her to church, teaching her things, when you should be spending your time teaching your own children their catechism or . . ."

"But I don't believe that catechism. I would be acting a lie!" she cried.

"It's still your duty to do it. We Catholics may be a hardheaded lot, but we think God gives the gift of faith if people steadfastly do what he commands. You might have received this if you were not so steadily set against it. Much as I have loved you, Faith, my Church comes first. If many more such incidents as this happen, no matter how I hate it on your account, I'll feel I have to insist on sending Rachel away. It is for our children's good, Faith. Do believe this!"

He was almost imploring her now, and it was at such times she found it hardest to stand up against him. But she hardened her heart.

"When you decide to send Rachel away," she said slowly, "I'll have a decision to make too. I have needed her."

She saw that he understood. He looked so pained that she could scarcely refrain from making another gesture toward understanding, but she could not think of anything that would have meaning for him, so she turned away.

Faith lay awake long, looking into the darkness, praying and trying to hear a word that would tell her what to do. Perhaps Neil was praying, too. But there seemed to be no right thing to do. As long as the children were reasonably happy and comfortable, they were better off as they were, even at the parochial school. She wished she could send Stevie for awhile to her brother, for whom he was named. He had spent a week with her mother and it had done him good. Steve had been a disputatious adolescent himself, carrying the tendency into early manhood, but settling down into an unusually reasonable man in his late twenties. He would understand his nephew, and so would Molly. But Neil would have refused flatly to allow the boy to go.

Several days after the Protestant rally, Faith had just finished a bit of mending and was putting the garment in a bureau drawer when she heard the little girls coming up the steps. It was still an hour before the noon recess and she was amazed to see them. Then she noted that Margie's face was dead white and Rachel was hurrying her toward the bathroom with motherly attentions. Faith followed and, after the child had vomited, carried her back to her bedroom and laid her, shaking, on the bed.

"Why, darling, what's the matter?" she asked, piling on the covers and sending Rachel for a hot water bottle. After a minute the child began to cry.

When Rachel came back she had the story from her, though she was timid about involving Stevie, and Margie had to supplement that part as soon as she could control herself. The fifth and sixth grade rooms were directly across the hall from each other and it was easy to see or hear what was going on in the other room if the doors were left open. The classes had just come back from the chapel and Stevie and some of the other boys must have done something Sister Veronica didn't like for she scolded them, and Margie saw her slap Stevie, who talked back. Two of the other boys talked back, too, but not as loudly. Margie had been sick with fear and disgrace. When Father Corrigan came out of the office with a big ruler and hit Stevie, the boy broke and ran. The other boys ran too. Father Corrigan, ulcers and all, reached the stairs in time to grab Stevie again, but somehow the youngster had swung himself over the bannister and dangled above the stair well with Father Corrigan holding his collar. He was far too heavy for the priest to manage at such an awkward angle, so he managed to kick himself free, dropped with a thud to the lower floor, then took off, with some help from his confederates. By the time Father Corrigan reached the lower hall, the boys were well out of immediate reach, and now no one knew where they were.

Nothing like this had ever happened at St. Aloysius, and the sisters were all horrified. They talked and talked about how people should respect the priest, and Margie was so ashamed she got sick and threw up all over the desk and the aisle. Sister Maria, who was kind, if she was stodgy, said for Rachel to take her home to bed.

When Stevie did not come home at noon, Faith called the other mothers. They, too, had heard of the trouble through younger children. One mother said that, when her husband got hold of his son, he'd give him a thrashing he'd remember all his life, for talking back to a sister and defying the priest. But the other mother said it was the last straw with her. She hadn't been satisfied with the school for some time and she thought they'd take her boy out and send him to public school. Her husband was a Protestant and had never been in favor of the parochial school. She was very talkative and explained that she was not a priest-ridden Catholic and, even if she did get excommunicated, she thought she'd manage right well.

Faith was sick at the whole business. She hadn't an idea how Neil would react, but she was sure he knew the moment she saw his face.

"Stevie home yet?" he asked.

"No. And I haven't a guess where he is. You knew he got into trouble at school?"

"Yes. Sister Veronica called me. Evidently he went clear off the hooks."

But he made no violent threats. He had been stern with the boy sometimes and, of late, unreasonable. He was not cruel and he had a horror of administering physical punishment. A few sharp spanks when the boy was small was about all he had ever been able to do. Usually he thought of some deprivation as a punishment. If possible, he tried to reason with his son. But on the school matter and attendance at Mass, he had remained adamant.

"If he doesn't come home in an hour, I'll look for him," Neil said. "Somehow I think he'll be back."

Within the hour Stevie came in trying to act as though nothing had happened, though he must have known the girls would tell. Neil was watching for him and, not letting him have a chance to talk with his mother, sent him at once to his room. Then he followed and Faith could hear their voices, Stevie's sullen and muttering, Neil's stern, but still trying to reason. It would actually be better if he talked back to his father, she thought. He would get more of the rebellion out of his system. When they came to dinner, Neil was very quiet and Stevie was still sulky. Margie had her dinner in bed and Rachel insisted on taking it up and eating with her. Faith found it difficult to keep a conversation going.

She went to Stevie's room afterward and tried to talk with him, but he fiddled with a map puzzle on his desk and refused at first to give her any satisfaction. He hated the priest, he said, and would always hate him. Sister Veronica was mean, but he hated her only by spells.

"What did daddy say?" Faith could not keep from asking, for she doubted that Neil would tell her.

"He says I've got to go back tomorrow and say I'm sorry, and that Saturday I'll have to go to confession and, if I don't, he's going to send me off to a military school that the Church has where boys have to behave.

If I do go back to school and say I'm sorry, it'll be the biggest lie I ever told. Everybody in our room hates Father Corrigan."

Faith was sure the boy had some plan in his head which he had no intention of telling, but she could not well ask if he was going to obey his father, for this implied the possibility of disobedience. So, worried though she was, she kissed him good night and told him she would think about his problem and pray about it, and he must pray, too. He must learn to control his temper, she said.

"How about a priest that can't control his?" Stevie demanded. But she knew his question was not intended in any way against her.

"Just because one person, even a minister or a priest, doesn't act right, is no excuse for us to do wrong, Stevie."

But words were useless and all she could do was to try to make the boy feel that she knew he had a problem and she was working on it with him.

It was even harder to get Neil to tell what he had decreed, but she was determined to have it direct from him and probed till she had a reluctant statement.

"I don't expect you to approve of my decisions, Faith," he said, "but you surely understand that, if the kid gets away with this, it'll be harder than ever to manage him. If I don't have to leave town early tomorrow morning, I'll go over to the school with him. It's gall and wormwood for him to knuckle under, but I can't see any way out."

"I called Mrs. Weyland before Stevie came home, trying to find him. She says they are going to take Bobbie out and put him in public school. They feel he doesn't get a fair chance at St. Aloysius."

"I know that's what you want to do with Stevie, but you might as well forget it. It would be tantamount to publicly defying a priest who has given years of devoted effort here and who is an old friend of the family. I'll grant he hasn't a knack for handling boys, but he's a priest and Stevie might as well learn what authority means one time as another. I've been too easy on him. I can see that now. And your attitude and naturally rebellious disposition may have something to do with it."

"His father isn't stubborn, or anything?" she asked with a smile that was a little like her old self, only more grim.

"I'm not saying he doesn't get plenty of bad traits from me, though I can't remember ever going into such a tailspin. I had too much respect for the sisters and the priests. Then I told Stevie he had to go to confession Saturday and that would start him off with a clean slate. It'll probably do him more good than anything else. Try to back me in this, Faith. Surely you care what happens to the kid."

"I care terribly, Neil. But I wasn't consulted as to the way the affair was handled. If we had followed my suggestion, he would have been in public school and this would not have come up. However, I'll not say anything against his going back if you go with him. I don't trust the temper of that priest. And I'm terribly opposed to forcing a child to go to confession."

"Confession is compulsory for all Catholics. It isn't exactly a pleasant duty, but I know of no more healing experience than the absolution when one has done wrong. Stevie knows right from wrong and this will do him good."

"If he could go to someone he likes I wouldn't mind so much. Some understanding person. But to have to confess to the very man who irritates him . . ."

Neil looked horrified. "You miss the entire meaning, Faith," he said sternly. "Stevie dislikes the man, Father Corrigan. He confesses to the parish priest. Because we happen to have just one man available, he is one and the same. But any Catholic knows there is no connection between one's personal feeling and the priest in the confessional."

"And every Protestant feels leery of a spiritual power that reaches its tentacles into the incidents of everyday life!" she retorted. "At your age you may be able to differentiate between the man and the priest. But Stevie cannot and it is harmful to force him to go to confession. Still, I'll not say anything against it if he goes willingly, or even with mild protests." She hated this last concession but the misery in Neil's face was hard to witness.

She read the look of distrust that followed the one of misery. Then Neil turned and went downstairs.

Late that night Neil had a call. He had to leave town before the family's breakfast on a serious business matter, and no one could take his place. As Faith placed his coffee on the table she asked, "What do you want me to do about Stevie? If I were handling the matter myself, I'd go over alone and talk with Father Corrigan and Sister Veronica. Then I'd know better what to do next."

She could see Neil did not approve of this.

"Suppose we just let it ride till I get back. I should be in Friday, if all goes well. I'll scratch off a note to Stevie and tell him I'm depending on him and take a chance. It's all I can do." Then, evidently sensing that he was handling the matter highhandedly, he added, with a hint of apology, "As long as I started proceedings, it seems better not to change hands in a crisis."

She did not argue the matter, She had not quite reached the point of taking a stand. Then, to her surprise, Stevie got ready for school as usual, put a book under his arm, and left. He did not mention the note his father had put under his door and Faith said nothing about it. Something told her that he had no intention of going to school but, since Neil was determined to take full charge, she would leave it all to him. She would give him one more chance to work things out.

Margie didn't want to go to school either, so Faith let her stay quietly in her room. Rachel debated the matter then decided to go. She mentioned changing over to the public school at the end of the term, and Faith said that perhaps she could. They would talk about it.

This was Wednesday. Stevie returned for lunch and at the correct hour in the evening, and left again as usual on Thursday. He repeated the process on Friday. Faith asked him how things were going and he said, "O.K." She was so sure he had not gone back that she did not press the matter. It was an abnormal situation because it showed the boy that she was a secondary parent at a moment when he needed to feel his father and mother spoke with one voice. But this was Neil's affair.

Friday morning Sister Veronica called to ask why he had not come back. She said Mr. Mackaig had promised to see that he did. She had been unable to reach Stevie's father at his office.

Faith explained briefly what had happened. His father had told him he must go back, then had been called out of town. As Stevie had left as usual each morning, she had assumed he was going to school. Sister Veronica said the law required her to report the absence by Monday, unless the boy returned. Faith expressed regret that the child had proved troublesome but added that the matter was in her husband's hands and he would be home that evening.

Then she went to the boy's room hoping to find some evidence of his plans. The only indication was an envelope from her brother which gave his return address. There were no other indications of his plans. At noon she asked Rachel a few questions and found that Glenn Hartford, the boy whose father had said he would whale him, and Stevie, were working in a shoe repair shop downtown. Out in the back room, Rachel thought. One of the girls had seen them. But she did not know which shoe shop it was.

Faith drove from shop to shop, asking about her son. Finally an Italian shop owner said, "I geev heem work. He needa money for Chreestmas."

Faith insisted that the boy come out in the car and talk with her. "I understand why you wouldn't go back to school, Stevie," she began, determined to establish rapport if possible, "but why did you need money? Tell me, dear. I want to help you if I can."

"How can you help me when daddy has all the say?" he demanded.

This was difficult to answer.

"I'm not sure he has all the say," she countered slowly. "In any case, I can help you more if I know how you feel and what you are planning."

"I'm going away," he said suddenly. "I had almost enough money to get there."

"Were you going to your Uncle Steve and Aunt Molly?"

"What made you think that?" he demanded suspiciously.

"I know you are fond of your Uncle Steve. You're his namesake and your Aunt Molly is your godmother."

"Daddy said she couldn't be any more because she had changed her religion. But I've changed mine, too."

Faith decided to ignore that statement. She made a desperate effort to be casual. "Of course, if you weren't going to be at home, I'd rather you went to see your Uncle Steve than anywhere else. But how is it, when daddy said he was trusting you to go back to school that you didn't go? We have always felt we could depend on you. He'll be terribly disappointed."

"I'm sorry about that part, Mother," Stevie said earnestly. "But I'm afraid of Father Corrigan when he's mad. He hates me. I know he does. And I hate him. Besides it would be a wicked lie to say I was sorry at confession if I wasn't, wouldn't it? And Daddy said I had to tell that lie or he'd send me off to a military school. I've got to do something bad whichever way I go. So I'm going to run away. And, Mother, don't tell him. Please don't. If you do I'll have to hide and manage all the harder, but I won't go to confession to Father Corrigan and I won't go to a boarding school. Not if they kill me."

His bravery was probably greater because he sensed she was an ally. In any case it was terrible that Neil had let the precious treasure of his son's trust slip through his hands. Now there seemed to be no other way out of the situation.

Faith swallowed hard, then said, "Stevie, if I could work it out, would you like to go back to California and live in the little cottage? Then you could go to public school."

"Mother, I'd love that! Could we really? Would daddy let us?"

"I'm not sure yet what we can do, Stevie. But you must have known that Protestants, as a rule, prefer public schools. I wanted daddy to let you change over when Father Donovan left, but I couldn't get him to see it."

"I know that, Mother. But daddy couldn't go to California because he's got to stay with his business."

"Nothing is worked out yet. Only I'm not going to let you be sent away from home unless it is to your Uncle Steve, and I'm sure your father would be against that. We could try it in California—this year at least. Rachel is homesick to go back, and Margie is so humiliated because she threw up at school that she gets sick every time I suggest she should go back."

Faith made the boy promise not to mention the California plan till she had time to talk with the girls and with Neil. She told him to tell the man he was working for that he would not be back, and she assured him she would stay by him through his difficulty.

"You mustn't think I approve of what you did, Stevie. I think you were very wrong and should be punished in some way. But Father Corrigan is not the man to be in charge of a school. Your father knows that as well as I do, but he thinks people should not object to what the priest and bishop want."

"He's priest-ridden," said Stevie.

"Why, Stevie Mackaig, where did you hear that word?"

"I've heard it lots of times," he said boastfully. "I wish dad wasn't that way. I like to have folks stand up to people."

She could see it would be no easy matter to show sympathy for the predicament the boy had got himself into and, at the same time, ward off recalcitrant remarks. But she must try.

She was glad the children were in bed when Neil arrived at nearly midnight. His first question was, "Did Stevie go back to school as I asked him?"

It was hard to answer. Neil would hate sending the boy away from home, but his pride was involved and his parish loyalty. The Mackaigs would convince themselves that it was what the boy needed, even though he would have to go with a bad report from the parochial school.

She decided that a definite statement was the only possibility. Tired as he was, she put it flatly before him. There was no time to lose.

She spoke rapidly, Stevie had played truant and had made plans for running away. A lie was involved whichever move he made. He had found a job to add to the savings from his allowance. "So I've decided to take the children and go to California for the winter, Neil. It will relieve you of any responsibility and you can tell Father Corrigan that I went against your wishes. It doesn't matter in the least to me what he thinks. Stevie has promised to be a good boy and, in a school that he likes, he's unlikely to give any trouble. Rachel is eager to go and Margie will be happier there than here, though she will miss you terribly." The sound of her own voice amazed her, for it was flat, decisive— not the pleading, apologetic tone she usually used.

"I have things pretty well planned. The cottage is empty. I'll leave here a day or so after Christmas. This will take care of the present and we can decide the future later. This isn't a good plan, but it's the best I can work out. If I allow Stevie to be sent to a military school, he will turn against both of us. It is better for him to be with one parent than away from both."

"You are assuming a terrible responsibility, Faith," he said frigidly. "If your child's salvation . . ."

"His salvation is much more assured in an atmosphere of love and confidence than in an impersonal place where he would have to take a poor report and be listed as an incorrigible at the very start!" she flared back.

He did not even answer. She knew he was utterly miserable for things had worked as much against him as against her. When first married they had come so merrily into this house. Ahead of them had stretched the lush fields of happiness. Now these fields had become barren wastes because they had not known how to build a spiritual home in partnership. When she thought of this the tears came and her heart changed to lead. But, if she should weaken, he would demand that she stay—not implore, but demand. It would have to be on his terms. These she could not meet.

The children were gleeful—they would be away from the hated school. They talked of California and wondered how many of their friends would still be there. Stevie kept out of his father's way and Neil made little effort to see his son. Evidently he had decided that his wife had made up her mind and he could no longer influence her decisions. He might even be a little relieved that he did not have to go through the misery of sending his son away from home, rebellious and frightened.

It was a sorry Christmas. Faith offered to go to midnight Mass with Neil but he refused her company. It would be a strain on them both, he said, for she would not be in sympathy with the service. He refused to acknowledge the times when she had made an effort to bridge the chasm. To him it was one thing if a Catholic, married without the Church, felt its pull and returned to it, even when done at heavy cost to a Protestant mate. But to him there was no such thing as the call of a Protestant faith. It could only be stubbornness. There was nothing analogous about the two cases. As for the Mass, she persuaded him that Margie should be allowed to go. It would not hurt her to be up so late just once. Finally he agreed to take the child along.

Her heart ached for him and for herself, and sometimes for Margie, who sensed that there was trouble. She would say, "Don't look so sad, Daddy! We'll be back." He would kiss her and tell her that he must do something else—read, or go to his office. Rachel was definitely relieved. Faith guessed that she sensed her Uncle Neil did not want her about. In a way this was understandable for there was some truth in the accusation that Faith lavished upon this child some of the spiritual interchange that should have been found in her own husband and children. So two of the children, at least, would be better off for a change.

Finally the car was packed and the children were inside, after saying their goodbyes to their father. When Faith reached for the handle of the door by the driver's seat, Neil whirled about and walked rapidly toward the house without a word of farewell to her. Perhaps he could not trust himself. Still she must not go off this way. Telling the children to stay where they were for she would be back in a minute, she ran back to the living-room. Neil was standing by the piano, his head buried in his hands. She had never seen him in such an attitude of grief.

"Neil!" she said softly, "Neil!" When he did not move, she pulled his hands from his face and tried to see clearly through her tears. "We have failed each other terribly. No matter who is really to blame, or whether we both are, we . . . we . . . Oh, Neil, I did once love you so much!" When, in his utter misery he said nothing, she went on, "I'm going back to our garden, Neil. And I'll pray that we'll both find love and God again. I'm not sure whether we first lost him, or lost each other."

When he made no attempt to kiss her, she put his long fingers to her lips, then used them to brush away her tears.

"I suppose the whole trouble has been jealousy, Neil. Jealous of loving God in a certain way, you might call it. I know you don't believe this but, Neil, even God himself can't be held in jealous, grasping hands."

Though he made no answer, she hoped he understood.

Chapter 14

THE little garden was stark under the brilliant sun. The dial which said, "Useless without a ray from heaven," told that it was noonday. Though there was still the big acacia and the wisteria vine, and the first shoots of spring plants were peeping through, it seemed a lonely place. The flowers on the inside of the wall were scraggly and the rough adobe was all too visible.

Faith walked slowly toward the little shrine, remembering that here she had first seen Neil cross himself, and it was then that she knew they walked separate paths toward God. She could not bear to look in the wishing well, because here Neil had dropped coins and they had wished that their love might last forever.

It was not a garden in which she could walk happily alone, yet it pulled her back, again and again. There was an adjoining building which was used as a home for retired priests, someone said, and a little chapel opened under the cloister, where the priests could say Mass without having to go up and down steps. One priest, in sandals and brown robe, often walked under the olive trees with his breviary. He had a sad but saintly face as though he had seen into the depths of human sin and suffering, and it had left its imprint. Sometimes Faith thought of talking with him, for he watched her with such kind interest. But always she left the garden without approaching him.

However, his eyes stayed with her, an invitation to admit her mistakes and sorrows. She knew that some day she would surely ask to speak with him.

From the first, life in the California beach town was quiet. Faith missed Alice Reredon and Uncle Jack and Aunt Kate. The children missed them all and spoke of them often but, being children, they readily adjusted to the changes. They renewed acquaintances with old playmates, found their old haunts, and rejoiced at their new freedom.

Steve changed, almost over night, from a sullen, recalcitrant boy to one who gave co-operation. He was much noisier than he had been at home and even more disputatious but, once he had voiced a loud complaint, he was usually amenable to reason. He liked school and did good work, if for no other reason than to justify his going to public school. Occasionally he would go to Mass at St. Anne's when Faith took Margie, but usually he refused. Faith did not insist. He joined the Boy Scout troop at the Methodist Church and was happy in it.

Margie, however, stayed by her Catholicism faithfully, though alone. She could go to Mass with one of the neighbors if Faith found it inconvenient to take her, but she always coaxed her mother to go along.

"I need someone to kneel beside me, Mother," she would say.

Faith, who knew so well that worship should be a shared experience, went whenever she could and knelt beside the little girl, praying that the child would find

God in such a manner that she could share him with others, all the while learning about him unafraid. Margie was not as thrilled with the change of schools as Rachel or Stevie. She liked the wide windows, with their views of "earth and sky and sea," and she found the lessons easier under the young teacher than they had been from stolid Sister Maria. But she missed seeing Sister Angela in the hall, and she thought the bright paper posters they were always making a tawdry substitute for the stories of the saints, the interesting Latin words in the missal, and the lilting poems of a romantic era.

Faith encouraged the children to write to their father. Stevie wrote occasionally, under protest. He could think of nothing to write about except soccer and swimming. Margie wrote more affectionately. She missed her daddy, and wished he would come to California. Then she would tell him about going to Mass, sensing that this would be the news he would wish to hear.

Faith took a part-time job in the office of the Methodist Church, which had grown till Mr. Budlong could no longer handle the work alone. This gave her a small check for her own use. Neil faithfully sent money each month, but she tried hard not to use it, and she had not asked for it. If she did not live with him, it was unreasonable to expect him to provide for her. Sometimes he suggested that Margie must need a new dress or shoes, or Stevie should have this or that. His letters to her were matter-of-fact and brief—more tender to Margie. He said nothing about their coming back, yet he did not seem to accept the arrangement as a separation. The girls spoke of it as a "visit," but Stevie declared he never wanted to go back, and Faith made no plans to do so.

But she was not happy. The strain of curbing her tendency to self-expression was gone, yet the years stretched ahead hopelessly. Though she had gained much in temporary peace, she had lost immeasurably, and in ways far beyond sexual, social, or financial matters. She had lost a dream. Neil must have lost this too. Each had a form of this dream. The difficulty was that these had not fitted into the same pattern.

She knew she could never go back on the old basis. Neil would have to listen to her side. He would have to believe that she felt the same call of her childhood teaching as a Catholic might feel. The few times they had tried to talk frankly he had always said, "There is nothing analogous about the situation. Protestants do not have deep-seated convictions. You're obsessed with an idea and have let it develop into an anti-Catholic bias and you call it a principle. After serious study, you made certain promises. You can't change your mind now."

At times she decided there was no use making another effort to heal the breach. Again it seemed she could not give him up, though she knew that this might now be beyond her to decide. If Neil's love for her were entirely gone, the sooner they brought the marriage to an end, the better. Neil could have his Church, live comfortably with his family, and none of his opinions would ever be challenged. She could have perfect freedom of expression if she stayed away from him. But without his love, freedom had a bitter taste.

One day she was driving by the Community Church down the beach, and remembered that here was the little chapel, furnished in memory of the baby she had lost. The doors stood open and she wandered about till she found, at a sunny corner of the education building, the tiny children's worship center. It was beautifully done, just as she would have had it. As she stood observing it, the minister who had come to her in the hospital, came through. To her surprise he recognized and greeted her at once.

"How do you like it?" he asked.

"It's perfect in every detail," she approved. "But you must have added something to the fund I gave you?"

"A little. Mostly work. A manual arts teacher in the schools made the little pews with material purchased with your check. So it went farther. And how goes it with you?"

She had a sudden impulse to talk with someone who must often be asked the questions which troubled her. It was easier to talk with Mr. Bishop, who knew something of her circumstances, than with Mr. Budlong with whom she worked each day. It seemed less personal and she felt the need of an impartial viewpoint.

"Not too well, Mr. Bishop. Some time when you are not busy I would appreciate it if you could help me think through my problem. Sometimes it seems that we cannot hope ever to make our marriage work."

"Have you time now? I'm at liberty."

He led the way toward his study, which looked out over a strip of beach, covered with new houses—pleasant little homes. Faith knew one could not tell about the lives inside by the bright-colored shutters or the thrifty ground-geraniums. Their home in Athens had always looked cheery from the outside.

It was difficult to state her dilemma, though Mr. Bishop seemed both interested and relaxed. She wanted to be fair. She had signed the prenuptial contract, then, almost immediately, had begun resenting the regulations. All warnings by her family had meant nothing to her because of her love for the handsome young man whom she was willing to marry at any price. The priest's instructions should have given her an idea of the domination that was indicated by the Church's claims, but again she had closed her eyes to the implications. As long as she could tell herself that this was an injustice of the Catholic Church and that it worked a hardship on her husband as well as herself, making him an innocent victim, one forced to insist upon compliance in the religious area, she had managed to adjust. Then came the death of her unbaptized child, about which he knew, her own serious illness, and then her gradual practice of exposing the children to some Protestant teaching, even while still taking them to Mass. Finally, she talked of her husband's nearness to death and his deep experience of the consolations of his church. From then on it had been a definitely divided path.

"Do you feel that your children are better off away from their father, hard as a broken home is, than to be with him and rebel against his religious teaching?" the minister asked.

"Stevie is much better off. Whether he will be so permanently or not is hard to say. But Margie adores her father and responds beautifully to Catholicism. A permanent break would be terrible for her. Neil has hinted that I must give up Rachel unless I force her to forego any participation in Protestant affairs that incites Margie to curiosity or envy. In other words, the family had to be Catholic. Now we have drifted apart till I have no idea how to heal the breach."

"Has he made any effort?"

"He helps financially. To him it isn't sinful, or even unreasonable, for him to demand that his family have the lion's share of the children's time and love. To him it is a part of their religious teaching. The hardest feature is that he does not believe I am sincere in my growing interest in my own church. He can understand a fallen-away Catholic's returning to his church, but not a revived Protestant."

"Could someone else talk with your husband?"

"I doubt if he would give them a chance. He knows what he thinks, or says that he does. He wouldn't listen to a minister or any other Protestant. I doubt if I could make a Catholic understand my viewpoint."

"You might, if you could find the right one. As a group they have been conditioned to think Protestants do not care greatly in these matters. Unfortunately, we have all too often given them reason to think so, either by weakly agreeing, or by keeping still in order to avoid friction. But, if you could find an understanding priest, I think it would be well worth your while to ask him to write, or talk, with Mr. Mackaig. It is worth real sacrifice to prevent a broken home."

"Our home was broken when we lived under one roof," Faith said sadly.

"If your husband is arguing that you do not actually care, that you have just built up a prejudice in order to get your way—if he's telling himself that just to convince himself he's not being unjust, I believe there's a chance he may grow to see your viewpoint if it could be well presented. A conscientious Christian, who is also a devout Catholic, has a problem with an unwilling mate. He'll feel less of a tyrant if he decides you are insincere."

"The hardest thing I have had to face is having my husband doubt my emotional integrity. Perhaps I mean religious integrity," she explained.

"As you well know, the Catholic Church tells its members what they are to do in case of a mixed marriage. They are to keep control of the children, insist on keeping the marriage in accordance with Catholic teaching, and to set an example of Christian living before the heretic mate. But the whole thing is predicated on certain responses from the non-Catholic. When, as in your case, the Catholic doesn't get the desired results, he doesn't know what to do next. The directions are all based on making a success of the project. It's a little like planning a difficult conversation with someone and knowing just what you intend to say, then having your opponent come back with unexpected answers. Catholics, like Protestants, are often thrown off their course by situations they haven't dreamed about."

"I know you're right," Faith answered.

"Still, it doesn't tell you what to do. And, unfortunately, I have no patent answer either. If your husband actually believes you have no rights in this matter, I would have little hope for a reconciliation. But if underneath he does love you and has let pride and prejudice get the best of him—even religious pride and prejudice—there is hope. Only he'll have to try to see your side. I still think an understanding priest is your best bet and, at the moment, I can't think of one to whom to send you. Let me think the matter over. In the meantime, there is always prayer. It is God's great gift to his creatures that we can carry every trouble to him. When we cannot make estranged loved ones believe in us, we can still pray for them. And, if the answer is not here, there is always eternity."

Faith rose, tears in her eyes. The minister's assurances brought back the comforting words he had used by her bedside years before: "When thou passeth through the waters I will be with thee, and through the rivers, they shall not overflow thee." But at times it seemed these rivers of grief would wash her off the rocks. Since her distress stemmed from religion, the very source of her comfort was tapped at the root.

She tried to word her gratitude for his counsel, but a lump in her throat stopped her. Mr. Bishop smiled understandingly.

"We do not know what is behind God's purpose for our lives, Mrs. Mackaig, but it may be that it is people like you and your husband—Christians who wish to serve him, yet are drawn across religious barriers to love one another, who will eventually bring the church of Christ, a broken body now, together again. You may have principles which you cannot sacrifice. You may even feel a bitterness that those who have not come up against such a wall as you have can never know what it is like. Yet these struggling unions may be an opening wedge in the wall that has divided the great communions of the Christian church. It is comforting to remember, also, that Jesus himself faced such prejudices when he said that 'the hour cometh, and now is, when the true worshipers shall worship the Father in spirit and in truth.' It is quite possible that, even at this minute, your husband may be praying for you and for a reconciliation, even as you are. That he may count beads while you do not is immaterial. Even if his prayers center solely around insistence that you become a Catholic is no matter. That he prays for you is what counts. The rest is in the hands of God, who does have infinite patience or he would have wiped us off this planet ages ago. I hope you'll come back and talk with me any time. I suggest you make it a point to meet Catholic people, especially those with a desire for mutual understanding. You will meet some prejudice, but there are Protestants of the same sort. One must always remember that some of our problems today stem from petty persecutions of a generation or two ago— more so, perhaps, than from the great conflicts immediately following the Reformation. There's a remarkable couple, I've been told—the Caldwells—who live back in the hills above the village. They've been making a study of conflicts—just what makes people get off on a bitter course, and how those who run against walls can handle difficulties. I don't know them, but I do wish you could get into a group like that. Better yet, I wish your husband could. Often just talking things out settles a world of difficulties."

But what if a person would not talk? She did not ask the question for she sensed that part of what Mr. Bishop was saying was conversation to help her cover inconvenient emotion. She managed to leave calmly but, once out of the village, she turned toward the beach and, stopping the car in a lonely spot, gave way to weeping. It was a luxury she could not enjoy at home. So she took some time to put her make-up on and comb her hair back into place. The children would be coming from school by the time she could reach the cottage.

But it was difficult to follow the suggestion about meeting Catholic people. There was St. Anne's, of course. But to meet people personally she would have to go to the sodality or altar guild, and her own church work took all her extra time.

One day she decided to drive to Laguna Beach for the day. A terrible restlessness hung over her and she was beginning to think that nothing pleasant could possibly ever occur again. There was not too much pleasure in going alone but she could think of no one in the village whom she wished to take along. I'm not good company, she thought. I'm a woman with one idea in my head—in love with a man who has shut me out and, like a high school girl, I can prattle about nothing else.

She had seen a little tea room, overlooking the ocean, in one of her drives through town. Now, with some effort, she found it. She would ask to be seated at a table where she could see the water. The immensity of it, the repetitiousness of its lapping, might soothe her soul. As she waited in the entry to be placed, she was struck with the familiar look of a woman ahead of her.

"Christine Marvin!"

"Faith Mackaig! How wonderful! We were going to drive out to see you the first minute Brooks could get off. Now you'll be my guest."

"It's so good to see you again. How is Athens? How long have you been here?"

"Athens is the same as ever. Brooks had an offer of a job in California that he thought he'd like, and wanted me to come down with him to see if I could be happy in California. We've been here three days.

225

There's something I miss but I'm not sure what it is."

"This country grows on you," said Faith.

"We got your address from Neil. When do you plan to go back?"

"I'm not sure yet."

The hostess came to seat them. Faith decided she might as well tell Chris her problem, but she did not want to plunge into the subject. After they were at the table she skirted it with, "Stevie got into trouble at the parish school. This seemed the solution."

"That mess at St. Aloysius, wasn't it? They've got a young priest now to take charge of the school. You weren't the only mother to be upset about Father Corrigan."

"How is Brooks?" Faith asked.

"Fine. But as cynical as ever. I hoped he'd get over it as he matured, but he hasn't."

"You didn't actually think you could make a Catholic out of him, did you?" queried Faith.

"Yes, I did, believe it or not. I thought when he saw how Catholics lived their religion, and what it does for us, he couldn't help it. But it hasn't worked out. If anything, he's worse than he was at first. He even seems to resent my praying for him."

"He can't stop you, though, can he?" Underneath her words Faith thought, I used to resent Neil's family praying that I would turn Catholic.

"No, he can't stop that," Christine agreed thoughtfully, "but it troubles me to have him feel so resentful about it. Especially when my family can't see why I don't convert him."

"Do most Catholics disapprove of their children marrying Protestants on the ground that they may lose their

226

faith, or actually want them to in hopes of spreading Catholicism?" Faith asked suddenly.

"Actually I don't know. I've heard both opinions. If they think the Catholic can win out, I imagine they may think it's a good thing. But most Catholics would be against having a weak one led astray, so in that case, they'd put up a fuss. Part of my difficulty with Brooks is that I can't hold my own with him. He's too quick-witted. Always asking me why I believe this and that. He says that to say I do because the Church teaches it isn't an answer at all—that it isn't my faith till I've made it that by thinking things through. I'd disrupt my whole thinking if I read the things he wants me to read. Maybe that's why he says as much as he does."

That's the way I did with Neil, Faith thought, but she said, "Brooks would be that way. He might even bother some Protestants. But a woman like my mother would be stimulated. There's nothing she enjoys like a religious argument."

"You've never felt you could go into the Church?" Chris asked a little wistfully, "I've always hoped you would."

"From my standpoint, I am in the church. Only my catholicity is more all-embracing than yours. But I couldn't be a Roman Catholic. That has made it hard for Neil. We're all in the same boat. If you are mated with someone who holds definitely opposing views on the most important questions in the world, both are placed in a wrong position. Oh, I know some of them manage well. Sometimes one goes over to the other's church, or they work it out. The family next door to me has four distinct religions, one Catholic, one Baptist, one Mormon, and one Christian Scientist, and it doesn't seem to ruffle any of them. Each goes his own way. They joke about the things that are mandatory or forbidden, and talk frankly about their beliefs. Evidently it isn't necessary to believe alike—just to avoid tension and keep a wall from forming. Sometimes I think the more you love, the easier it is for the wall to grow."

Chris had a sweet, sensitive face. She wanted to live as a good Catholic Christian should live, but Brooks put obstacles in her path. Neil, too, would have been a good Catholic Christian in the right atmosphere. Neither could be their best with Protestant mates. And the Protestants could not be good Protestant Christians, witnessing to their belief in the priesthood of all believers, when they had denied that priesthood and had stifled the expression of their witness.

"I believe you have something there," Chris said. "Naturally I'm the confiding sort that spills everything on my mind. But I'm becoming as secretive as a turkey hen hunting a place to nest. I hate to be laughed at and many Catholic teachings are hard to defend without special training or vocabulary. Things that have helped me all my life, Brooks can make seem like childish drivel."

"Religion should be lived and enjoyed," said Faith, "not defended and argued about. Probably that's the trouble with both of us."

"That's so. Though I've been married to Brooks all these years—and I still love him just as much—I haven't the slightest approach to his mind. It's absolutely shut against the best books I can give him. He just laughs at me for caring. All I have left is prayer."

When the waitress had taken their order for dessert, Faith said, "I'm sorry you and Brooks have trouble with this interfaith business, but it may make you sympathetic with my situation. Frankly, Chris, I'm not at all sure that Neil and I will ever go back to living together again."

"Why, Faith! Everyone has said you were the one couple that could make it work. Oh, I'm so fond of you both. I can't bear to have you part." Her voice was almost a wail. "Have . . . have you ever thought of talking to some good broadminded priest? I know Catholics talk as if tolerance were a worse sin than adultery, but actually, some priests are real understanding."

"They'd all say I made the promises and they can't be abrogated. They wouldn't consider the gift of faith could be Protestant faith, would they?"

Chris didn't know the answer.

"If you told them it was a choice between breaking your marriage off altogether or an arrangement that seemed to you more on a basis of equality . . . still, I don't know. It's a horrible choice, isn't it?"

"It's fantastic," admitted Faith. "The sacrament of marriage is presumed to give you grace to endure each other's limitations. Maybe it does when those limitations are ill temper or drunkenness or brutality or adultery, but it didn't do a thing for Neil, who hasn't one really base trait in the world except . . ."

"Except being pigheaded about his religion," Chris finished, laughing a little.

"That's it. The irony of it all is that he may even rather I pulled out altogether than to change the status quo. It makes me ill to think of it. It will ruin both our lives."

"There must be some way," Chris kept saying. "Wouldn't it be easier to live together and scrap now and then than to break up?"

"Neil just won't haggle. He retreats within himself. I don't want to leave him; I love him. Except for this wall, I could be the happiest, most devoted wife in the world."

"Does he know you still love him this way?"

"He would say that, if I did, I'd show it by giving in. But it is wrong, Chris, to promise you'll not try to transmit to your children the finest ideals and hopes and thoughts of your mind!"

Chris seemed puzzled. "I had never thought of Protestants reasoning that way," she conceded.

"When Ann Forbes signed the antenuptial contract, you thought her folks shouldn't make her promise not to become a Catholic for she might change her mind. Yet the Catholic Church asks us to make similar promises, and sometimes we change our minds. It seems to depend on our experiences and reactions. If I were terribly religious I suppose I would say it depends on the way God leads us. Yet a Catholic would not think God had anything to do with inspiring Protestant convictions."

"What a muddle it is!" Chris sighed.

"When you saw Neil did he . . . did he look well?"

"I wasn't going to say anything about this, Faith, but now you've said what you have and asked point-blank—Neil is thin. The thinnest I have ever seen him. He really doesn't look well, but he insisted he was. Do

230

you suppose that when he's alone he doesn't cook the things he should have?"

"It isn't the food," Faith answered. "He can go to his mother's and have wonderful meals whenever he likes. He's a good cook himself and he's never skimped on food. Eats out a lot and at the best places. He probably isn't any happier than I am, and it has told on his health."

"Faith, you people must get together again. I'm going to pray and pray about this. Don't worry. I'm not going to pray that you'll turn Catholic. I'll just pray that somehow God will show us what he wants us to do. That's a prayer that can't hurt anyone, can it?"

Faith laughed, more naturally than she had for some time. "You darling! Pray anything you like and use all the beads you need. My mother used to say no matter what people prayed, we could be sure of God and his providence, and that this was the biggest comfort people could have!"

"I hadn't thought of it just that way but actually that is Catholic teaching, too."

"Chris, I have to go. The children will be getting home from school and they like to have me there when they arrive. But do come and see me. Plan to stay all day. And tell Brooks I want him too."

She was almost happy again as she drove home. Perhaps something could be worked out. If Neil still cared, surely he would try. But, if he didn't, then there was no use.

There was a letter in the mailbox when she reached home. She always looked longingly for the slightest word from him, yet she was more miserable for several days after hearing. Sometimes it was just a sentence with a

231

suggestion of his stubbornness, or an allusion to his convictions. Sometimes it was the lack of anything personal whatsoever. He wrote seldom, always claiming that he could not find time. Usually the letters were addressed to the family. This one was. It was noncommittal, flat, and almost businesslike.

The tone of the missive left her so depressed that it was all she could do to summon a measure of cheerfulness to greet the children when they came from school.

Chapter 15

FAITH had just finished baking cookies and packing the jar as the children expected it to be done, when she saw a car drive up to her gate. It was Christine. Faith ran down the path to greet her. She showed her through the house and garden.

"It's adorable," Chris said enthusiastically. "So quaint and different from your other place."

Faith insisted they have coffee and sample the cookies.

While they were eating, Chris said, "Faith, I do wish you had been with us last night. If I had realized where I was going, I'd have come clear down here for you. This Mr. Caldwell, who is showing Brooks about this new job, is a Quaker. He's an unusual man. He's married to a Catholic woman, and they each had money in their own right. But they got off on the wrong foot and almost had a divorce. Then they realized where they were headed and tried a new tack. They believe in facing every problem and talking it out, no matter how touchy it is. From their own difficulties they've branched out and now they ask in people who have conflicts, to have informal chats in their home. It's a lovely place up on a hill between here and Laguna Beach. Sometimes the questions they discuss are national problems. Sometimes local ones. They say it takes skill and patience to learn to say what you think and not start feathers flying, but they believe in it. Even Brooks was impressed. He's talked about it ever since."

"They must be the people Mr. Bishop mentioned."

"Who's Mr. Bishop?"

"The minister of the Community Church in the village below ours. He mentioned the Caldwells."

"I asked Mrs. Caldwell if I could bring a friend to see her and hinted that the problem was like her own. She said to bring you. You'll go, won't you?"

"You mean just the two of us?"

"Certainly."

Faith considered. She must not refuse any opening. "I hate to air my affairs, even as a theoretical case, but I do need help."

"You won't mind Mrs. Caldwell. No one would. You should have seen the mess last night. It seems there's a new public school going up in an area that's already got a parochial school. The Catholic school has been using a near-by park for a playground. They bought some equipment and did a good deal to fix it up. Then the women's club, that seems to be dominated by a strong Protestant, bought some more apparatus. Now it looks like the logical place for the children from the public school to play. It belongs to the town. But the Catholic sisters think they have squatters' rights. Then there was a complication about a road going through that I couldn't quite get, but it added fuel to the flames."

"Were there many there?"

"About ten or twelve. Most of them were honestly searching for a Christian solution. At first one Catholic woman spouted off and was rather nasty and the club president took it up. I had a feeling she meant well but couldn't get her ideas across without offending people. But Mr. Caldwell stepped in and the first thing you know, they were all stating their views, but searching for a common denominator."

"I wish I'd have heard it. I know just stating your case and knowing that people are listening often helps."

"Doesn't it? The funny thing was that Brooks and I seemed to have more in common this morning than ever before in our lives, yet we didn't discuss one personal thing. I tell you, the whole evening was educational."

Faith decided she must see the Caldwell house and this extraordinary woman who was willing to give so much time to soothing tensions.

"I wouldn't have so much confidence in this thing," Chris continued, "if it hadn't affected Brooks. Anything that he listens to has to have cold-blooded sense to it. Believe it or not, when we got back to the hotel, I told him some things I'd kept under my hat, like money I'd given to the Church, and going to Mass during the week if he was out of town. And he didn't leer once. Just said it was too bad we'd allowed things like that to keep us apart and said what a becoming hat I'd bought yesterday. And he made love to me as he hasn't for years."

"Oh, that's wonderful," said Faith, rejoicing that Chris was happy.

"Of course when I said something about how I hoped some day he'd see things more the Catholic way, he said to lay off that. He thinks it's the type of mind you have and says he could never swallow so much that was supernatural. But he kissed me and I felt comfortable about it. I can't remember discussing religion in years when I didn't feel like I was tied in a bow knot."

The women drove together to the Caldwell home, following a road that zigzagged above the ocean. Chris was enraptured and wanted to stop at each bend to look out over the water.

"I can see why you like to live here," she exclaimed.

"I'd be happy anywhere if Neil and I could make a home together. One reason I love it here is because this is where we met."

Mrs. Caldwell greeted them graciously. She was a large woman, with a warm smile and penetrating eyes. She asked them out to the sun room on the west of the house. Faith had expected to feel shy and self-conscious, but the older woman was so natural, so interested, yet without any of the curiosity that often accompanies concern, that she found herself settling comfortably into a deep chair.

Chris introduced the subject. "Mrs. Mackaig has the reverse of our situations, Mrs. Caldwell. She is a Protestant, married to a devout Catholic. I told her how impressed Brooks and I were last night with the effort made to see into other people's minds and understand what causes friction. Faith and Neil Mackaig are dear friends of ours and we cannot bear the thought of their home breaking up. I thought you might be able to answer some questions."

"If I can't, perhaps I can find someone who can. Have you and your husband gone to anyone about this?"

"Oh, no!" said Faith quickly. "My husband thinks discussion is likely to degenerate into quarreling, especially on matters of religion. I thought at first that we couldn't talk because we didn't know each other well enough. Instead, it has grown more difficult all the time."

After a minute's silence the older woman asked, "Would you be interested to know why I feel such concern over problems that are not mine?"

When her guests expressed interest, she began: "I met my husband in Arabia. He was there as an engineer and I was visiting an uncle who was working on the same project. Almost at once we fell in love and began planning our marriage. There was a war in the offing and several events pushed us toward marriage faster than we normally would have gone into it. I knew the teachings of my church but none of my relatives were at all interested in religion. I doubt if they realized how many worlds apart Quaker and Catholic teaching can be. We both knew what we believed, yet I was much interested in his interpretations. I took it all in greedily, refuting him when I could. I felt my conception of God was broadened by listening to him and was amazed that certain devotional books from his desk were in keeping with what I had been taught and helped me greatly. Then the war situation became worse and we saw that, unless we were married at once, we might be separated. He had to go to Constantinople on business. My aunt offered to go with us, and we could be married in the office of the American consul. We knew it would be only a civil ceremony but he said if I wished a religious one, we could have it later. There was little time to plan and we did what he wished. It was three months before we were where a priest could marry us. When it was too late, some of the impediments came to the fore. Neither of us had known that unbaptized people, however Christian, are infidels in Catholic nomenclature. I could feel my husband's resentment and I was dismayed myself. I couldn't think how to explain such terms and, because I couldn't, I felt I must defend them. I find that this terminology, however trivial the matter may seem to a Catholic, often irritates Protestants. Perhaps, like many other obsolete expressions, used in all religions, it should either be changed, or people everywhere should be educated to understand what it connotes to Catholics. I am sure most of them mean no insult when they use it. But most of the feeling blew over in time and it was not till we had children and were settled next door to a very devout Catholic woman that friction began. She felt she must warn me about the difficulties a Catholic had with an unbaptized husband. She felt I should urge him at least to be baptized. This he refused so definitely and rudely that I was crushed. I simply couldn't understand a man with religious scruples against baptism!"

She paused for a moment and Faith commented, "I can understand this. My uncle and aunt here in California were birthright Quakers and they felt that water and wine and symbolism of any sort detracted from worship. It was the Spirit that mattered."

"But some of us are sacramentalists and need certain devices to direct and inspire us. My husband could not see this. Before we knew it, we were growing apart. I became apprehensive for fear he would make definite statements of his belief, or as it sometimes seemed to me, his unbelief, before the children. I didn't mean to nag but I came to the front like a mother hen guarding her chickens. Only I was guarding my husband's children against what I thought was his heresy."

"What did he do about it?" Faith asked.

"At first he protested, then said almost nothing. I should have been aware something was wrong, but my neighbor kept harping on the danger to the Catholic Church when a Catholic partner allowed herself to be swayed by a Protestant mate. Perhaps I took his silence for agreement. It seemed normal to me that a Catholic should be apprehensive about how things would work out and might even regret a marriage that handicapped her. It never entered my mind that Protestants reacted the same way. In fact, many of my Catholic friends insisted that, if one was firm enough, the Protestant came round in time. If they didn't talk, it was a sign they had no answers."

"Believe me," Chris interpolated, "I didn't marry one of those silent, suffering Protestants. It's hard for me to imagine there is such a race of people, after living with Brooks."

Everyone laughed.

"Maybe talk is the best way out in the long run," said the older woman. "Anyway, about this time there was an agitation against parochial schools in the state where we lived and the matter came up for a vote to close them entirely. I spent a great deal of effort on the defensive side. I knew my husband was interested in community projects as well as his business, but he said less and less all the time, and was home very little. He was always gone in the evening. Beyond giving me a generous check each month, and being home for an occasional meal, we seldom saw each other. One day it struck me that I was virtually a widow. I became lonely beyond words, but I hadn't the faintest idea how to retrace my steps. If there had been quarrels, I could have apologized, but there was no controversy. Nothing one could put a finger on. I had lost my husband, but I didn't know when or where, or altogether why.

"The school controversy in our town came to a climax. My nerves were tense for I was sure the Catholics were getting an unfair deal. I talked a great deal about it but I couldn't get my husband to respond. Then I decided this might be the cause of his silence and I dropped the subject when he was at home. But when a general community meeting was called at one of the public schools, I went. I felt the Catholics would be inadequately represented and there were not too many in the community who could express themselves forcibly, yet with dignity."

The younger women settled in their chairs.

"I was late getting there, so found a seat at the rear in a poorly lighted corner. The chairman outlined the points of controversy, then said he would call on a man who had taken deep interest in the public schools and had contributed much to the community, both in time and funds. Then he introduced my husband! I had been so busy with my own aspect of the dissension that it had never occurred to me to ask what he thought. I certainly had a jolt that night. If I were to analyze his arguments I doubt if, even now, I would agree with him. But he spoke well and I was proud of him. I knew he was trying to be fair, and many did not make that effort. But what hit me so between the eyes was that I had been so busy with my own cause, that I hadn't thought of his having one. The thought that he was working on the other side and hadn't breathed a word to me told me that I was lost—up till then I had prided myself that, matrimonially, I was holding the winning hand. I slipped out early and was home before he got there. It was several days before I could figure how to get us into a give-and-take conversation. When I finally asked him to take me for a ride so we could talk, he looked as though he had been accosted by a strange woman. Looking back, I can scarcely believe that two people, once so close together, could grow so far apart."

"How did you get together again, when you believed so differently?" Faith asked.

"It wasn't easy. Especially when there were certain things which each of us considered as principles—things we could not give up. But we started with one premise. When we were in Moslem country, where Christians were few and far between, we had seemed quite close to each other. It was our churches, which should have drawn us together, which actually pulled us apart. Once we had helped one another by trying to enlarge our conceptions of God. On the point of God as creator we believed much alike. We were both eager to establish the oneness we had lost, only now we were both shy and self-conscious. But Mr. Caldwell would keep coming back to the fact that we must start with our idea of God. Each of us had picked up some concepts from our early training. I kept falling back on authoritarian teaching. He felt a refusal to think an idea through and make it one's own was refusing to use the mind God had given. We were worse off than those couples who quarrel about concrete problems and allow the abstract to ride. Neither he nor I could be satisfied with surface answers."

"That's partly our problem," Faith acknowledged, "Just settling something temporarily, won't do for either of us any more."

"Do you feel the antenuptial contract was explained clearly to you before you agreed to it?" Mrs. Caldwell asked.

"Y-e-s. At least, I don't blame the priest. He was a charming, fluent person, and very intelligent. I was very much in love and determined to marry Neil Mackaig. And these regulations seemed reasonable to the priest or he wouldn't have been a priest. He couldn't have understood my viewpoint, even if I had expressed myself, which I was too wary to do."

"Are you sure he couldn't?" Mrs. Caldwell asked, laughing.

"He was a man. And he had taken a vow of celibacy. Under no circumstances could he be a mother, so he couldn't possibly know how frustrated I would feel," Faith contended. But she felt no tension with these Catholic women and she even smiled as she spoke. Then, afraid she was trying to make too good a case for herself, she added, "You mustn't think that I feel I had all the right on my side. I'm sure that, at the time, neither of us realized how much of an outsider I would feel in the family, or how repressed when I couldn't explain my beliefs to my children." Then, because she felt the keen sympathy of both her listeners, she sketched the story of her married life and the unhappy ending to it which she seemed unable to avoid.

"I don't want to break up my home, but in a way, it is already broken up," she finished. "I don't know what to do."

"There is no one cut-and-dried solution," Mrs. Caldwell acknowledged slowly. "For years I have been studying this question with great concern. I would certainly discourage any devout person of one faith from marrying into a different religious group. Yet young people will continue to do so, and some will establish happy homes. Occasionally one can accept the other's religion. If this can be done sincerely, it may work. Too often it is a device and with too many reservations. More of them end with the silent treatment. The more concerned people are with the deeper responses of religion, the more difficult the answers. You say that your husband is a very ardent Catholic?"

"Very. A perfectionist. If he cannot keep both of his children in the Catholic Church, he'll be weighed down with a sense of sin. No matter what the obstacles, he feels he must succeed."

Neither Mrs. Caldwell nor Chris had an answer for this. Perhaps neither one wished to step beyond the formula which the Catholic Church had outlined. Marriage was a sacrament which gave sanctifying grace, enabling a man and woman to live together in holy matrimony, forgiving, loving and sustaining each other far beyond the responses of sexual attraction. She believed that too, but only if the man and woman accepted the grace bestowed. Mere words and motions could not make a sacrament.

Both her listeners must know that Protestants did refuse to keep the antenuptial contracts on occasion and that many kept them unwillingly, or solely because of love for the Catholic mate. Some were constrained to return to their earlier training. Some, who had no convictions, were filled with resentment for no reason that they could explain. She wanted to ask them if this seemed reprehensible to them and, at the same time, it seemed a noble thing for a wandering Catholic to insist on the blessing of the Church after a mistaken idea that she could live happily with a civil marriage. But, even with such frank and delightful people, she hesitated.

Mrs. Caldwell insisted there must be some way through even such a reason-defying difficulty as one concerned with the conception of truth. God was over them all. The greatest benefit one could give a loved one, particularly an estranged loved one, was to bring him to the throne of grace. She promised to pray for this herself. Chris promised, too, but she could see no immediate prospect for a reconciliation without open conversation.

Faith kept coming back to the most troublesome part: "But, if he can't forgive me for changing my mind?"

"Then, my dear," Mrs. Caldwell said, "he is refusing God's forgiveness. He knows this, no matter what absolution he is given."

"Maybe he doesn't actually know he doesn't forgive. What then?" Chris asked.

"We could all be in that category to some extent," Mrs. Caldwell granted. "But I doubt if he would insist, even to himself, that he had forgiven, if he refused an attempt at reconciliation. I'll try to think of some priest to whom you could talk, Mrs. Mackaig. And we'll all pray, by whatever method is natural for us, that God will lead us, and will bring you and your husband together again."

As the younger women were leaving she repeated, "Remember, we must all pray faithfully. If we do, God will guide you. I may have picked up some Protestant expressions on the way," she added, "but my husband is such a strong Protestant and I have had to see my youngest daughter become a member of the Society of Friends, and now she is in Europe working under the Service Committee."

Faith caught the words "How wonderful" before they escaped her lips. Something told her that this great service to humanity would be difficult for a Catholic mother to take, when sponsored by a non-Catholic group.

Instead she said, "Then you will understand something of how my husband feels when our son insists he cannot be a Catholic. I think it is wonderful for you to concern yourself with my problems and those of other people who have no more claim to your time than I have. Do believe, Mrs. Caldwell, I'm not trying to place all the blame on Neil, or even on his church. It's the wall between us that is wrong."

"I'm sure of that. And love is the only force I know which can eradicate a wall and the disfigurements it leaves upon a landscape."

Chapter 16

FAITH felt more alone than ever when she realized that Chris and Brooks had gone back to Athens. Even if they did move to California, no change was contemplated till autumn. Yet the hours with Chris had done her good and she knew her friends would go back to Neil with a report of the family. This seemed closer than the flat, newsless letters they were exchanging. Faith was certain some definite approach must be made. One could pray, but one must also work, and pulling themselves together again over the wall was not easy.

Ten days after Chris left, Faith decided to go back to the garden where she had first known she loved Neil. There would be the place to pray. Its quiet would soften her will, its age would remind her of the permanence of spiritual things, its loveliness would assure her that her love for Neil had once been a holy, ennobling emotion and make her more ready to try reconstructing the lost dream.

There were few people in the garden—a pair of young lovers holding hands by the wishing well, an older couple sunning themselves by a bright blue jug covered with geraniums, the saintly-faced old priest with his breviary, down by the stone table in the far corner under an olive tree.

Under an olive tree . . . there Christ himself had prayed. Not only the hour, but the thought, Faith mused, is ill that severs those it should unite. Not God— he could not sever people. Not truth, for he was truth. But God, or truth, could never divide them. It was their conception that made the wall. She must pray that the wall would be torn down. Not that the garden would be defiled, but that the wall would be obliterated.

I will understand that Neil cannot think differently. I must believe in his sincerity. And he must believe in mine. Dear God, help us! He feels that he must not see things my way or he will lose something more precious to him than wife or children. I will believe that it is more than pride, that it is a great necessity for him to approach God in this particular way.

She went into the little chapel with its stone and dirt floor, its backless seats and ancient, faded images. There were no kneelers, but she dropped on the stones, concave with use, and the words of her petitions, wet with tears, came from the great repertoire of faith: the Psalms and the Gospels. O God, who made us to love each other . . . Thou who art the author of peace and lover of concord, in knowledge of whom standeth our eternal life . . . who settest the solitary in families . . . reunite us somehow . . . keep the thread that binds us unbroken till we can work out a plan. . . . Show us Thy way, O Lord. Lead us in a plain path. And, if for reasons we cannot see . . . Thy will . . .

She had to stop with that for she could not meet the challenge honestly. When she finally rose, the old priest was standing by the door.

"Are you in trouble, my daughter?" he inquired gently.

"I am in terrible trouble," she answered, "And I need counsel."

"Do you wish to make a confession?"

"Not in the usual sense, Father. I am a Protestant, but I am married to a Catholic and our religious differences have become a wall between us. If I could talk with some Catholic who would help me."

"If I could do so?" he offered.

"Could I tell you in my own way? Somehow I feel that you would understand."

"I shall try, my daughter. Would you care to sit under the olive tree? We would not be disturbed."

"Could I tell it as an allegory, Father? I could do it better that way." He nodded and she began: "The first time I saw this garden was with my husband when we were first lovers. I had grown up in an all-Protestant community and the most common Catholic practices were unfamiliar to me. I knew of them as history and through literature but I hadn't encountered them in my life. Perhaps that accounts for my growing thought of the Catholic Church as a garden, a very beautiful garden, yet with a. . ."

"Speak frankly, my daughter. Concealing your own feelings will not solve your problem."

"My husband loved the garden, more than anything else in the world, and he wanted me to love it too. He showed me its rarest flowers, though he felt that no one could catch its fragrance perfectly except those who had walked in it a long, long time, or who were born within its walls. But I saw the great beauty, the delicate flowers by the pools, and the gnarled old trees whose roots went back to the apostles, lovely things I had never seen before. My husband told me that the people inside the garden spoke a poetical language those outside couldn't understand in full. They called it the poetry of God, and they spoke it reverently. There was a high wall around the garden, but from within it was graciously hidden with flowers and I was scarcely conscious of it. I supposed that I could go and come in and out of the garden as I liked. Perhaps my husband thought so, too. I am sure he believed that one day I would love it as he did, and learn to speak its language."

"But you didn't?"

"Sometimes I almost did. Then something would happen to keep me back. I would see the wide open space outside, the green fields and valleys leading up to the mountains in the spiritual country where I had grown up. If I went inside the wall, I had to renounce these things. And I knew that the distant views also led to God, but by another pathway."

"Did anyone inside the garden tell you they did not?" the priest asked softly.

"Not absolutely. But they said on the free way people wandered about without purpose and with no roots. They were often quite scornful of it."

"And the people outside the garden?" the priest asked again, still softly. "Were they ever scornful?"

"Oh, yes. Very. From the gateway they could see only the narrow paths, and some of the regulations nailed on the trees. They didn't know what was inside, and they couldn't understand the language. A few went in and brought back lovely cuttings from the plants. But some of those inside the wall didn't like this, either. They said the plants belonged only to them."

"And you thought they should be more generous?" queried the priest.

"I thought there should be a give and take," Faith insisted. "When the gardeners from outside the wall brought their cuttings and wanted to exchange, the gardeners inside would hold their noses and refuse even to smell the offerings. Sometimes people on the outside said the garden would finally die. Others said to leave it alone. They talked on both sides of the wall. Sometimes I agreed with one, sometimes with the other side."

"You felt yourself on slippery ground?"

"Very slippery. I would be almost to the beautiful gate where you could see the azaleas growing by the pink pillars of the cloisters, then I would see someone else go inside and they would tie a bell on them and say 'See, we have a new inhabitant for the garden!' Maybe the new person would be very happy and seem to feel at home but sometimes they were lonely and sneaked back out under cover of darkness. Sometimes the new ones wore monkey suits and chattered till even the people inside must have been annoyed with them."

The priest threw back his head and laughed aloud.

"My dear young woman, you'll never know how much of the grace of God it took for some of us to tolerate those chatterers!" he said. "They threw our poetry off rhythm. Their clacking drowned out the songs of the lilies of the valley, which were the saintly little nuns, with white coifs. Verily, they were a pest!"

They were both laughing a little, though Faith was near to tears. Here was a Catholic, a devout Catholic, who seemed to understand her problem.

"I couldn't be belled like a cat," Faith continued, "or be gloated over as though I had been won by conquest. Besides, the wall seemed to be growing higher. People from both sides poured on more concrete. I knew that people from within, even those who wore the sacred garments, sometimes slipped out of the gate and would not go back, though this was a secret and those inside were not supposed to talk about it. But the people outside knew it and often they were very glad."

"Did you rejoice too?"

"Sometimes. Occasionally I was ashamed of this and asked God to make me feel right about it. If they lost the way altogether, I was sorry. If they found an open road, where they could see God without obstructions, I couldn't help thinking they were better off. This must have been the way the garden was before the wall became so high."

"So you became disheartened because the lives of the people inside discouraged you?"

"For a long time I went back, again and again. The paths were like a game where you spin an indicator and it tells you to go so many steps forward. If you do the wrong thing, you get a penalty and have to make up the points. Sometimes there were extra credits of your own or someone else to give you a faster spurt. I didn't like that part and I don't think my husband liked it too well either. But he felt he must not say anything against the garden. It was sacrosanct."

"Were you married in the garden?" asked the priest, careful to keep it in allegory.

"Yes. But just before the marriage the people outside suddenly began telling me how difficult the wall was, and how I couldn't jump over just anywhere, as I had been used to doing. I worried some for fear I'd have trouble going one way toward God, walking with a free stride and trying to see him everywhere, while my husband could see him only in the garden and he had to walk so carefully for fear of stepping on the flowers."

"Did it work at first?"

"In a way. But I'm an uncaged spirit and I couldn't renounce what I believed. The worst part was that I had promised my children could live in the garden with my husband. That put me outside alone, and the only way we could get together was for me to join them. Every year this became more impossible. I felt my husband used the garden as a shield. He hid behind its wall. If I had wanted to take a stand, I had no support, which made me appear bigoted. So even the sweet little lilies of the valley seemed to lose their sweetness, and the language of God was spoken with an—an. . ."

"An Irish accent?" he asked.

"How did you guess?"

"I was born in Cork. I have lived all my life in the garden and have given it such humble service as I could. The noise and clamor has probably troubled me more than it has you. But continue, my daughter."

"I began to see the wall in a different light. Instead of being a sheltering barricade against winds that might have hurt the flowers, as my husband said it was, it had become an ugly barrier that divided families. It meant I must not tell my children there was a lovely, free way to God. I had never been so lonely before. Though he was not separated from the children, I think my husband was lonely too. Sometimes I hated the garden. I even wanted to toss a bomb into it. But, if I had been able, I wouldn't have because . . . because. . . ."

She was almost in tears. The priest finished for her.

"You couldn't because you knew the lilies in the garden were nourished by the blood of the saints," he said softly, "and after the banners and the shouting and the parade of the first of the seven deadly sins, the Church will still live on, because it cannot fail!"

She put her head down and began to cry, sobbing as she had not done in months. The old priest did not disturb her.

When she looked up again he asked very gently, "What were the people outside the wall like?"

"They were a motley crew," she explained, forcing a smile through her tears. "Some ran around in circles, pretending they were happy and shouting they were having a good time. Some got together in little groups and tried to worship. Some built shrines. Some had very austere services and wouldn't allow music for they thought God was tone-deaf. Others had tin whistles and cheap instruments, and the louder they blew them, the better they thought God liked it. Occasionally a group built a fence around themselves and put up signs like 'You can't thumb your way to heaven. The gospel train is the only sure track.' But most made no boastful claims. They thought that all who tried would find God."

"Even without indicators?"

"With just a few sure ones. The paths were hard and not too clearly defined, but many were happy and sang as they marched along. The nearer they got to the top of the mountain, the more they joined hands and the easier the climbing became. It was a beautiful sight. But I couldn't get my husband to look, and he forbade our children to do so, or to hear about it." The priest nodded. "The worst feature of all is that we hurt each other. It doesn't matter who persecuted whom the most in the sixteenth century, or even a hundred years ago. The people who loved God are with him now, whichever side they were on. But we still persecute each other.

My husband was cruel about our children, though he is kind in other ways. And I hurt him—sometimes purposely. It's all been because of the wall. What is God going to do with us, Father? So mixed up in our ideas of him, and so determined to make others conform to our pattern!"

"It's an age-old question, my daughter. And you know the Church's answer."

"But that doesn't settle my problem. I was told the Catholic Church teaches that, if a person cannot believe its teachings, even one who is a communicant, that it is his duty to leave the fold. Surely, on the same basis, one who has promised certain things, thinking she did believe, would have a right to a change of mind."

"I doubt if you could get any Church authority to so rule. The provision about leaving the Church is to discourage hypocrisy. The gift of faith is freely given, if greatly desired. I also doubt if the way God is approached is the basis for many family difficulties. It is an interwoven factor, no doubt." He was silent for a moment, then asked a number of penetrating questions about where she was living and what the family was doing.

Faith answered as honestly as she could, stating that her husband was an exemplary man, his family a gracious, Christian household, and that much of the time she had not been too unhappy about the parochial school. Her listener seemed to appreciate Stevie's reactions. Perhaps he had been in charge of a school and had been like Father Donovan. She tried to explain that it was not a rebellion against a mode of worship but against claims of authority that troubled her as a Protestant.

"You want me to say," he replied after a time, "that you should be released from your antenuptial promises. I doubt if the Church would ever do this for anyone. It would be tossing aside a duty to perpetuate the truth. This right belongs only to the Catholic Church. It is seldom the Church makes an attempt to police homes to see that the contracts are kept, but she prays they will be, and she never waives her claims. Any compromises you can make must be with your husband. If he has been unreasonable, that is his to correct. But he has certain duties too. It is not my place to judge you or him. But I can tell you this—there is one argument the Catholic Church cannot refute! It is the sincere, devoted life of a Protestant Christian. We cannot answer that any more than Protestants can find an explanation for the saintly devotion of a sincere Catholic. If one, or both of you . . ."

"Had been saints, Father? But we weren't. Maybe there's just no way. . . . ."

"I wouldn't say that. God gives us grace for the asking. He also expects something of us. You must not leave one stone unturned to hold your home together. Do your part. Write your husband. Urge him to talk frankly with you. Confess your own shortcomings. Demand the very minimum. If possible, make no demands at all. Above all, tell him you still love him and your children and wish to make them a Christian home. Will you do this, my daughter?"

"May I ask one more question before making a promise?"

"Certainly."

"If I can get my husband to come to California, would you talk with him, or with both of us? If you heard his side, you might be able to help us more. I seem to have great faith in you."

"Have faith in God, my daughter. It is he who gives grace to help us through such difficulties. But I am happy to be an instrument in his hands."

"I'll write my husband at once. It can't do harm and it may do good."

"And remember 'More things are wrought by prayer than this world dreams of. Wherefore let thy voice rise like a fountain . . . day and night.' You know this?"

"And I believe it. I'll try to get Neil to come here and we'll pray together. I do thank you, Father. Please pray for us both!"

"God bless you, my child."

The path that led back to the highway, around a tiny point of hill, seemed to disappear in a burnished ocean. The path of her life was equally elusive. It might end in the glory of a sunset, or it might drop into an ocean of loneliness.

But on one point they were all agreed. All believed in prayer.

Chapter 17

THE letter could not be written hastily. Each morning after the children left for school and again after they were in bed at night, she worked on it, re-writing to make her meaning clear. Neil must not mis-understand. Still, if he were determined to do so, it would be better to be certain. When it was finally ready to go, she was not satisfied, but had become convinced that, if she waited to satisfy herself, she would never keep her promise to the priest. Before sealing it she re-read it for the twentieth time. So much depended on how it sounded to Neil.

"Dearest Neil,

This will be a long, serious letter. I am praying that you will read it in the spirit in which I am writing it. First I must tell you that, regardless of what you decide, I have always loved you—from the day when we were first in the old garden together and much, much more when I go back there to pray for you, and for us. No other man has ever had a thought from me. If it had not been for the wall that grew between us—a wall whose foundations we did not lay —we could have had one of the happiest homes in America. Except on the one matter of religion alone, you were courtesy and kindness itself. I shall always remember gratefully the many gracious things you did so naturally.

I know now that I wronged you in making the antenuptial promises. Perhaps more than I wronged myself. Remember the night when I first protested having a Catholic wedding? You explained that, without it, you should not have the sacraments of your Church and, cut off from them, you would be a different person. You said that, in such a case, I would not want you.

But what neither of us knew was that, if I gave up the inherent benefits of Protestantism, one of which is its vocal witness, that you would not want me, for I, too, would be a different person. That is what has happened. My people tried to tell me this but I was too much in love to grasp their meaning. We both thought that, if I could attend a Protestant church, take Communion, have a part in its activities—all of which you encouraged me to do—I would be happy.

But there was something in Protestantism that I lost just as surely as a Catholic who makes concessions loses the Sacrament. Protestant theologians talk about 'the Word rightly preached' being a sacrament. They are thinking of sermons from a pulpit. But it means something more to me and, I presume, to all Protestants who know its value. It means the right to say what one thinks about God, to share one's religious heritage, to do what we call 'witness to our faith.' I could not do these things. I tried to live in a sort of spiritual claustrophobia, refraining from singing the grand old hymns as I went about my work; I bit back my interpretation of a kindlier God than I could feel through Catholicism. If political issues had religious implications, I had to be silent for fear I would arouse a doubt in the children's minds that the Church was always sinless.

So my seethings were like water behind a dam, piling up and becoming dangerous. I know many Protestants have no such trouble. They say what they think or they adjust to keeping quiet, just as some Catholics manage to live apparently happy lives without taking the Sacrament. But with the years I became just as reconverted to Protestantism as any fallen-away Catholic who comes back on her knees. You may not understand this, Neil, but do try to believe it.

I should have told you these things when they first began to happen. But I loved you so madly and always I hoped that the next issue would be the last. When I began taking the children to Protestant church school I hadn't the slightest idea of undermining Catholic teaching. Always there are some Catholic children in any Protestant group and often, I am sure, it does not interfere. In Margie's case it has made no difference. She lives in a beautiful, imaginary world where saints and angels watch over her, and God himself is very near. I am sure our little daughter is much closer to him than either you or I have been able to get the past few years. We have both been defending our specific roads to God instead of living vital Christian lives. We have been no help to each other. But Margie is a devout Catholic Christian. Because she has wanted someone to kneel beside her, I have often gone with her to Mass.

Stevie is still rebellious about going to church and I have not urged him much. Occasionally he offers to go with me. He insists he is going to be a Protestant when he grows up. If he is to be won back to the Catholic Church it will have to be by someone who can show him its beauty for at the moment he is too recalcitrant to find an appeal in authority. He does well with his Scout work and is making excellent grades in school. But he needs you, Neil, as all boys need a good father.

When Steve and Molly were at our home in Avalon last summer they asked me about the possibility of adopting Rachel. At the time I felt so lonely spiritually and found her such a comfort that I said little. It seems they are unlikely to have children of their own and hope to adopt several, and plan to choose children the ages of their friends' children. Rachel has always appealed to them. She is the best adjusted child I have ever known, going faithfully to Mass with Margie and to church school at the Methodist Church with me. She accepts my statement that God is so far beyond any conception that anyone can have of him that each church has only a small part of the vision. Such a child should be consulted about where she wishes to live, but she is devoted to both Molly and Steve and might like the idea.

As for us, Neil, I think we must make some decision for another year. If we are to stay here, I should take a full-time job and contribute the greater share toward the children's expense and all of my own. Either you should have your family where you can love and enjoy them, or you should not be burdened with them.

On the other hand I cannot live with you and bear children who will be the fruit of my body but cut off from my soul. The work about a home becomes a drudgery if all the spiritual is extracted from it. We would have to find some way of sharing our experiences, some better way of making family decisions.

I do not want a divorce, Neil, but, if this is the only way out, would your Church annul the marriage for you so you could marry again, on the basis that I did not keep my agreement? Surely they should not blame you because, if anything, you tried too hard.

The other day I went back to the old garden where I first knew that I loved you. I prayed a long time in the little chapel, then talked with the old priest who walks under the trees saying his breviary. I told him I couldn't honestly keep all my antenuptial promises but that I did feel I was wrong in concealing from you the direction things were taking, even though I did it for love of you and because I wanted family peace. He said little, but advised me to write you, and promised to talk with us both if we cared to come to him.

Neil, we have so often wondered at the stupidity and impatience of people who could not hold the Church together in the sixteenth century and at how they persecuted each other. But it doesn't matter now about that. What matters is that we still persecute each other. In retaliation for what I suffered I have hurt you, sometimes intentionally and more often, I presume, unconsciously. Even now I hardly know whether I grieve more for your suffering or for my own. We let our beautiful dream go up in the smoke of a theological battle.

But tell me what you want me to do now. Shall I plan to stay on and take a job? Shall I tell the children? So far they think of this as a 'trip.' The cinerarias and lilies are almost gone and summer is nearly here. I must make a decision. Try to forgive me, Neil, and understand how I feel, for I have loved you and you only, and I did try to make our marriage work. Somehow I failed. I am praying for you with every breath I draw—for you and for me and for our children.

Faith"

She tried to compute how long it would be before she could reasonably expect an answer, and she struggled to steel herself against disappointment. If he wrote coldly, noncommittally, she would take it as a No. Sometimes she had a flash of horror that he might try to take some action that would get the children back to his people, though she could think of no legal basis on which he could do this. Or he might write a bitter, upbraiding letter. Or suppose he didn't answer at all? Then she would assure herself that he would respond as he always had to her advances in the earlier years of their happiness. God must answer such fervent prayers as she had been making when they could not be petitions for something that was wrong.

It would take the letter two days air mail to reach him. If he were out of town when it arrived, it might be a week before he would read it. He might wish to give his answer some consideration. If it took him as long to answer as it took her to write her letter, it would be ten days before she could possibly hear, yet she began counting the hours after the fourth day.

When the eighth day had gone by without a response she began condemning herself for having written. Good man that he was, Neil was too hard to yield to dramatics. Perhaps her letter sounded maudlin to him. It was a tragic thing to lose love from one's life and to break up a home. He might say, "If you care, keep your word. Make it work."

Then there was a telegram. The message read:

ARRIVE INTERNATIONAL AIRPORT, INGLEWOOD, MAY 20 5:45 IF POSSIBLE MEET ME ALONE   MUST SEE YOU ONCE MORE   NO COMMITMENTS NOW

signed

NEIL

She told the children, briefly. There was no other way. Margie was rapturous and Rachel politely cordial. Stevie's joy was tempered with apprehension. She wondered how she could put it across to Neil that Stevie had felt he needed her and resented it that she was powerless against the one great decree—"the Catholic Church teaches." He had even taunted her that she did not have a mother's authority. She put the thought from her mind. It was not one that would help in an adjustment.

The children spent their excitement in helping put the house and garden in shape. Faith bought a tiny green bonnet of the shade Neil liked best. With touches of bronze and brown and the green of crisp lettuce, she looked well, except for the telltale shadows under her eyes.

She told the children not to expect her back from the airport at any certain time. She and their father would eat before coming home. It might be late and they must not worry. In case of an accident, she would phone. She told herself that all was well.

The huge airliners spiraled up and down over the runways—from Honolulu, New York, and Japan. But Neil had to come from a still farther point. He had to come from the ages, moving past the early reformers, for whom he had such bitterness, past Geneva and Wittenberg and Canterbury. He would remember those who had died with a crucifix at their lips but he would refuse to see those who sang hymns among the flames. He must walk through Irish bogs and hear the wails of those oppressed by a Protestant government. He must stop at an Atlantic port to note that his grandfather had been a foreigner, an Irishman. That some of the same limitations struck at Scottish and English immigrants, he would have dismissed as an idle excuse.

Mrs. Caldwell knew that people had suffered on both sides. Molly knew it, even when she was still a Catholic. Lots of Catholics knew it. Even Chris. Of course Chris considered the idea of silent, suffering Protestants, overpowered by noisy, aggressive Catholics, as a myth. Anyone would after living with Brooks and his family, who were, like Brooks, verbose and argumentative. They made their witness in season and out of season. It might not be radiant or inspiring, but it was sincere, open, and often annoying. Any concessions Chris, as a Catholic, had wormed out of them had been paid for hour by hour, and none of them could have been throttled with less than a garrote. And through all this Chris tried to be fair.

But Neil?

She saw the figures that told his flight number as the huge plane came to a stop and the steps were wheeled into place. She held firmly to the strong, meshed wire. She saw him when he stood in the door

266

of the plane, then he was at the top of the stairs, waiting to go down. A little redhead beside her waved frantically to a sailor who was just behind Neil and the sailor returned the greeting, but Neil looked straight ahead. Once, on the ground, he stopped to pick up something for an elderly woman.

He wore gray, as he so often did, and he was very thin, but still the handsomest man at the airport. He was handsome in a stern, puritanical way. Strange about this admixture of Puritanism in him, as though it would be a flippant matter to rejoice in the Lord. But you couldn't pin that on Catholicism. There were plenty of Protestants whose religion gave no comfort.

Neil walked quickly, but without evidence of making haste. Physically and spiritually he knew where he stood and where he was going. He has not changed, Faith thought. He cannot change. She knew what his tie would be like, even if it were a new one. It would be striking, but not garish. It would be right.

What did the words of the telegram mean? "See you once more. No commitments." Must he think it over for a time? Would it be decided by what she said, or by what concessions she could make? "Oh, God, help me neither to antagonize him, nor to deny my conception of Thee! Oh, help us both!" she prayed fervently as she waited.

Perhaps it was all a pattern. Neil had grown hard, brittle, as she had become rebellious. Was it as difficult to be always right as to be sometimes wrong?

He was in the underpass now. She could almost hear his step. In a minute he would reach the stairway. He would turn left. He would look up. He would see her face through the meshed wire.

But it was not the meshed wire that was between them. It was the wall—the wall made of conceptions of truth. Men before Pilate, and after him, had asked "What is truth?"

To Neil it was a revealed, encased, static quality. To her it was a light on a far-off mountain, the glint of an ever-unfolding hope.

He had reached the steps and was looking up. He saw her through the meshed wire.

And the wall was still between them.